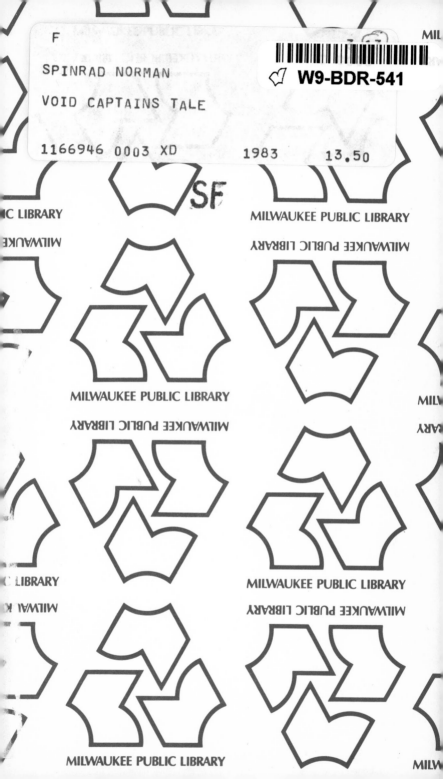

the
VOID CAPTAIN'S
tale

the
VOID CAPTAIN'S
tale

Norman
Spinrad

TIMESCAPE BOOKS
distributed by
Simon and Schuster
New York

Copyright © 1983 by Norman Spinrad
All rights reserved
including the right of reproduction
in whole or in part in any form
A Timescape Book
Published by Pocket Books, a Simon & Schuster
Division of Gulf & Western Corporation
Simon & Schuster Building
Rockefeller Center
1230 Avenue of the Americas
New York, New York 10020
SIMON AND SCHUSTER is a trademark of Simon & Schuster
Use of the trademark TIMESCAPE is by exclusive license from
Gregory Benford, the trademark owner

Designed by Eve Metz
Manufactured in the United States of America

1 2 3 4 5 6 7 8 9 10
Library of Congress Cataloging in Publication Data
Spinrad, Norman.
The Void Captain's tale.
I. Title.
PS3569.P55V6   813'.54   81-21334
AACR2
ISBN 0-671-43483-7

Fur mi Kameraden de todas partes
No mondo nostro,
No spirito uno,
J'essaie esto Traum futuro
In an anglish sprach
De nuestro Lingo.

——— *1*

I AM GENRO KANE GUPTA, Void Captain of the *Dragon
Zephyr*, and mayhap this is my todtentale. Of necessity,
it is also the tale of Void Pilot Dominique Alia Wu, but
she is gone into the Great and Only, and I lack both the
art to present her point of view in the late 20th Century
novelistic mode and the insight to say in what sense her
tale goes on.

So this tale must not be presumed to mirror any consciousness but my own. Indeed, so acutely aware am I of
my own imperfections as a subjective instrument that,
were I a Sea Captain of Old rather than a Void Captain
of the Second Starfaring Age, I would be sorely tempted
to adopt the literary mode known as Ship's Log, in which
Captains even less versed in the tale-teller's art than I
scribed terse laconic descriptions of daily events, reporting everything from the ship's position to occurrences of
tragic enormity in the same even, stylized, objective
prose.

Thusly:

On the day that Void Captain Genro Kane Gupta assumed command of the *Dragon Zephyr* in orbit around
Earth, he engaged in an unwholesome exchange of name
tales on the sky ferry to the ship with the Void Pilot
Dominique Alia Wu.

On the day of the first Jump, he conversed with her at unnatural length afterward.

After the third Jump, they performed a sexual act.

On the ninth Jump, Void Captain Genro Kane Gupta neglected to dump the vector coordinate overlay into the Jump Circuit Computer prior to activation of the Jump Circuit. The consciousness of Void Pilot Dominique Alia Wu left its material matrix and did not return, though the *Dragon Zephyr* somehow survived this Blind Jump.

The ship is now marooned about a score light-years from the nearest habited star, without a Pilot. This is the last Log entry I shall make before I call for volunteers.

One must admit that this mode achieves a certain power of understatement, the wu of an unselfconscious artifact crafted entirely by functional imperative.

But like any product of an unselfconscious mechanism, it touches not the spirit. It does not explain how a man could come to sacrifice himself and his ship, his center and his duty, to an unwholesome passion for the unattainable, nor does it enable the audience to judge for itself whether this be a romance or a tragedy or an evil farce.

For that, a mode that admits of its own subjectivity is required, and besides I have neither handscriber nor book leaves with which to produce an artfully pleasing ersatz of an ancient Ship's Log. So I am encoding an admittedly personal tale on word crystal in our contemporary manner in the wan hope that by doing so, by attempting to tell the story without excluding the storms of the spirit, I may in the end come to gain that insight in the telling which failed to inform the acts in question. In the unlikely event that this account should reach another human spirit, I ask that you decode it first into print, so that some small reflection of lost objectivity be retained.

Having made this miserable and pathetic apologia, I shall henceforth abandon all pretense of objectivity and speak my final tale from the heart as if I were recounting it into the sympathetic ear of a fellow being.

Thus I shall now proceed in the conventional manner with the tales of my pedigree and freenom.

My father, Kane Krasna Alda, was a Void Ship Man Jack without desire for command. Rather for him the attraction of starfaring was the rhythm of the via itself—the shipboard opportunity for solitary contemplation, and the long planetary layovers he chose to take, which enabled him to savor fully a multiplicity of worlds. While he was a rounded man who practiced several Ways from time to time as a matter of civilized course, his goals were esthetic rather than spiritual. He traveled widely to enrich his store of sensory data rather than approach the One through its multiplicity, and he used his shipboard solitude not for spiritual meditation upon all he had encompassed but for the practice of many sensory arts.

He practiced the eternal arts of painting and sculpture in many styles and with a multiplicity of tools and materials. He composed music conventionally on sound crystal but also on a silver flute, of which ancient instrument he had achieved considerable mastery. He crafted world bubbles and the tiny organisms within. None of his works achieved commercial validation or critical incorporation into the stream of the art, but then, he chose not to offer them up for such.

His freenom, Kane, he chose homage a Karl Kane, a semi-legendary figure of the First Starfaring Age, an artist of visual images, who, upon completing a thirty-year voyage from Earth to Novi Mir in one of the slower-than-light torchships of the period with an oeuvre of completed works that supposedly put him in the class of Leonardo, Hokusai, and Bramjonovitch, packed his works and himself on the next torchship leaving the planet and disappeared into legend.

My mother, Gupta Lee Miko, never left Arcady, the planet where she was born, where she served as a judicial arbitrator when she met my father, and where she so serves still. Arcady is a rather pastoral planet of soaring mountains, broad plains, and placid crystal seas; moonless, without significant axial tilt or orbital eccentricity, its habitable regions are lands of eternal autumn briskness, the heimat of a people similarly cool and clear and brisk. Justice on Arcady has been likened to a clear blue light proceeding from a center of platonic logic, and this is the consciousness that my mother has always sought to maintain, ironized by a gemutlich perception of the merciful impossibility of ever achieving this goal absolute.

Her freenom, Gupta, she chose homage a Sanjiro Gupta, an ark administrator of the early First Starfaring Age, who left the system of Sol with a consignment of stellar colonists dredged up from the deepest political dungeons of a consortium of sponsoring national governments, and arrived three generations later as the guiding memory of the sanest political system of the day, the forerunner of our modern transtellar society. Though this model colony ship society did not long survive planetary dispersion, and the proto-Lingo that had evolved soon began to break down into its constituent sprachs, it was Sanjiro Gupta who tossed the first pebble of modernity into the dark pool of that chauvinridden age, whose time-amplified ripples are the social mantra of our day.

My parents met on Arcady of course, on one of his open-ended planetary sojourns. Though she was ten years his senior and their consciousness interface was mutually recognizable as ultimately unstable from the start, their pheromone profiles matched chemical objects and desires so mutually that amour was inevitable.

Since each was a person of caritas and both understood the transience of their passage together, a mutual agreement was conceived to commemorate it with a child, namely myself.

My father remained on Arcady with my mother as agreed until I was six. While my father's Lingo was dominantly nihonogo and the sprach of my mother more deutsch than anything else, the parental sprach they evolved together was heavily anglic. I grew up speaking this, and my Lingo is an anglish sprach to this day.

On my sixth birthday, my father resumed his wanderlebe, returning to Arcady at long irregular intervals from his starfaring. Since the rhythm of their time together was long and intermittent and since their love song had a pre-designed end, my parents were able to maintain a mutual caritas long after amour had faded, despite their basic psychic dissonance, and my upbringing was satisfyingly complex.

From the intermittent appearances of my starfaring father, I naturally acquired an image of the romance of travel, and, more subtly, the yearning to achieve a broadness of psyche, to become a man who was more than a functional description of his work.

The influence of my mother tempered this romanticism and subjectivism with a certain respect for logical detachment, with the belief that a truly centered person would always retain a cool, clear void in the eye of his storm.

Even then I was probably not entirely unaware that in this dynamic I was merely choosing my own psychic sprach of the social Lingo of our Age, finding for myself in my own carefully naive way the specific expression of the general image of menschkeit.

Which for me became the desire to be a Void Ship Captain even before I passaged through my wanderjahr to adulthood, though of course I spent the traditional year or so aimlessly wandering through the mondes and demi-mondes of the habited star sphere anyway, sampling molecules and charges, masters, adventures, and hardships, wandering women and vagrant vias. Like everyone else, I passed through adolescence as a child of fortune, but, unlike many, I never felt the seduction of an eternal wanderjahr as the ultimate incarnation, and, unlike most, I wasn't reluctant for this golden summer to end.

After a seemly interval searching for the true essence of my being, which I had long since found, I entered the Academy of the Stars, and graduated as a general officer of Void Ships after an unexceptional and unexceptionable apprenticeship.

My freenom, Genro, I chose upon graduation, homage a Genro Gonzago Tabriz, a famous Void Ship Captain of the early Second Starfaring Age, who had attained almost three centuries of age, spent most of that time as a Captain of Void Ships, visited most of the habited planets of his day, and planted colonies on a score more. When advanced age finally caught up with him, he recorded what is still considered one of the most artistically satisfying todtentales ever told, then flew a small scoutcraft in a downspiraling orbit about a black hole, sending back his impressions continuously in the haiku mode until he reached the event horizon, where, so the legend might be crafted, he exists as an eternal human haiku even today.

I did not, I think, choose Genro as my freenom out of my romantic admiration for the life that the man had led and my desire to emulate it—which of course existed—but for the finished work of art that was its end result. Though at the time all I probably understood was that Genro had been all that a Void Captain should be, that Genro was what I wished to someday become.

Only the Genro that I now am can begin to appreciate the irony of the choice of freenom of that naive young man.

—— //

Now that I have properly introduced myself, one tale-telling mode would have me recite my exploits and adventures and glorify my rise to Captain before proceeding to confess the story of my fatal obsession, thus rendering what might otherwise be a mere tale of perverse passion into formal high tragedy. Another, less classical, mode would proceed at once to my exchange of name tales with Dominique Alia Wu.

As I sit here in my cabin encoding this onto word crystal before screwing up my courage to face crew and passengers once more, I can hardly summon the hubris to paean what glory I may have attained prior to that karmic nexus, but on the other hand my prior experience shipping with close to three score other Void Pilots seems both relevant as a background of generality regarding my previous congress with the creatures, and necessary to recount if I am then to convey the absolute uniqueness of the Void Pilot Dominique Alia Wu.

At the time that I assumed command of the *Dragon Zephyr*, I had been a Void Ship Captain for eight years, had served as second officer for four, and had served the usual junior apprenticeship for three. Thus I would estimate that I would have shipped with some three score Pilots before I met Dominique, a good twenty percent or so of those extant within that timeframe.

Dominique Alia Wu was the first and only Pilot with whom I ever exchanged name tales, let alone amour.

For those who have neither crewed on Void Ships nor traveled extensively as Honored Passengers, this total lack of social intercourse between Captain and Pilot may amaze; for those who have, only my crossing of this interface will be anything but a restatement of the obvious.

Of course there can scarcely be any citizens of the Second Starfaring Age who do not think they know something about the Void Pilots who make our transtellar civilization possible. In functional terms, the Pilot is the human component of the Jump Circuit, the organic element of our star drive, who, cyborged to the Jump Drive by the Harmonizer and actived by the Primer Circuit, navigates the ship through the space-time discontinuity of the Jump and out the other side the requisite number of light-years in the right direction.

There is no falsehood in this, but none of the inner truth either.

Alas, literature and, to a lesser extent, the pictorial arts have archetyped the Pilot as the mystical, sensual belle dame transhumaine of the spaceways, and this is a lie both so enormous and so cunningly twisted around the truth that it forms an all-too-necessary foma at the heart of our transtellar weltanschauung.

To dispose of the trivialities of surface with a surface refutation: few Pilots choose to be beautiful and none are sexual sports between Jumps. Far from it. They are as divorced from the sphere of human desire as it is possible for a member of our species to become.

"Pilot" is an ironic misnomer. Far from the mastery of ship and vector that the word implies, a Pilot is merely the psycho-organic resistor in the Jump Circuit, a living module of circuitry in a far larger mechanism. The Primer induces a specific configuration of psychesomic orgasm in the nervous system of the Pilot. The vrai

Jump Drive, the actual propulsion system, is entirely a mass-energy device, which enmeshes the ship in the psychoelectronic matrix of the Pilot's psychic reference state, the fields synergized by conventional inorganic circuitry. Once this synergy is achieved, the Jump "begins." At the other side of a quite literally immeasurable temporal discontinuity, the ship "comes out" of the Jump an average of 3.8 light-years away and most often roughly along the desired vector.

For what happens within this timeless moment, not for any romance of the spaceways or altruistic desire to serve the species, Pilots surrender all else.

When they lapse into occasional coherency on the subject of their beloved Great and Only, Pilots claim that the interval of the Jump is both timeless and eternal, like the orgasm itself, that all else is shadow, that true union with the Atman is achieved, und so weiter.

Whether this is subjectively true or not and whether this subjective truth transcends phenomenological reality, it has very real phenomenological effects on both the recruitment parameters imposed by reality upon our Void Ship fleet and the social role or lack of same of the Void Ship Pilot in shipboard dynamics.

For obvious biological reasons, a Pilot must be a woman; the male psychoelectrical physiology is simply incapable of platform psychesomic orgasm. Less well known are the rigid psychic parameters, which evolved through a process of trial and error over half a century. The Pilot must be a willing volunteer. The Pilot must possess what in ancient days would have been called an "addictive personality," which here translates into a willing surrender to the Jump and all that it implies—the ultimate coeur addiction on a metaphysical level. The Pilot must be incapable of ordinary orgasm at the touch of congruent flesh, though the causality direction here is sometimes disputed.

So outre and specific are the psychic parameters for

Pilots that the fifty billion population of the habited planets supplies us with no more than two hundred of these rare creatures on duty at any given time, to the great detriment of interstellar commerce and exploration. These are almost entirely recruited from the demi-mondes and mental retreats where those whose wanderjahrs led not to the finding of the true self but to the losing of same live out their lives in obsessive addiction to no particular charge or molecule. Indeed this may be why such bas-kulturs are not merely tolerated but glorified by popular culture and subsidized by corporate entities and magnates, though the circularity of this causality would no doubt be fiercely denied by all concerned.

So the Pilot-recruit is a nonorgasmic terminal addict recruited from a spiritual vacuum to willingly surrender all to the ineffableness of the Jump. Aimless vagabonds of the spirit, alienated from their own bodies, willingly offering up the last ghost of their humanity to the Jump Circuit.

And the Jump makes them worse. The physiological price is severe; the required twenty-four-standard-hour recuperation period is the true speed limit of interstellar voyaging, and the average Pilot burns out after ten years. Typically anorexic to begin with, the Pilot loses all interest in the esthetics of nutriment and must be dripfed during the recuperation period. Needless to say, personal grooming and cleanliness have an even lower priority in the Pilot's scheme of things.

So while they are considered officers of the crew with the privileges of same through long tradition, they mingle not with the crew or the Honored Passengers, by both an almost equally long tradition and their own chronic physical enfeeblement. Of all the Pilots I have shipped with, only Dominique Alia Wu ever crossed the walls of this unstated purdah or even acknowledged anything but indifference to its existence.

Perhaps now you will be ready to understand why the

notion never broached my consciousness that Dominique was in fact my Pilot when first I saw her on the sky ferry up to the *Dragon Zephyr* from Earth.

In one sense every Void Ship voyage is a new command and in all senses one's crew is never the same twice, but in the case of the *Dragon Zephyr*, this was doubly so. The module I had dubbed "Dragon" was not only new to me, it was new to service, straight from the circumlunar fabrik; by one of those mathematical oddities, there was also not a single member of the *Dragon* crew with whom I had shipped before.

So what with an enlarged number of technical reports and crew tales to go over in a command assumption rite not expanded beyond the usual week, my consciousness had been warped toward a necessarily speeded-up mode. I seemed to be just barely on time for everything, and in fact I found myself dashing on board the sky ferry rather at the last minute.

There were only two empty seats available by then: one beside a rather obese and untidy-looking fellow wearing the blazon of the Flinger crew, and the other beside a slim but attractively proportioned woman, plainly but smartly dressed in a functional pale-blue voyaging costume, with a cap of short brown hair, bright dark eyes, and an eagle-visaged profile. Naturally, I chose the beauty over my fellow beast without noticing the decision in my haste as anything but pheromonic esthetics.

Only when I had strapped in, stretched out, and performed a brief breathing exercise to relax my tempo, did I fully notice my seatmate, who sat staring out the port at what seemed like nothing in particular.

What I had perceived in my distracted mode as conventional beauty was now revealed as something far less boring. The body within the form-revealing voyaging costume was not a slim, boyish figure but rather that of a buxom voluptuary honed down to its bare functionalism by the practice of some martial or yogic art, or feverish dedication, or both. Her features were not paradigms of stylized beauty in any cultural mode with which I was familiar, and the plain cap of brown hair was seemingly a deliberate anti-dramatic gesture.

Yet the gestalt had brio, presence, a beauty not of feature but of inner transmutation. Her dark bright eyes were the crown of a curving aquiline nose that served to highlight their intensity, her mouth seemed an ideogram of ironic internal dialogue, and the lack of grand coiffure served to focus visual attention on the inner fires rather than on external fleshly harmonies of form.

Of course I was well aware that this perception owed a good deal to the chance congruence of her pheromones with the chemical ideal engraved in my genes and I thought little more of it at the time, my thoughts still primarily focused more on taking command than on this frisson of passing glandular attraction.

At any rate, before I could contemplate initiating a conversation, the warning chord sounded, the luzer was lit, and the sky ferry surged upward atop a pillar of luz, a stream of densified photons pushing it to orbital velocity at an even three gravities—smooth and silent, but still not exactly conducive to artfully casual discourse, and nothing passed between us until the ferry was in the process of matching orbits with the *Dragon Zephyr*.

Though all Void Ships are assembled for their voyages out of the same eight basic module classes, no two, even of the same general function, are exact duplicates—appropriately emblematic, it is sometimes said, of the coding mode of the DNA molecule.

Indeed, the shape of the core module, the *Dragon* in this instance, all but turns this fanciful metaphor into a parody of itself. With bridge, crew quarters, sick bay, Jump Drive machinery, and Pilot's module all contained in the ellipsoidal body of the *Dragon*, and the spine trailing behind like an erect tail, the core module did indeed resemble a giant silvery spermatozoon; the yang, the male, the propulsive principle, ejaculated from the electronic phallus of the Flinger to fertilize the stars with human genes.

Fortunately, perhaps, the metaphor breaks down at this point. Rather than burying itself in some massive ovum, the prow of the *Dragon* was the bow of the *Dragon Zephyr* configuration itself, with the various modules gestalted as the *Zephyr* slung close against the spine of the core module like a variety of huge metallic sausages.

The *Dragon Zephyr* was a free-market merchant conveying a mixed cargo of freight and passengers to Estrella Bonita. This was a planetary system about two hundred light-years or a mean twenty Jumps from Earth—four habited planets, three gas giants, and any number of mineral-rich rocks. A system long on economic opportunity, short on labor, and with enough outre flora, fauna, and impressive scenery to attract the grand tourists and their floating cultura.

So on this outward voyage, the *Zephyr* configuration consisted of ten dormodules, each storing a thousand immigrants in electrocoma; twenty freight modules hauling lucrative luxury goods and classic Terrestrial cuisinary items; a stateroom module for fifty Honored Passengers; and the congruent Grand Palais module.

To the untrained eye, this superficially asymmetric assortment of cylinders of different sizes and masses secured to the spine of the ship in no discernible formal pattern must seem random, but in fact each Void Ship configuration must be carefully balanced as to both mass distribution and congruence with the Jump Field aura.

This balance is checked and rechecked endlessly to ensure against either excessive stress during conventional acceleration or breach of integrity of the Jump Field aura, and the assembly crew was giving it one final check before turning the ship over to my command as we maneuvered toward it from several kilometers out.

An aura of pale rainbow brilliance suddenly enveloped

the ship, turning it into a shimmery silhouette of itself— the configuration was in fact congruent with the field produced by its Jump Drive generator, as by now all knew it would be. This final test was more a salute to my arrival than anything else, the equivalent rite to the ancient seafaring custom of piping the Captain aboard.

But my seatmate's face twisted momentarily into a mask of what seemed like fear. Or anger?

"Don't worry," I said soothingly, "it's just the final test of the Jump Field congruence, and all is in order. Is this your first stellar voyage?"

She turned to regard me with curled lip and angry eyes. "Hardly," she said. "And I ken the procedure. But time-honored stupidity becomes not sage, ne?"

Her ferocity aroused something primal in me, but what she was saying made no sense. "Time-honored stupidity?" I inquired.

She didn't answer until they had turned off the Jump Field and we resumed matching orbits with what was once again entirely a conventional mass-energy construct. And she let out a sharp sigh of what seemed like bitter relief before she spoke.

"Contra disaster, test the Jump Drive, ja?" she said scathingly. "Sans a Pilot in the circuit, vrai? So as to court the greater disaster, no?"

"Greater disaster?" I asked in mystification and in a certain mood malo. From whence this contemptuous anger?

"A *Blind Jump*, mon cher dummkopf! Pilotless and blind in the Great and Lonely, a current they no se comes and carries them away."

Now at least I understood what she was talking about. The "Blind Jump" is of course part of the romance of starfaring; the belief, or the thrill of tempting the belief, that ships have vanished in mid-Jump into the Great and Lonely, passengers and crew translated from matter and energy into the Void beyond the void. Since it is the ingenious nature of this folkchose that its truth can be neither proven nor disproven, and since Void Ships inevitably do disappear without a trace over the centuries and light-years, no Void Captain could utterly deny the possibility.

But it is surmised, indeed all but proven, that such a hypothetical Blind Jump can occur only when the Pilot dies in mid-Jump, in the exact instant of psychesomic orgasm. Either that or a malfunction in the Jump Circuit computer somehow causes it to fail to impose the vector coordinate overlay on the Pilot's psychic matrix.

However, in either case a Pilot must be in the circuit. Without a Pilot in the circuit, the ship will not Jump, and a ship that does not Jump obviously cannot Jump Blind.

"I can assure you," I said, "that such a thing is impossible."

A wordless snort of derision. "So the Blind Jump, it is impossible, upon your word of honor?" she said, bending her Lingo closer to my anglish sprach, the better, perhaps, to convey her contemptuous sarcasm. "Ships have never vanished, and a dead Pilot in the circuit is nothing?"

Her arrogance was more than beginning to disturb me. What had I done to offend her? Whence this vehemence on a topic of casual conversation? At the same time, there was something sensually fascinating about the very vehemence that was arousing my own ire. Her psychesomic metabolism seemed turned up to a pitch of barely controlled fever. Her eyes burned, her tongue stung, her body seemed to radiate an attractive excess of prana, and I was sure that this was more than my pheromone receptors coloring my perception. It seemed to me that whatever this mode was, it was not generated by any reaction to me, but by her own internal essence.

This perception allowed me to recenter myself, to stay my reactive anger. "I didn't say Blind Jumps were impossible," I told her. "Or at least I didn't mean to. All I meant was that there's no danger in testing the Jump Field without a Pilot in the circuit. Without a Pilot in the circuit, the ship cannot Jump, and if it cannot Jump, it can hardly Jump-Blind."

She half-turned in her seat. Her anger seemed to transmute into something else as she studied me with an open, slightly mocking stare. " 'There are more things in heaven and earth than are dreamt of in your philosophies,' " she said. An eldritch trick of perception occurred in the next moment. As she continued to stare at me, the irony seemed to vanish from her face and the humanity from her eyes, as if a mask had been removed—or donned?—and I found myself looking into two opaque marbles set in the face of a fleshly statue, classically Greek in their archetypal emptiness. As if the animating consciousness had gone—elsewhere.

It—whatever it had been—lasted only a moment, just long enough to make me shudder. Thespic art? Vibrational control? Or merely an artifact of my own sensorium?

"The Great and Lonely is the One and Only," she said. "The order you see is a dream, mon petit. Only chaos is real, outside the law."

"The laws describing the totality of mass-energy phenomena are quite real, have been fully elucidated for centuries, and make any such thing as a Blind Jump without a Pilot in the circuit impossible," I told her angrily. "I can assure you of that."

"You assure me? *You* assure *me?*"

Her arrogance, her patronization, and the pheromonic ambivalence of my reaction to it, finally produced an outraged strut of masculine pride. "You may consider yourself a seasoned stellar traveler," I told her. "But I've been starfaring for fifteen years, and in fact I happen to be Genro Kane Gupta, *Void Captain* Genro Kane Gupta, commander of the ship you're about to board!"

Whatever response my endocrine system might have

been expecting, it was certainly not the one that it got. She seemed to choke back some snide species of laugh. She cocked her head at me as if in amusement. A measured devilment seemed to replace the fire in her eyes.

"You will now spiel for me your name tale, Captain, bitte?" she said more quietly. "And after, if you wish, I will be most pleased to declaim mine."

Though I deluded myself not that our discourse had suddenly harmonized into a genuine exchange of courtesies, I could hardly refuse a request for civilized introduction from someone I had just boasted my name and rank to.

So, while she listened with no apparent keen edge of interest, I told the tales of my paternom, my maternom, and my choice of freenom in what was probably an unduly terse and not very artistic style.

When I told the tale of Genro Gonzago Tabriz's haiku-trailing eternal spiral down into the black hole, intensity of attent seemed to sparkle back into her eyes, but when I had finished, she regarded me with a strange blank uncertainty.

"An admirable pedigree and a choice of freenom not without more satori than you suppose, Captain Genro," she said enigmatically. "At your pleasure, my name tale is now yours to hear. But if you will the sparing of the experience, I withdraw feelings of offense now. You may wish the absence of the burden."

"Burden?"

"Verdad."

"What burden can your name tale possibly impose on me?" I asked in bewilderment.

"That you cannot know till you have heard it, ne?" she said sardonically.

"Speak to me then the tale of your name," I said, feeling I had been trapped into hearing something I had every intention of hearing in the first place. "I accept full responsibility."

She laughed—cruelly, I thought—and her expression grew stranger and stranger as she spoke, distant, abstracted, and yet seeming to study my face for any passing reaction with ironic amusement.

My name is Dominique Alia Wu.

My father, Alia Smith Per, was a man of mighty argent, a rich merchant of biologicals, both import and export, on Ariel, but that describes him not at all. His mother originated the enterprise, and while she lived to maintain it, his life was one grand golden wanderjahr of magnificent indulgence of the sensorium, long years of floating orb to orb in the cultura of the Honored Passengers and passionate pursuit of samadhi through its bioelectronic matrix.

But exit la mama de oro via a flying collision and my father must return to Ariel to sustain that which sustains him or have the courage to continue as a child of fortune sin dinero.

Choosing that discretion which is no part of valor, he returned home to la vie bourgeoise, a merchant by day, a tourist of the ecstatic by night, and nowhere a center.

His freenom, Alia, he chose upon assumption of this duality, in foolish wistfulness, homage a Alia Haste Moguchi, merchant princess of the late First Starfaring Age, who, in her quest for wealth, spent her life in pursuit of same at a sublight crawl but stumbled upon the planetary ruins of We Who Have Gone Before, and thus found the key to mass-energy transcendence in the service of her own greed. Thus did my father seek to justify to himself and beg a boon of fate.

My mother, Wu Jani Martin, was also born on Ariel, but not to the silver. During her wanderjahr of the customary duration, she experienced much samadhi, or the shadow of same, and upon her return to Ariel, sought to survive as a teacher of inspiration, on the white light of her essence.

Her freenom, Wu, she chose upon embarkation on this via, homage a an endless line of boddhis who had chosen this freenom back into the mists of dawn man on Earth homage a the purity of being they sought to attain, the clear consciousness of the unselfconscious act, the embrace of the Void.

My mother and father met on Ariel, in a casa de amor in the seacoast playland of Carondole, sehr romantic, ne? For one path of the many that my mother followed was that of the tantric ecstasies, and my father considered himself a maestro of these arts, though his ultima thule might fall short of the perfected mystery.

The magic of amor, quien sabe? These two, who each in the mirror of the other should have seen a halfling, and via that vision the halflings in themselves, against all logic made for each other a sexual fascination, and out of that, a period of caritas, and out of that, me, and out of me, a bond of honor which survived both the cooling of the fires and the war of the spirit which consumed the ashes.

Upon my nativity, my father conferred upon my mother in a license of honor the irrevocable droit to draw upon his treasure as she saw fit, and when their differences sundered them when I was twelve, the same on me.

So my kinderhood on Ariel was one of material whim and psychic smorgasbord. Chez mama, satoric disdain for the things of the world in luxurious asceticism; chez papa, professions of dedication to that from which he had turned away and the selfish obsession altruistique that his kleine cher be truly free to follow her own way.

From my mother, I received the quest for the absolute, and contempt for everyone I've met who thinks they have found it. From my father, dinero dripping from my jeweled fingertips, and the assumption that the road of excess leads to the Palace of Wisdom.

In this karmic state did I commence my wanderjahr as

soon as it was possible, and with lust, grand passion, and gelt did I dance that camino real. Through amour, the exotic, and the perfume of decay did I seek to balm the wound in my father's soul in his stead. Through molecules and charges, disciplines and arts, perfect masters and those far from, and even the study of the nonhuman enigmas, did I seek to find that which my mother thought she had.

The result, naturellement, was an endless nada receding before me in flesh and locales, in mondes and demi-mondes, in the floating cultura and the mystic wastelands, drugged with experience, unable to fly. Your typical lost child of fortune, ne, were it not for the studies and ways, which, though unable to show me the Way, were puissant enough to never let me forget just how lost I really was.

My freenom, Dominique, I chose homage a Dominique Noda Benares, a person who died in the gifting, perhaps a person of no consequence, and certainly someone you would despise. . . .

She paused, not so much I think for effect, but out of the sudden realization that she was going too far. These tales of her paternom and maternom were like regurgitations of bitter bile, not a name tale in the civilized mode. In the demi-mondes of aging children of fortune or in the groves of mental retreats might such be considered fair introduction. Yet in their raw red pain, their uncivilized darkness, lay their power and fascination, which only a corpse could fail to perceive.

"I would spare you the tale of my freenom, mon cher," she finally said.

"You have not spared me the suspense, and you know it," I told her. "You wish me to ask to hear it and thus absolve you of the imposition you truly wish to make. Very well then, spiel me your tale."

Emotions seemed to flicker after each other in her eyes—shock of recognition, anger, respect of a new sort, bitterness. But her mouth remained a sneerish ideogram, a challenge to my acceptance of her challenge. "Tres bon, then," she said. "Meet your shipmate, mein Captain."

My freenom, Dominique, I chose homage a Dominique Noda Benares, a Void Pilot who died after the eighth Jump on the Void Ship *Feather Serpent*, ten Jumps out of Wunderwelt headed for Han and at least three Jumps from anywhere else.

I was an Honored Pasenger on the *Feather Serpent* on that voyage, and as is known, under such circumstances, the Void Captain, for want of any better hope, appeals to altruism and honor, points out that the alternative is slow death by marooning in any event, and asks virgin females as it were to sacrifice themselves upon the altar of the Jump Circuit.

Such a longtime Honored Passenger as myself, versed in the lore and no little of the functionality of starfaring, knew quite well that such Pilots of desperation almost never succeed, and that ships such as ours were almost certainly doomed.

Nevertheless, it was not some naive child of fortune who volunteered to brave the Great and Lonely but this open-eyed and knowing sophisticate. With the clarity of mama, I saw that this was a wager I could not lose. On one side, certain death when the air ran out, and on the other, either triumph transcendent or the status quo ante. With the passion mystique of papa, I lusted after this ultimate confrontation with existence. Chez moi, I felt I had always Jumped Blind.

Thus did I find myself and my freenom. Thus did I trade all for the Great and Only. Thus did I become your Void Pilot, Captain Genro; thus the name tale of Dominique Alia Wu.

Her laughter rang in my ears. Once again, that eldritch frisson of perception as the humanity seemed to flee from her eyes into places unknown, as her features seemed to stylize into a No mask of themselves.

I froze, I flashed hot and cold; I must have actually gaped in amazement and horror at this grand coup of outrage.

Pilots, or my image of Pilots: pallid, slack-jawed, ill-smelling creatures hardly capable of social intercourse at all, the necesary unseen fleshly module in the machinery of function.

What unseemly rubicon had I been tricked across? Now I had spoken with my Pilot, the comfortable arche-type had been shattered, and I knew that I had indeed heard a name tale that would prove a burden. Though we spoke no more on the sky ferry, the deed had already been done. Captain Genro Kane Gupta had exchanged name tales with Pilot Dominique Alia Wu, and that much was already irrevocable. Tiny tendrils of relation-ship had already begun to insinuate themselves through the stone wall of wisely crafted custom that should have stood between us.

NATURELLEMENT, I saw not my Pilot again before the first Jump. Time, as well as custom and my own determination, forbade it. Indeed, taking over my new command, preparing the ship for acceleration, and then matching orbits with the Flinger, all within four hours, so totally occupied my attention that I didn't even have time to meet the Domo of the Honored Passengers before we left orbit.

To the virgin starfarer, six officers may seem a somewhat inadequate crew for a vehicle transporting over ten thousand humans and three thousand tons of cargo, but the same person thinks nothing of fabriks of equal size and complexity with only one human maestro. Actually, the reverse is true: a six-officer crew on a Void Ship like the *Dragon Zephyr* has a high redundancy coefficient.

The bridge crew consisted of Argus Edison Gandhi, Computer Interface or Second Officer; Mori Lao Chaka, Man Jack or Third; and myself, Void Captain, or First.

Upon leaving the Academy, every starfaring officer first ships as Man Jack for a period, learning the systems of the Void Ship and how to repair them in an emergency from a functional craftsman's point of view. After achieving distinction as Man Jack, an officer then does a tour as Interface, becoming the maestro of the ship's machineries from a control position. Only after mastering the duties of both Third and Second Officer may one aspire to Void Captain and command. Thus Argus could perform Mori's duties in extremis and I could double for both of them. And of course Argus had reached the stage of her career where command should not be beyond her should heroism demand.

The virgin Honored Passenger is also sometimes discomfited to learn that round-the-clock bridge watches are not maintained, and may first be startled to encounter all three bridge officers in the Grand Palais at the same time. But since a Void Ship between Jumps is in effect lying dead in the deep starless void, there is no reason to burden the crew with pointless duty or the ship with excess personnel, and there is no reason why we may all not take our ease in the floating cultura.

Of course this hardly applies to the Med crew; these three are kept more than busy during the inter-Jump periods tending to the recuperation of the Pilot, their role in the floating cultura being traditionally filled by their dedicated absence.

Paradoxically, the single period of idle repose for the Med crew is the period of maximum activity for the bridge crew. As the Void Ship is warped out of its holding orbit, matches orbits with the Flinger, and eases itself carefully into Go position, the Man Jack must constantly monitor all systems for acceleration-generated deviations, and the Interface must deal with the mathematics of the subtle trajectories while the Captain tends to the intangibles of command.

But since the Pilot at this point has not Jumped since the last voyage and need not be inserted into the Jump Circuit for several hours, it is customary for the Med crew to come to the bridge to observe departure; since this is the only time the entire crew will muster during the voyage, the departure becomes rite as well as functional procedure.

The design of the bridge itself enhances this artful homage to the ancient seafaring esprit. An elliptical wedge forming the upper bow of the *Dragon*, its curving outer wall is one seamless tele screen, handsomely crafting the illusion that one rests upon an open forward deck looking bowward into the depths of the starry sea.

The Second Officer sits at her Computer Interface facing this grand panorama, casting data readouts and reference grids upon it at the Captain's command. To her left is the chaise of the Man Jack, empty now as Mori scurries and worries over her brood of systems monitors curving along the forward bulkhead.

My chaise, with its master controls, enhanced height, and carven brass embellishments, is fastened to the deck just behind them, the ceremonial throne of command.

Behind me, a small temple pew as it were: four spartan courtesy chaises for the rest of the crew, all but the traditional empty chaise of the Pilot now occupied by the Med crew Maestro, his Man Jack, and the Healer.

"Prepare to leave orbit," I intone, and the ritual begins.

"All systems secured for orbital maneuvering," Mori called out, hovering over her bank of readouts.

"Orbital exchange profile computed, . . ." Argus said, touching a control point, ". . . and ready to dump." A red control point on my own console winked on, inviting my command.

"Display maneuvering grid."

The illusion of open starry space surrounding us was faulted by a red gridwork of spherical coordinates centered upon a green crosshairs signifying the ship's axis of acceleration.

"Dumping orbital exchange profile," I announced, touching my first red command point. The maneuvering command was now transferred from my command holding banks into the orbital control computer, and another of my red command points became active.

The moment of high romance, such as it was, had arrived. "Exchanging orbits," I announced, conscious of a certain thespic self-indulgence as I touched the command point.

Auditory sensors provided an ersatz confirmation of the *chuff-chuff-chuff* of a horde of tiny reaction thrusters, and the starfield jitterdanced into a new alignment with the reference grid. A sapphire slice of the Earth below lit up the far right edge of the great tele screen with its gegenschein glow. A louder, more authoritative ersatz *chuff*, and the crosshairs bow of the *Dragon Zephyr* began to cleave the wine-dark sea in a ponderous glide, a foamy wake of stars streaming in slow motion over us as we rode into a higher orbit.

At this moment, I had always been accustomed to flowing into the romantic seafaring metaphor, the Captain slowly inching his ship out of harbor, gazing eagle-eyed into the voidy sea surrounded by the full muster of his admiring crew.

But this time, for some reason, my role in this happy rite had a somewhat hollow feel. My consciousness was focused on the functional, not its greater metaphorical glory. I was too aware that all I had really done was feed a command computed by my Interface into the orbital maneuvering computer, that the drama of conning my ship as the starfield eased gracefully into new configuration was illusion, that we were moving along a ballistically inevitable curve as beyond my control as kismet. For some reason I cared not to contemplate, this in turn focused my awareness on the psychic pressure of the unseen empty Pilot's chaise behind me, mocking me with the reminder that soon enough I would lose even this thespic ersatz of true command.

"Flinger on the grid, Captain Genro," Argus called out, and there, tiny in the distance but nominally centered in our crosshairs, was a tube of silver filigree lace, a phallic cobweb rapidly growing in size as we eased into our leading orbit before it.

"Read out closing velocities to dead stop, Interface," I ordered.

"Five thouand meters per second . . . 3,700 . . . 2,000. . . ." Digits flashed in yellow beneath the crosshairs as that which had seemed far away, fragile, and small rapidly became closer, fragile, and enormous.

"Fifteen hundred . . . 1,000 . . . 423. . . ."

The Jump Drive itself is not exactly a precise propulsive instrument; a final Jump that puts a Void Ship within half a light-year of the target system is bon suerte indeed. Fortunately, the mass-energy discontinuity of the Jump affects not the ship's velocity relative to the quotidian universe: a Void Ship emerges from one or ten or a hundred Jumps with the relative velocity with which it began; conservation of momentum in mass-energy reality is not disturbed.

Since no amount of corrective Jumping will place the ship cozily within the target solar system, a high relativistic velocity is needed to effect final rendezvous within a reasonable subjective timeframe. With the gravitic compensators insulating the ship from any gee stresses, losing this velocity on final approach via severe ballistic breaking maneuvers is no problem, but generating it from a dead stop in space would require an economically crippling amount of onboard reaction mass. Therefore it is more than desirable for a Void Ship to enter its first Jump with near-light speed.

Voila, the Flinger.

"Two hundred ten . . . 175 . . . 80 . . . 17 . . . 0. . . ."

"Zero relative velocity," I announced ceremoniously. "Orbital exchange perfected."

Now the *Dragon Zephyr* sat motionless in space facing into the circular mouth of an enormous yet ethereal tunnel half a kilometer in diameter and a hundred kilometers long. Constructed of nothing more substantial in material terms than a framework of cryowire hoops supporting equally thin longitudinal members, the Flinger tube seemed as much of an abstraction on the tele as the maneuvering grid projected upon it, vast in scale, yet barely extant.

"Patch Flinger Control," I ordered. An amber point lit up on my console as Argus established a com channel.

"Flinger control, this is the *Dragon Zephyr* at zero relative velocity in orbit 2.3 kilometers out. Request guidance interface."

"*Dragon Zephyr*, this is Flinger control," a vaguely female voice answered. "Coordinates and zero velocity confirmed. Computer patch confirmed and locked in. You may proceed with your insertion procedure."

Another touch point on my console glowed red. Needless to say, conning a Void Ship the length of a tunnel a hundred kilometers long and a mere half-a-kilometer wide by manual maneuvering, while not humanly impossible, would be tedious and problematical. So when I touched this command point, the Flinger control computer took over the conning of the ship via its synergy with our own orbital maneuvering computer and I was reduced to the role of human safety backup to the automatics—a perception that this time around somehow seemed new and unsettling as they proceeded to turn the ship end for end and draw it stern-first smoothly and surely down the bore of the Flinger barrel toward Go position.

The far end of the Flinger was capped by the field generator and the Flinger control complex. A system of orbiting solaires beamed power to the field generator in the form of luz densified from the local stellar source; this in turn was used to electrify the gridwork Flinger barrel, creating a powerful cylindrical magnetic field in the manner of a particle accelerator. At Go position, the *Dragon Zephyr* would be encapsulated in an electromagnetic bubble of opposite charge, which in turn would be accelerated electromagnetically by interaction with the field, flinging the ship within it into the void at near-light velocity.

Now the ship was being drawn down the Flinger bore by a slow-motion reversal of this selfsame process, receding down the latticework corridor like a fly slowly being drawn into a spider's web.

"Go position," Argus called out as the *Dragon Zephyr* came to a dead stop, its stern less than a half-kilometer from the "bottom" of the Flinger tube.

"Confirm internal gravity at one gee."

"Internal gravity confirmed at one gee," Mori called out from one of her consoles.

"Assume departure position," I told her. "Activate internal com systems," I ordered Argus.

Mori seated herself beside Argus. Another amber point glowed on my console. The climax of the departure rite neared. Now the Honored Passengers could listen in on the bridge conversation and watch our departure via the teles in their staterooms or the Grand Palais module. At this point, many Void Captains choose to address some salutations to the Honored Passengers, even at times a haiku composed in honor of the occasion, as I myself, in other moods, have done. Now, however, my tongue seemed tied, and I left the unfelt poetry of the moment to the wu of unselfconscious functionality.

"Flinger control, this is the *Dragon Zephyr*, awaiting Go command release."

"Dragon Zephyr, this is Flinger control. You have Go command release. Bon voyage, Captain Genro."

A red touch point lit on my console; the final, not strictly functional, bon chose of the ritual. Now the Flinger control patch was reversed, and I commanded the energies of the Flinger from on board the ship, a symbolic transfer of the ship's destiny to my lone hand.

Following the rite mechanically to its final conclusion, I positioned my finger above the touch point with a mimed gesture of thespic pregnancy, though somehow it all seemed hollow now, like a Way degenerated into mere religiosity. Before me, the starfield was framed by the latticework tunnel of the Flinger barrel, dwindling away in perspective to a small distant circle of stars marked by the crosshairs of the maneuvering grid laid in over the approaching immensity of the deep void.

Focusing on this as best I could, I chanted the word "Go!" with as much grandeur as I could muster and touched the glowing red point.

For the merest instant, the purest augenblick, the great latticework tunnel blurred into the apparent solidity of tremendous relative motion, the stars in the central circle dopplered through blue into violet and beyond, as we seemed to hurtle forward into an unreal universe of ultraviolet pinpricks through black velvet keening into eye-killing transvisibility.

Then we were floating, apparently motionless, in the still, silent cosmos of multicolored stars as the tele's spectral compensator circuits cut in, recreating the illusion of crystal starry night, annihilating all sensory connection to our headlong near-light-speed crawl through the god and awful void which had already put the womb-world of men far behind us.

The rite ended in a spatter of formal applause, which, in that moment, seemed as empty and transparent to me as the tele's tranking illusion. I ordered Mori to put her consoles on internal automatics, gave Argus leave to secure the bridge, and rose from my chaise to accept the customary nods of approval from the Med crew, rising from their own chaises behind me.

But as I ushered the crew out of the bridge, as I led them in the usual fashion to the usual departure fete in the Grand Palais, as I put this functional duty behind me and went to fill my symbolic role in the floating cultura of the Honored Passengers, I found my consciousness focusing not on the five who accompanied me but on the one who did not. On she whose place in the departure rite had been an empty chaise, whose role in the floating cultura would be equally defined by her absence. On my Void Pilot, Dominique Alia Wu, who would remain, or so I then thought, the unseen center of all these rituals and machineries, the invisible hub of our karmic wheel, the center which was void.

——— IV

As I sit here reviewing what I have just encoded onto word crystal, I ponder whether the scene I have just attempted to render has been infected with my present knowledge of what was to occur later, an uncrafted employment of the time-honored literary device known as foreshadowing. Or had my spirit already been warped by that single chance encounter on the sky ferry? Worse still, is psychic time, like the absolute time of pure mass-energy science, a circled serpent biting its own tail, so that future events color past perceptions, moving us along the inevitable skein of maya via ballistic trajectories of deterministic inevitability?

But in that direction lies both paranoia noir and the guiltless psychopathy that denies destiny and will in favor of surrender to all-absolving karma.

So I will plead not the excuse of karmic inevitability and return to my narrative of conventional linearity with but a passing attempt to illumine the strange mood of the Genro of that timeframe with the hindsight of this.

Which is to say that even as I led my crew down the *Dragon*'s spinal corridor toward the Grand Palais module, I do believe that I had some dim gray awareness that the void I had felt within the departure ritual, the ennui of resentment I had sensed within me for the first time toward the surrender of true functional command to the automatics, had somehow to do with the impingement upon my Captainly persona of the being of my Void Pilot.

There is no time during the voyage when the Void Captain is not in total command of his ship, or so we are taught at the Academy. The Captain commands the orbital exchange and the Flinger insertion; it is he who gives the Go command and trims vector preparatory to the first Jump. It is he who commands the Jump itself—

—then the ship is several light-years away from its previous locus, and command is resumed after a discontinuity of literally no time at all. I could count on a mean average of twenty Jumps between Earth and Estrella Bonita, three weeks during which the moments I was not in command could not be measured by man's most subtle timepiece, indeed might be said to have no duration at all.

Yet those twenty odd moments were in an absolute sense all that mattered.

As long as the Void Pilot remained a protoplasmic module in the machineries and nothing more, the illusion of total command could remain complete. But once my Pilot had acquired a name in my consciousness, a name with tales attached to it—in short, humanity and a personality—I could no longer entirely blind myself to the fact that I too was in a sense a protoplasmic module in a complex of automatic machineries, a subjectivity cyborged to the objective mechanism of the ship. Did not all my commands in truth amount to naught save the activation of computer-generated programs, programs that I myself had not personally crafted since my tour as Interface?

When then was I truly in command in the ancient seafaring sense?

Even then, as I led my crew into the Grand Palais, I

believe I had achieved—if it is not too rich an irony—an enhanced perception of the inner wisdom of the custom of sequestering the Captain from personal contact with his Pilot, a foreshadowing in real and not literary time of worse things to come.

But this dark mood lifted as soon as I made my first entrance of the voyage into the inner world of the Grand Palais. For here was the other sphere of my Captainly duties, and one that admitted not of mechanistic distancings or excessive objectivization of my central role in its subjective reality.

Indeed, absolute perception of our objective reality was exactly what it was designed to avoid.

In objective reality, five dozen humans were to spend the next three weeks sealed in a series of metal canisters, insulated from the absolute reality of the absolute cold, absolute lifelessness, absolute immensity, and absolute indifference to the human spirit of the deep void between the stars. Long experience, dating back to the dawn of the First Starfaring Age, had shown that naked exposure to the psychic reality of the void was as deadly to the spirit as naked exposure to the physical reality would be to the flesh.

In those bygone days when starfaring meant generations spent in a single voyage, it was soon learned that only ships large enough to be worlds entire could sanely convey their human cargo from star to star, indeed that further, only carefully crafted shipboard cultures would prove viable: those in which rite, art, festival, entertainment, indeed interior architecture itself, were all designed to concentrate consciousness on the world inside, and to avoid excessive true awareness of the absolute reality without. Vast transparent vistas of the starry glories, while technically feasible and esthetically satisfying in an absolute sense, proved ultimately destructive to the soul. Consciousness liberated from ritual, custom, and role, while part of the general philosophic bravery of the age, proved too naked and vulnerable in the face of true chaos; indeed, our current acceptance of the quotidian metaphors for the absolute as necessary psychic artifacts is thought to date from this confrontation of total clarity with total necessity.

Apres the Jump, with voyage times reduced to weeks instead of generations and the electrocoma storage of passengers reducing the subjective duration to zero, it was first assumed that Void Ship crews could endure the naked absolute. Indeed many did. But too many did not.

Thus the institution of the society of Honored Pasengers and the Grand Palais, not out of desire to increase the profitability of the voyage—for a long time these fares were subsidized at a loss—but out of the necessity to create for the crew an interior world not merely of artifact but of culture, not merely of thing but of spirit; rich enough, complex enough, *human* enough to focus attention on the reality within rather than the void without.

Only later, when starfaring became the ultimate pastime of the rich and the wanderer, the seeker and the ennui-ridden, did the fare rise far beyond the point of economic profitability, did ship vie with ship in the luxuriousness of its Grand Palais and the hedonics to be found therein, did figure and ground reverse themselves, did the floating cultura and its endless fete become its own raison d'etre, did Captain and crew become personas in a system of shipboard dynamics designed as much for the savor of the Honored Passengers as for the mental centering of the ship's officers.

The *Dragon Zephyr* configuration contained one standard stateroom module quartering fifty Honored Pasengers, the domo, and the staff of ten freeservants. While this mandated a single Grand Palais module of standard volume, the Grand Palais *Zephyr*, like all such modules, was a sui generis and idiosyncratic work of art within its standard cylindrical shell.

The main passage from the *Dragon*'s spine debouched directly into the grand salon deck, following the usual esthetic logic. What was a functional steel safety door on the outside was abstracted filigreed brasswork on the inside and opened onto a dramatically lit pink marble platform for grand entrance sake. This in turn was the capstone landing of a short curving flight of marble stairs down which all who entered must promenade in full sight to reach the main floor of the salon.

The main floor itself was a rather cunning sort of integrated environmental sculpture in assorted polished and occasionally carven hardwoods, carpetings of many different textures, hues, and designs, and plushed cushions sensuously curved in rather anthropomorphic shapes. There were no furniture, consistent floor, or ornamental sculpture as discrete elements; rather chaises, conversation pits, tables, wooden sculptures, cushions, und so weiter flowed and metamorphosed into each other, indeed seemed to evolve out of each other in an organic whole of many subtle levels, sublevels, and gradations in an artfully chaotic multiplexity seemingly as convoluted as the human brain.

Hanging high above in the vaguely burgundy shadows of the overarching ceiling was a huge mobile chandelier of multicolored crystals lit from within, a dazzlingly complex dance of orbiting elements softly dappling all below in an ever-changing prismatic pavane. In addition, small spots, glowing globes, candled sconces, and holosimed fires added dramatic highlights, subtle counterpoints, circles of brilliance, to the overall spectral complexity of the whole.

Across from the main entrance, a kind of ramp or balcony began at mean floor level, spiraling twice around the zebrawood walls before disappearing through an archway high above us. This was scattered with tiny cafe tables and chairs whose legs were cunningly crafted in an asymmetric manner to remain level against the subtle pitch of the ramp for those who preferred an observatory tete-a-tete to direct participation. Visual artworks in various modes formed a mini-museum along the walls of the ramp, which also triplexed its function by leading to the vivarium above, which was both the "top" deck of the Grand Palais and its esthetic piece de resistance.

The departure fete was in full flight as I paused on the entrance platform with the full muster of my crew behind me. All the Honored Passengers were in attendance in their finest plumage; freeservants emerged via the lift from the cuisinary deck below bearing silver trays of hot viands to augment the scattered cold buffets; floaters of beverages circulated among the revelers, fumes of assorted intoxicants perfumed the air; focused musics in various styles harmonized into an overall fugue from this aural overlook. The essential ambiance of the floating cultura was in full flower. Our Domo, Lorenza Kareen Patali, had thusfar done herself proud.

This was hardly surprising; for although I had never shipped with Lorenza before, her repute was wide in more modes than one, and her name tale was au courant among Void officers and floating cultura alike.

Her father, Patali Ktan Abrim, had been that rarity, a Void Captain who had cunningly invested his wage in mercantile realms, and who upon retirement chose to join the floating cultura itself as an Honored Passenger. Her mother, Kareen Mirne Mois, had inherited vast wealth as a young child of fortune, had chosen to spend it in the floating cultura, had met Patali Ktan Abrim five years before his retirement while an Honored Passenger on his ship, the *Star Phoenix*, had thereafter been an Honored Passenger on every ship under his command, and no doubt had decisively influenced his ultimate choice of retirement venue.

Lorenza Kareen Patali had been conceived by this pair on the *Unicorn Garden*, had been born on the *Flame Mountain*, had been raised to womanhood in the floating cultura by her parents, who voyaged together to this day, and prided herself on never having set foot on a planetary surface.

Her freenom, Lorenza, she chose upon her first appointment as Domo de Grand Palais homage a Lorenzo the Magnificent, a perhaps legendary doge of the perhaps legendary terrestrial city of Venice, famed in lore as a patron of art, opulence, and decadently magnificent hospitality.

It was gossiped among officers that Lorenza Kareen Patali sought after her own Void Captain with whom to recreate the love story of her parents. It was said she possessed the wealth to confer the boon of eternal Honored Passenger status on whom she chose; it was also said that she had never shipped with a Void Captain who had not become her amour in flesh as well as metaphor.

This apocrypha certainly lost no credence in my eyes at the sight of the woman slowly and dramatically mounting the stairs toward us in a flourish of her flowing garments, playing to the hushed revelers below with full consciousness of her thespic beauty.

Tall and sinuous, long of limb, petite of bosom, she wore a long train of some silvery gossamer gathered into an artificial waist just below her bare breasts by a wide dirndl so encrusted with multicolored gems that the color of its matrix material remained a mystery. From her shoulders flowed a long, high-collared cloak of black velvet veined with traceries of silver thread. Her nipples were capped by silver brooches upon which blazed huge rubies lit from within. Her long blood-red hair was helmeted above her head, secured in place by strings of Tartanian snow-pearls. Her skin was a preternaturally lustrous black, her features thin, delicate, but dramatically chiseled, and her eyes a lucent sapphire blue.

Even in an age when a woman's appearance could be an entirely self-crafted work of art, indeed perhaps *because* mere genetically inherited beauty could be simulated at whim by the biocosmetician's skills, Lorenza Kareen Patali's fleshly persona was outrageously audacious in its outre concept and entirely stunning in its successful execution.

"Salutations and greetings, Captain Genro Kane Gupta, and welcome to the fete," she said in an intimate purr that yet carried for effect to the far reaches of the salon. She held out her hand for my greeting; I took it, raised it in the general direction of my lips, but did not kiss.

"Bienvenidos, Domo Lorenza Kareen Patali," I replied with equally thespic formality, pitching my salutation to encompass the Honored Passengers below, and turning my head to face them. "Salutations to your Honored Passengers, from your Captain and your crew."

Following the ritual with punctilio but also with a certain detachment of attention, I introduced Interface Argus Edison Gandhi and Man Jack Mori Lao Chaka in that order and in those functional terms as protocol dictates. Each in turn bowed briefly to the salon, to the Domo, to the Captain, and then descended individually, basking for a moment in the full attention of the floating cultura before being absorbed into it; Argus with a certain would-be Captainly hauteur, Mori with the more forthright enthusiasm of the junior officer.

"Your Med crew, Maestro Hiro Alin Nagy, Healer Lao Dant Arena, Med Man Jack Bondi Mackenzie Cole . . ." These three I introduced all together as a functional unit, and as a triparte unit they descended the stairs together with more perfunctory bows, metaphoric of the Med crew's role of dedicated detachment from the voyage-long fete of the floating cultura.

"Allow me, my Captain," Lorenza said ceremoniously, hooking my arm in hers.

"My pleasure, Domo Lorenza," I replied formally, and we descended arm in arm into the fete, which, with the customary stylization of hushes and flourishes, resumed its previous pavane of varied amusements ere we had reached it, allowing Captain and Domo their traditional interval of initiatory acquaintance.

The origin of the duet of Captain and Domo played out for the delectation of the floating cultura is lost in the distant mists of starfaring's antique social evolution, but its post facto rationale in shipboard dynamics is taught at the Academy.

As the Captain serves as the apex of the crew, so does the Domo serve as the apex of the Honored Passengers. The Captain, the yang, maestro of the propulsive, the exterior, the objective component of the voyage, derives his hierarchical pouvoir from his functional position atop the structure of the crew; he is defined by his authority to command. The Domo, the yin, maestra of the nurturative, the interior, the subjective component of the voyage, derives not pouvoir but puissance from her psychic position as the focus of the Honored Passengers' collective desire; she is defined by her ability to please her clientele with artistically, libidinally, and socially satisfying ambiance.

Thus, the multiplex dualities of the voyage—the yang and the yin, the propulsive and the nurturative, the objective and the subjective, the hierarchical and the democratic, pouvoir and puissance, the exterior and the interior, the cold, dark void without and the bright, glittering complexity within—are embodied and metaphored in the Captain and the Domo.

Ideally, their duet d'amour embodies the higher unity that transcends these dualities of maya, expresses and confirms the ultimate source of social, psychic, and spiritual energy in the dialectic between yang and yin, objective knowledge and subjective desire, that phenomenon of the interface between that is both spiritually subjective and a biological mass-energy reality—the libidinal tension, the prana, that some identify as the life force itself.

On a less metaphysically exalted level, the ritualized affair d'amour between Captain and Domo serves to maintain the necessary psychosexual distance between both Captain and Domo and the ever-shifting patterns of lustful liaison that dance to the sybaritic music of the Grand Palais. While both Captain and Domo are free to indulge their caprices d'amour from moment to moment with Honored Pasengers of the floating cultura, their traditional voyage-long liaison—sometimes mere useful metaphor, frequently not—maintains their roles as archetypal embodiments of the overall shipboard dynamics of yang and yin and prevents them from forming liaisons of the heart with those to whom they must remain living but psychically distant metaphors if dynamic balance is to be maintained.

Thus are we taught at the Academy. In the unofficial lore bandied by officers, elaborate jocularities are derived from the notion that in Captain and Domo do the opposite worlds of bridge and Grand Palais maintain cordiality in the face of inherent psychic differences, even as men and women, through the aqua regia of sexual congress.

Truth be told, I have long believed that the custom is one of those inner mysteries of archetypal drama whose highest function is to remain forever beyond the final analysis of the actors involved.

And my curious reaction to the fabled and dazzling Lorenza Kareen Patali did little to disabuse me of this paradoxical conviction.

It goes without saying that my organism was lustfully magnetized by this persona of all fleshly desire, whose every detail was magnificently crafted to evoke just this response; the diaphany of her gown, the jeweled brilliance of her rubied nipples thrust upward by the tightly cinched dirndl, the velvet texture of her ebon skin, the sapphire sparkle of her glowing eyes, even her rosy musk, which seemed all but designed to accord with my pheromonic ideal of womanly savor.

And as she conducted me on the customary grand tour of the Grand Palais module, which she had crafted, both traditional archetype and personal attentions served to focus the full puissance of this feminine armamentarium on the conquest of my masculine desire.

"Do try some of this wine, Captain Genro," she said, handing me a goblet off a passing floater. "Tres piquant, and rather a rare vintage." The goblet was antique gold-reddened cut crystal; the wine, though red, was cold, with a strangely refreshing, bitter afterbite; and her eyes regarded me over the lip of her own goblet with frank speculation.

"Tu tambien," I said with the expected gallantry, though of course she *was* also a rare and piquant vintage, which I knew almost as well as she did.

She laughed, took my arm again, and danced me about the grand salon, displaying for me the artifacts and effects she had gathered, displaying me as well for a brief choice selection of the Honored Passengers who had chosen to voyage under her esthetic direction, all the while contriving to brush briefly against me with thigh and shoulder, private glance and perfumed breath.

As much, of course, for the Honored Passengers as for myself; this too was a grace note of the total effect, which, I had to admit, was as well crafted or better than any I had experienced on previous voyages.

While the Domo is neither chef nor interior designer, composer of music nor vintner, dramaturge nor colorist, she is the maestra who directs and blends the products of these diverse arts into the whole that is the Grand Palais, the total voyage-long fete, the overarching ambient artform that will exist for this voyage alone. The style of the duet d'amour of Domo and Captain is also an element of this design—sometimes a chase, sometimes a series of dramatically feigned assignations, sometimes a complex rondole involving Honored Passengers in supporting roles, occasionally a true affair of the heart.

Here, it seemed, Lorenza was playing to her own legend as seeker after a true eternal life-mate, would-be seductrice of the Captain into the via of the floating cultura.

While the Honored Passengers to whom I was fleetingly introduced seemed a typical cross-section of the floating cultura—aging children of fortune possessed of unearned wealth, merchant princes and princesses on holiday or permanent vacation, stunning specimens of male and female beauty traveling as companions to the rich, successful artists enriching their input, less successful practitioners gifted with the voyage by patrons, assorted tropical pilot fish of the wealthy cherished for their entertainment value—there seemed to be an unusually high proportion of repeat voyagers, Honored Passengers who chose to follow Lorenza Kareen Patali from voyage to voyage rather than flit from Domo to Domo sampling eternal variety in the more usual mode.

A few of these—a tall, somewhat anguished-looking merchant from Heimat, Korma Ori Sandoval; an ancient jeweled femme named Sandra Roche Pandit; Picasso Lar Colin, a flashily dressed painter of some repute—seemed wistful suitors for Lorenza's attentions. but others, exchanging fey glances with her, examining me with deliberately feigned coversion, commenting upon her brushes and touches against me in subtle ideograms of body language, seemed connoisseurs, as it were, of the mystique in which Lorenza had wrapped herself, followers of the perhaps deliberately endless tale of her search for the Captain of her desires.

I began to wonder if this romance attached to the name tale of Lorenza Kareen Patali was not part of the total persona she had crafted for herself, a deliberate touch of psychic piquancy to enrich the ambiance that was her artistic metier, as much a conscious artifice as the chandelier of light-casting crystal, the bright-blue eyes set in ebon skin, the illumined ruby nipples, the high-sculptured coiffure crusted with snow-pearls.

Thusly pondering, I began to wonder whether there was *anything* of essence within the artifice; whether this dazzling persona that so aroused my fleshly desire contained a being whose dimension extended into hidden realms of the spirit, or whether Lorenza Kareen Patali had become entirely the creation of her own consciously crafted mystique, that and nothing more. I do not know why hypothesized perception frissoned my animal appreciation of her libidinal attentions with a moue of contempt.

Following this tentative nuptial display for the delectation of her Honored Passengers, Lorenza conducted me on a somewhat perfunctory tour of the decks "below" the grand salon, apparently saving the vivarium that crowned it, the piece de resistance, for last.

Immediately below the grand salon was an entire deck devoted to the cuisinary arts. In the center was an elaborate larder, cellar, and food preparation complex presided over by Bocuse Dante Ho, a truly great chef maestro with whom I had had the pleasure of shipping twice before, master of the daring blend of contrasting cuisinary styles. Arranged in truncated wedges around this hidden hub were no less than four dining parlors in contrasting modes.

There was a great dining hall done in brass, dark woods, massive stone fireplace, crystal chandeliers, and blue-and-white brocade containing an immense circular table of carven mahogany around which the entire complement of Honored Passengers and crew could be seated for formal banqueting. A second parlor was divided up into a dozen small curtained booths for intimate dining. A third was arranged in the Han floor-sitting mode—immensely ancient decorative wall hangings, low, round red-and-black-lacquered tables around sunken braziers, an abundance of plush bodyform cushions. The fourth and plainest was deliberately severe; long tables of white wood with matching benches, floor of gleaming black tile, matte white ceiling, walls covered with stylized floral designs in bright primary colors—a pleasant enough refectory for strictly functional fressing.

Beneath the cuisinary deck was a deck devoted to the dramatic arts, thespic and musical, living and recorded. Central to this complex was a circular theater suitable for both live performance and display of the ship's large library of holocines. Around this central core, libraries of word crystals and traditional leaved books, a small chamber for intimate musical performances, a room suitable for public exhibition of the erotic arts, a storage closet boasting musical instruments spanning three thousand years of history and a multiplexity of cultural modes, a cloud chamber for light and air symphonies.

Throughout this tour of the lower decks of the Grand Palais she had wrought, Lorenza assumed a certain formal distance like a maestra of production conducting a prospective investor through the machineries of her fabrik; not, however, without the stray touch of thigh on thigh, the taste of perfumed breath on words uttered nearer than aural function demanded, her arm linked in mine all the while.

Only when we had reached the nethermost region did she grow more openly intimate. The "lowest" deck of the Grand Palais module was given over to a seemingly chaotic maze of dream chambers opening off a convoluted tunneled passageway that curved and wound around them like the interior of a great coiled serpent. The organically rounded walls of the tunnel glowed an erotic rose, a hue picked up and made palpable by the perfumed mist that filled it. Many of the chambers were already occupied, and while the interiors of most of these were screened from our view by light curtains, the sighs and moans, the rhythmic rustlings, were allowed to suffuse into the rosy ambiance of the passageway, surrounding us with the music d'amour, inevitably drawing us deeper into each other's body spaces.

Lorenza pressed her side lightly against mine and slid the arm that had been hooked in mine around my waist; I protested not.

"Let me show you what dreams and pleasures are presently available," she said close by my ear, close enough for me to feel the tickle of her breath upon it.

Side by side, virtually cheek by cheek, we peered into an impressive variety of vacant dream chambers—zero-gravity wombs upholstered in vulval pink, holoed in fire, englobed in the illusion of boundless black; simulacrums of bosky groves and grassy dells from half a dozen planets; cunning illusions of grandiose landscapes; rooms and chambers from many epochs and worlds; even a pool of some viscous rainbow fluid undulating in slow motion under enhanced gravity.

"And your pleasure, Captain Genro?" she said, slipping around to face me. "Which of these dream chambers would you choose to share?"

"I cannot answer that," I told her.

"Por que no?" she asked, her bright-blue eyes staring into mine, beacons of illusory meaning in an otherwise unreadable and entirely composed countenance.

"Because it's not a question one can answer in the abstract. It depends upon with whom."

She laughed, perhaps all too perfectly. Lightly, she snaked her hands into my hair and drew me into a short, tight embrace, a brief, deep kiss. Her mouth tasted of mint and roses; her jeweled nipples and gem-crusted dirndl embossed my flesh with patterns of delicate pain.

"For the sake of argument, then," she said huskily, drawing away but leaving her arm draped around my waist. "Which dream chamber would now be yours?"

"And yours?" I asked, challenging her with my eyes, feeling the heat of her calling to me, and yet acting out my role in this erotic pavane with a certain annoyed detachment.

"All this is mine, cher Genro," she said, leaning forward with utter precision so that the hard-jeweled tips of her bared breasts stung my chest like electrodes. "You will find me an amour of considerable variety."

"Will I?"

"In time," she said with a sublime frankness that went beyond arrogance. "But now we should finish our little tour, oui?" She ran her fingertips lightly over her dirndl, her breast brooches, her complex coiffure; a series of erotic self-caresses that both aroused my fleshly desire and focused another part of my attention on the complex artifices of her carapacelike persona. "Beauty, alas, does not always allow for function, and I am currently dressed for the former."

For a moment, lust, annoyance, and something else not easily identified synergized within me into a desire to tear away the artifices of that persona, strip her naked, and have her not in some chamber of illusion, but there in the functional passageway. But of course that was unthinkable, and besides, I wondered whether, once the wrappings had been peeled, there would be anything within.

So, without demur, and with a formal little bow of gallantry, I allowed her to lead me back to the lift, which took us directly back to the grand salon itself. The fete was in full flower; many of the Honored Passengers showed the effects of civilized intoxicants; discoursing with extravagant gestures, silently absorbed in contemplating islands of music and patterns of shifting light, caressing each other genteely in private alcoves, or staring into each other's eyes across the small private tables set along the observatory ramp that led up to the vivarium.

Argus glanced at me covertly from the center of a small group of admirers as we crossed the main floor to the debouchment of the ramp, obviously playing at officership with this self-selection of Honored Passengers, perhaps fantasizing her future as a Void Captain. Half-

way up the spiral of the ramp, we passed young Mori, her
eyes shining as she held hands across a table from a
handsome young man with a great mane of leonine curls.
Shipboard dynamics appeared to be proceeding nominally, at least where my charges and Lorenza's were
concerned.

"And now, mon Captain, the piece de resistance,"
Lorenza said as we reached the pinnacle of the ramp, a
light-curtained archway beyond which was hidden the
vivarium that capped the Grand Palais module. "I venture to warrant that even a seasoned voyager such as
yourself has never quite experienced its equal."

Indeed, vraiment, sans doubt! While all Grand Palais
modules have their vivariums, and while I had seen
many fine specimens of the genre, I had indeed never
experienced quite the equal of what lay beyond that
light curtain.

As I had expected, we stepped forth into a cunning simulacrum of nature, an interior garden under
an overarching dome. Tall, full-leaved trees of half a
dozen species had been thickly planted all around the
circumference, screening off the walls, destroying any
unseemly sight of periphery or horizon, artificial or otherwise. Jagged peninsulas of this circumferential forest
grew out randomly toward the center of the vivarium,
perfecting the illusion of a shaded dell in an endless
wood.

The garden floor was thick black loam; here mossed in
green velvet, there obscured by undergrowth fringing
the solitary trees scattered about the open space, small
islands of cropped lawn elsewhere, black baldnesses
framing artful arrangements of rock outcroppings, brilliant carpets of fungus scattered everywhere like spilled
jewels. There was a pool dappled with green lily-pads
and bright violet blooms. A shallow, winding brook bur-
bled over miniature rapids and tiny waterfalls. The distance between trees had been carefully calculated to

support a lacy overhead canopy of lianas, vines, Spanish mosses. The air was warm, moist, and fragrant with veg-etative abundance just this side of rot. Stone benches anciently patinaed with moss and wooden seats crum-bling away were the only visible human artifacts, these seeming to be subsiding into the landscape or growing organically from it.

Two things raised this vivarium from craft to some-thing approaching genius—the fauna and the sky.

Insects buzzed torpidly over the pool where frogs croaked their overfed hunger; bright-blue, red, and yel-low sauroids, tiny flashes of color, zipped through the undergrowth; shy little rodents darted across our path. And the birds! The air was alive with the song and color of hundreds of minuscule finches, like schools and shoals of tropical reef-fish taken to the skies.

And the sky itself, beyond the thin overhead canopy, was that of late Earth evening, a deepening blue directly overhead, purpling toward black in the direction of the unseen horizon, where, in the "west," a smoky orange slice of sun flared somberly as it set through the obscur-ing foliage, streaking the sky with streamers of mauve, deep pink, and rose.

We walked for long, silent moments along the edge of the brook, beside the forest pool, serenaded by the birds, steeped in the eternal sunset. Few Honored Passengers were in evidence, and these for the most part solitaries absorbed in themselves. After a time, we found an iso-lated stone bench highlighted in a magic circle of rose-colored light that poured down through a small break in the forest canopy.

"You asked me which dream chamber I would chose to share," I said, drawing Lorenza down beside me. "Now I have found it."

"Here?" she said with a moue of distaste, if not of sheer alarm. "In the dirt and shrubbery perhaps, or on this bed of stone? Que drole, Captain Genro! You are of course not serious. In any event, I am hardly dressed for

the sharing of such a bizarre fantasy, even should it arouse me to ardor."

"Of course," I said ambiguously, staring at this creature of jeweled and crafted artifice, this woman who prided herself on never having set foot on a planetary surface, and wondering how she had brought such a place into being. And why. And whether for her this was merely an exercise of technical craft, sans spirit. And how it could be possible for one to coldly create such art while remaining indifferent to its own essence.

Now it was growing noticeably darker; the sky above us was deepening to black, the sun had disappeared behind the forest wall, and the last faint rays of gauzy light were peeling back from the body of night.

"Night follows day here?" I marveled. "You have arranged that as well?"

"Naturellement," she said evenly. "It is the logic of the form, is it not? Projected on the dome is a holocycle; at times there are clouds for sunrise or sunset, the program is randomized a la brute nature."

From behind a copse came the intrusive sound of human footsteps, and a moment later came the most intrusive of all possible human apparitions—Hiro, Lao, and Bondi, my Med crew, wrapped in some technical conversation, darker birds of omen, harbingers of another reality.

"—remarkable parameters—"

"—we shall see after the first Jump—"

"—could last another ten years—"

"Ah, Captain Genro," Maestro Hiro Alin Nagy said by way of greeting, his swarthy face a mask of abstracted concentration under a short cap of black hair. "We were just discussing the med profile of our Pilot, an amazing specimen. . . ."

I could feel Lorenza tensing beside me; a new aura of chill seemed to emanate from her, and this did not seem a matter of persona.

"Domo Lorenza," Hiro said formally, apparently from

the look of him picking up the same vibration. Here was another aspect of the Med crew's alienation from the floating cultura, a subtle pariahhood that even I at this moment could sense.

"We were just returning to the sick bay in any event," Lao said uncomfortably. A slight gray-haired man of advanced years and sensitive brown eyes, he at least seemed unhappily aware of the unwelcomeness of their presence.

"Indeed yes," Hiro said obtusely. "Soon it will be time for our first Jump."

With that, and perfunctory bows, the three of them departed. But the spell of the garden, if only in my own consciousness, had been broken. With a furtive look above, Lorenza rose from the bench.

"It is time we too departed, ne," she said. "I must see to my Honored Passengers, and you . . . you, mon cher, will soon have your duties to attend to as well. . . ."

Following the line of her glance, I saw that above us the sun had fully set, and all at once the stars had come out, and not via the slow stepwise pinpricking into visibility of a simulated planetary night seen through a misty and comforting curtain of atmosphere.

No, the holoed illusion had vanished entirely, and the dome now functioned as a direct tele, its only concession to artifice the spectral compensation circuits. Now the full metallic brilliance and icy black emptiness of the naked void itself howled in upon this ersatz garden, upon we poor ostriches hiding our heads in the sands of illusion from the full and terrible perception of that infinite night through which the shadow world of the ship presumed to pass.

V

"**J**UMP DRIVE GENERATOR activated on standby . . . parameters nominal. . . ."

The first red command point lit up on my console.

"Jump Circuit electronics activated . . . parameters nominal. . . . Harmonizer circuits activated on standby . . . parameters nominal. . . ."

One by one, the amber ready points lit up before me as Mori scurried along the bank of monitors rimming the curving front wall of the bridge. As she scrambled back and forth before the chest-high monitors, her eyes fixed on her instruments as she chanted her part in the ritual, I understood for the first time, or at least had the unique perception, that these consoles had been so arranged as a piece of psychic engineering.

After all, they could more conveniently have been heaped up around the Man Jack's chaise; there was no purely functional need to string them out along the curve of the bridge's "bow" like a retaining wall. Indeed, this was an inefficient arrangement that forced the poor Man Jack to hop about from one to the other like a slavey.

But without this curved retaining wall of instruments, this fence between us and the lip of the abyss, this foredeck railing, if you will, the three of us would have been vertiginously planted on the bridge deck surrounded by a sea of stars with nothing to keep a random breeze or a fumblefooted stumble from spilling us over the edge into the infinite void.

Naturellement, in reality the starry sea was but a color-corrected tele image; we were not on an open deck but in an enclosed capsule, and there were no galactic breezes or waves about to sweep us away. The mind understood this, but now, close on to the first Jump, with no projected maneuvering grid to fracture the totality of the illusion, the spirit could begin to wonder.

". . . Primer circuit activated on standby . . . parameters nominal. . . . Pilot in the circuit . . . life signs within acceptable parameters . . . checklist completed, and all systems ready for the Jump."

Mori glanced back at me expectantly, her young face bright with anticipation, her eyes eager yet professionally cool. "Take your Jump position, Man Jack," I ordered from my Captain's throne, feeling a certain tightness in my voice, the usual building of tension.

Mori took her seat beside Argus, who now began her own brief speaking part in the ritual.

"Ship's position and vector verified and recorded . . . vector coordinate overlay computed—and on your board, Captain Genro!"

Two more red command points lit up on my console, and now I had reached the peak moment of total command. "Dumping vector coordinate overlay into Jump Circuit computer," I announced, touching the first command point.

Now the vector coordinate overlay that Argus had computed was programmed into the Jump Circuit Computer: a specific solution to the equation that related the mass-energy universe to the co-extensive non-Einsteinian psychesomic space of the Jump, which would guide—or force—the mindfield of the Pilot and the congruent mass-energy phenomenon of the ship through that ineffable Great and Lonely and out the other side in more or less the right direction.

All my ready points remained amber. I touched a second command point. "Jump Field aura erected."

Three soft musical notes sounded throughout the ship, the traditional announcement of an impending Jump. Now the *Dragon Zephyr* was entirely englobed in the complex energy field known as the Jump Field aura. My ready points all stayed amber, indicating that the Jump aura was in the proper configuration without breach or waver, that the Jump Circuit electronics were still functioning nominally, that the Harmonizer was ready to tune the ship's Jump aura to the Pilot's mindfield, impressing the higher psychesomic coordinates on the lower mass-energy pattern that was the ship, pulling it into the Jump as soon as I touched the final red command point.

As I always do, as all Void Captains surely must, I paused for a long contemplative moment, taking a slow intake of breath as my finger poised just above this point of ultimate command.

What actually happens during the Jump? A schematic description is possible. When I touched the command point, the Primer circuit would boost the Pilot's nervous system into total psychesomic platform orgasm; simultaneously, the Harmonizer would sync the Jump aura with this psychoelectronic configuration, the Jump Circuit computer would overlay this combined field with the vector coordinates, and—

--the ship Jumps.

But what happens during the Jump? What does the Pilot do, what does the Pilot experience, in that eternal nanosecond of psychesomic orgasm?

An electrophysiological description of psychesomic orgasm is possible. The Primer circuit simultaneously stimulates the Pilot's nervous system to sexual orgasm, nirvanic fugue, alpha wave peak, vagal spasm, adrenal

flush, and about twenty other less drastic electrophysiological cusps. And keeps her there for something less
than a micromininanosecond of objective time, for the
timeless subjective eternity of the Jump.

But what happens there in the discontinuous Great
and Only? How does the Pilot Jump the ship? How does
the vector coordinate overlay usually enable her to Jump
it in more or less the right direction? Why do the lengths
of the Jump vary with such total unpredictability?

A psychoelectronic theory of the Jump more or less
exists. In psychesomic orgasm, the electronic hologram
in four-space that is the Pilot's psyche becomes co-
extensive with the space-time hologram that is the total
eternal universe, existing in this hypothetical Jump
space for a literally timeless moment co-extensive with
eternity itself. The vector coordinate overlay somehow
serves as an "anchor" to four-space, pulling Pilot and
ship back into what we are pleased to call "the universe,"
several light-years more or less along the computed
vector.

Or so we are taught at the Academy. By this process
do we mighty Captains con our ships between the stars!
Do you begin to appreciate the true discontinuity between Void Pilots and quotidian humanity?

Then consider this ultimate mystery of the Jump: the
process itself was developed from a cryptic device found
in the neat and perfect ruins left by that long-vanished
race who identified themselves only as We Who Have
Gone Before, after thirty years of experiments on a
purely trial-and-error basis.

So as I sat there on my throne of command, my finger
poised to initiate this literally timeless process beyond
my true comprehension or control, I held my breath for
a long moment, staring out into the sea of stars, the
infinite universe of matter and energy which we are
pleased to call the void, and for the first time, that awesome vista seemed no more an absolute reality than its

image on the great tele before me. The tele image was a color-compensated mask beyond which lay the naked universe itself; was this not in turn a mask of matter and energy, the final veil of maya, behind which lurked, beyond which lurked . . . ?

I blinked. I forced myself to exhale slowly and completely. Even as I first realized that it was there, I forced myself to banish the name of Dominique Alia Wu from that corner of my consciousness where I suddenly found it lurking, the human personification of that mystery, the psyche behind that functional glob of protoplasm known as the Pilot wired into the circuit that ended at my fingertip. I perceived a new level of the time-honored wisdom that isolated the Pilot from human intercourse with Captain and crew; now that it had been breached, however briefly, I saw that she had already perturbed the equilibrium of my spirit, the focus of my will to put her through the Jump.

I stared intently into the starry sea, using it as a mandala to center my being on the moment at hand, to banish these dark musings. I was the Captain, this was my ship, and here was the realm through which I would now sail her. "Jump!" I shouted, and as of old, I played the time-honored and futile Captain's game of trying to perceive the starfield's shift as I touched the command point.

And as of old, failing. One instant the stars were in the previous configuration, and then in another, no motion, no blurring of image, no instant of discontinuity that the human eye could record.

We were elsewhere. We had Jumped.

Argus projected a gridwork across the naked countenance of these new stars. Ghost images of other starfields flickered rapidly across the tele, doubling vision, tripling it, as the computer sought to match reality with the perspective patterns in its memory bank. In less than a minute, this process ended as one of the memory images locked in, synced to the master image of the reality without.

Numbers flickered across the tele, then held. Mori let out a wordless cry of approval.

"Four-point-oh-one light-years," Argus said proudly. "Radial deviation from nominal course .76 percent. We couldn't ask for a better Jump, Captain. Congratulations."

"Thank you, Interface," I replied somewhat hollowly, wondering, in truth, who was really being congratulated for what.

Wandering under the bright morning sky of the vivarium not long after that first Jump, inhaling the life-redolent air, listening to the converse of the twittering finches, observing small groups of Honored Passengers walking, conversing, assignating, and in general acting very much like strollers in any planetary garden, I wondered, perhaps for the first time, why they all chose to be Honored Passengers in the first place.

To travel from star to star? But that was achieved more easily and at far less cost by the ten thousand the *Dragon Zephyr* carried in electrocoma; go to sleep at your point of origin, awake at your destination with no passage of subjective time, and with nil expenditure of lifespan in the bargain. To experience the adventure and romance of sailing the starry main? But Honored Passengers hardly deigned to admit awareness of the ship's passage into their consciousness; everything in the Grand Palais, like this planetary simulacrum, was designed to deny it.

Of course I knew full well that the true answer was to enjoy the endless fete of the floating cultura itself; people chose to be Honored Passengers for the ambiance created for them by Domos such as Lorenza. But if the floating cultura was its own tautological raison d'etre, why then did it need the venue of Void Ships to exist?

Could not all this as easily be called into being on a planetary surface or an orbiting pleasure palais?

Obviously not, since no such phenomenon existed. There must be an inner reason, some subtle and deeper psychic need buried within these seemingly straightforward devotees of the hedonic arts, a call from the void to their spirits of which they were consciously unaware, which, paradoxically, they spent their endless voyages both seeking and fleeing.

Truth be told with hindsight's vision, these musings were no doubt the externalization of the roilings and bubblings beginning to stir the deeper waters of my own being. Why had *I* devoted my life to this selfsame starfaring? To share the vie of the floating cultura in the only way feasible to my economic station? To experience the variety of the far-flung worlds of men? To encompass the exhilaration of command? To gaze from my Captain's throne into the starry seas and know the full soul-stirring glory of confronting the void absolute?

All this had always seemed well and good, but now, although I knew not why, it was beginning to seem like another veil of maya, a tissue of illusion that was beginning to shred. Like some primal lungfish confronting the interface between sea and air for the first time, I could dimly sense some evolutionary force urging me onward into the fearful unknown.

"Ah, Captain Genro, I surmised that here you might be found."

Lorenza Kareen Patali had appeared around the next bend of the brook, seated on a stone bench amid a brightly plumed entourage, reminiscent, in that moment, of the flock of tiny finches twittering in the willow above it. Four men in suits of green, crimson, ice blue, and white, the latter two sporting cloaks of contrasting brown and black; a short, buxom blonde woman of ripening age in a suit of gold with high, tight black boots, and a tall, spectrally thin woman magnificently clad in a knee-length gown crafted of some arcane material perfectly simulating the tail plumage of a male peacock.

Lorenza herself was attired in understated contrast to both her companions and her previous persona. Halter and shorts of white silk and calf-high white boots, all plain and unadorned, were her only garments, but these, set off against her velvet black skin, created a stunning harlequin effect. Not a jewel was in evidence, and her long hair flowed over her shoulders and breastbone in artful disarray.

Whether this effect was calculated for my benefit I knew not; certainement, it aroused a less ambivalent desire than her previous style, sufficient to burn away my complex mental mists in the fire of unalloyed sexual lust.

"Come sit beside me," she invited amid the flutterings and rustlings of her standing flock, whom she introduced in a chirping of syllables that passed through the forefront of my attention without leaving a significant memory trace.

Similarly, the ensuing idle discourse made scant impression at the time, still less in memory's recollection. Two of the men, Seldi Michel Chang and Peri Donal Jofe, green- and white-clad respectively, were obviously longtime devotees of Lorenza's voyages; amours of one time or another—as, I surmised, was the woman dressed as a peacock. The other woman was a light composer of some obscure renown, and the men in blue and crimson were traveling merchants. The talk of connoisseurship—the vintages of the Grand Palais's cellar, comparison of Bocuse Dante Ho with other chef maestros of renown, who had worn what at the departure fete, amateur critiques of various holocines, the psychic effects of sundry drugs, und so weiter.

In this refined discourse I took little active part, nor, really, was such expected of me. The true interest, the inner dialog, lay, for Lorenza, myself, and our audience, in the placing of her hand on my knee, the covert stage glances between us, the languages of our bodies as the pavane of assignation was played out in public for the amusement, delectation, and perhaps somehow the reassurance of our Honored Passengers.

Now I took an unselfconscious pleasure in the playing out of my Captainly role; perhaps there was as well reassurance for myself as I allowed sexual magnetism and the ritual of the cultura to sync the focus of my being into the expectations inherent in my persona, banishing the tension between inner and outer man. Or perhaps banishing, for the moment, the inner man himself to the subworld whence he had intruded upon my tranquillity. Thus the wisdom of properly crafted ritual—and its folly.

After a time, our audience detected that the first movement of the piece was over, and, with bows, hand kisses, exchanges of glances and body signals, they made their departures, whispering and gossiping their way among the trees, perhaps inspired to intrigue d'amour of their own by our archetypal example.

Lorenza arose, drawing me to my feet by the hands, stretched in languid invitation, gazed at me with those sapphire-blue eyes. "You have noticed, have you not?" she said.

"How could any man have not?" I replied gallantly.

She laughed a bit perfunctorily; a moue of impatience seemed to form on her lips. "I mean that I am more suitably attired for amour," she said, touching a finger to the fastener between the cups of her halter, another to a strip running down the front of her shorts. "A touch here . . . and here . . . and voila, the inner woman."

"To please your perception of my taste?"

"Por que no?" she said, shrugging. "As I informed you, I will prove an amour of considerable variety. At another time, you will grant me gallant reciprocation, ne?"

"Certainement," I replied, glancing about. The vivarium, though, was relatively crowded at this juncture; seclusion for long seemed unlikely, and public performance less than genteel for this occasion. "I venture not to suggest this natural venue."

"You have now a choice of dream chambers?"

"Your stateroom and yourself would be dream enough for now," I said. "I need not alloy with fantasy such an enticing reality."

She wrapped her arm around my waist and drew me close. "For now," she said, "like this ship, I am under your command. Later, I shall school you in the sensory refinements."

And so, our bodies pressed together, our arms around each other's waists, we promenaded out of the vivarium, down the ramp to the main floor of the grand salon, across it, up the display stairs to its entrance, through the passageways of the ship, to her private chamber. All under the approving gaze of multitudes of Honored Passengers, freeservants, and even Mori, who favored me with an engaging smile.

Of what transpired between Void Captain Genro Kane Gupta and Domo Lorenza Kareen Patali in her stateroom, there is much to say and little. Lorenza's body sans its final scant bits of concealment provided but one slightly unexpected frisson of surprise—the hair of her pubes matched the red hue of her long mane. As to whether this verified the naturality of her tresses, or, more likely, the subtlety and completion of her artifice, I retained too much gallantry to inquire. Lorenza nude differed not in total effect from Lorenza clothed, and to say that both were beautiful is to belabor the obvious.

Like any conceivable Domo, indeed like any woman of the floating cultura, she proved well schooled in the techniques of erotic performance and adept at their execution. Whatever my personal or psychic limitations, I have always cultivated the arts of civilized sexuality as well as being a natural man of no less than normal animal energy, and I think it accurate to say that my repertoire and performance thereof was, at the least, adequate to the occasion.

Together we enjoyed chingada in several configurations, amour de la bouche in equal measures, the delicate diddling of the pain-pleasure interface with no little satisfaction, and in between the less orgasmic-oriented arts of erotic massage and digitation, achieving both a satisfying prolongation of libidinal tension and an abundance of orgasmic completions.

That is the much and this is the little: that during the entire passage d'amour we practiced not those higher exercises of the tantra which seek to harness the libidinal energies and fleshly possibilities in the service of a communion of the spirit. Thus while it might be fairly said that our practices of the erotic crafts left little to be desired, it cannot be said that our duet achieved the level of true art. At the surfeited conclusion of our exercises we were no less strangers and no more lovers.

Nor, do I think, did either of us seek such higher union. Whatever the pheronomic congruences that might have drawn us together on a biological level, the psychic extension of our passage d'amour lay not in the personal sphere but the social, not in any tropism toward emotional intimacy but in our fulfillment of our roles within the shipboard dynamics of the floating cultura. The Void Captain and the Domo had successfully completed their nuptial dance; if our congress attained anything beyond the purely physical, it was this.

Afterward, we lay there on the bed quenching our thirst with dry white wine, conversing idly as we might have after sharing a well-prepared meal.

"You are quite skilled in the oral sequences, Captain Genro. I was for the most part pleasantly unable to anticipate your pauses and changes."

"Not so much through creativity on my part, I think, but due to the spontaneity of your responses, controlled, and yet with a randomness never quite predictable . . ."

"Ah, tres gallant! But one who dances well with one partner may not with the next, who in turn may perform brilliantly with a third . . ."

"To our synergy, then," I said, clinking glasses.

Und so weiter. Truth be told, once my lust had been slaked and my Captainly role performed, it was not long before I desired nothing so much as to end this unsatisfying coda, to make my exit in a harmonically benign manner. Thus I was not as perturbed as I gallantly pretended when the stateroom's annunciator interrupted these civilized banalities.

"Captain Genro . . . Captain Genro, please contact chef Bocuse Dante Ho."

"What could Bocuse want of me?" I muttered in puzzlement to Lorenza. "Surely it must be a matter for the Domo. . . ."

Lorenza shrugged in equal puzzlement as I patched through to the cuisinary deck. "This is Captain Genro . . ."

"Bocuse here, mi Captain," said the chef maestro's agitated voice. "We have here an altercation between one of my freeservants and an officer. Unheard of! Scandalous! Shit! Merde! Caga! This cannot be countenanced! You must make fini muy presto!"

"What is the problem, maestro?" I demanded.

"This officer is demanding service. It is an uproar! Grossity! I cannot create under this catastrophe!"

"What's the *problem*, man?" I snapped. "Who is this officer and why is a demand for service creating an uproar?"

"Who is this officer *is* the problem, Captain Genro. It is *the Pilot*, here in my province, and demanding the preparation and service of culinary unspeakability!"

___ VI

THE UPROAR ON THE cuisinary deck, when I arrived there with Lorenza, was perhaps not quite the catastrophe that Bocuse had painted, being confined to the sparsely occupied refectory, but I could immediately see that undoing this unprecedented knot of custom and protocol was going to take a Gordian stroke.

Dominique Alia Wu sat alone at one of the long white tables in this most starkly functional of the four dining rooms, her hands balled into fists on the tabletop before her. She was dressed, if that is the word, in a plain blue sick-bay gown, and her short brown hair had not seen a comb. There were deep black circles under her eyes, the skin of her face was somewhat greenly pale, her mouth was curled into a snarl, and, in short, she would have presented a most unwholesome spectacle at any feast.

Standing across the barricade of the table from her was Bocuse Dante Ho, a thin, elegant, dark-haired man unsuccessfully trying to calm himself, and one of the Grand Palais's freeservants, a blond young woman in full flush of outrage. Fortunately, this particular dining chamber seemed not popular at this hour, and there were only half a dozen Honored Passengers in attendance at this unseemly altercation.

Before any and all could assail my ears, I held up my

hand in a gesture of both peace and command, putting on a stern visage of Captainly ire, and demanded of Bocuse: "Why was it deemed necessary to summon me to your venue, chef maestro? And please reply with the clarity and calm of which I know you to be capable."

Bocuse could be seen to be making a strenuous effort to contain himself; indeed, it seemed to me that his jaw-clenching and deep breathing were at least partly for thespic effect. "This . . . *personage* demands service of my staff and myself, Captain Genro," he said thickly. "She has refused the request of my freeservant to be gone, she has gone so far as to deny my own authority to effi-cate her removal, and . . . and she has invoked the cuisin-ary privileges of an officer! Moreover, mon Captain, the viandry barbarism she demands I produce—*pfah!*"

"This is so . . . *Pilot?*" I asked Dominique Alia Wu sharply.

"That I wish to be fed nourishment for my body? Ja-wohl! That I have the droit legal as an officer of your crew, certainement, nicht wahr? As for the barbarism of my alimentary request, de gustibus non disputandum est, ne? Besides, who better than I to judge my body's nutritive requirements? If medical verification is re-quired, secure the opinion of Maestro Hiro. I will not have my nutrients prescribed by this oaf!"

"*Oaf*, is it, you vile creature?" Bocuse shouted. "Im-becile, the art of Bocuse Dante Ho is famed throughout—"

"Quiet!" I roared. "Contain yourselves!"

Immediately, Bocuse presented me with a mask of sweet reason. "My apologies, Captain Genro. I should not have allowed the rantings of this creature to inflame my passions, this I contritely acknowledge. Pero, a kilo slab of semi-raw steak of beef encrusted with melted cheese, garnished with three fried eggs, accompanied by boiled haricots soy—does not the gorge rise? To be washed down with a beaker of milk, no less!"

The gorge rose indeed. "This is truly the meal you requested?" I asked Dominique, surmising that Bocuse was indulging in his customary hyperbole.

"My organism requires massive intakes of protein and calcium," she said, glaring at me. "This meal supplies it. But if it will end this farce, this artiste de cuisine may drown it in a sauce of his own choosing. For me, it is mere fuel, I concern myself not with esthetics."

"Merde! Sacrilege! How am I to contend with this attitude?"

"These culinary niceties are hardly to the point, are they, Genro?" Lorenza said, interjecting her secondary authority as Domo for the first time. "If we may discuss this together for a moment . . . ?" she said, drawing me aside. "You cannot allow a . . . a *Pilot* to disturb the harmonics of my Grand Palais," she told me sotto voce. "To insult and distract a truly great chef maestro. You must banish her from the Grand Palais permanently and forthwith."

"I'm afraid I can't do that, Lorenza," I told her.

"You're the Captain, are you not?" she snapped at me, eyes flashing, mouth twisted—in short, displaying more genuine emotion than during our entire passage d'amour. "Your authority is absolute."

"But she is the Pilot and technically has the rights of a ship's officer."

"Pah! It is unheard of for a Pilot to exercise them! Look at her, without even the minimal attention to grooming, and no doubt her odor matches her appearance. Observe the discomfort of these few Honored Passengers. What if she were to demand the right of attendance at banquet?"

"What if she were to refuse to enter the Pilot's module?" I pointed out unhappily.

Lorenza's tightened jaw fell. Her lips trembled for an augenblick. "Then . . . then you would force her, no? You are empowered to . . . to . . ."

"A ship will not Jump without a *willing* Pilot in the

Circuit. Long experience has established this unfelicitous fact."

"Then . . . then what will we do?" Lorenza's change of expression and her use of the plural pronoun seemed to indicate that at least her displeasure was no longer focused on my person.

I shrugged. "Under the circumstances, there is no alternative save to exercise the diplomatic arts and effect a compromise."

We returned to the suspended tableau of confrontation. "Custom and contractual droit leave me no alternative," I told Bocuse. "I must order you to fill this officer's request and to honor all such requests in future."

"This is an—"

"However," I interrupted loudly, "this meal will be served behind curtains in the chamber of booths, not here." To Dominique I said harshly: "I will join you at table, and we will discuss some necessary matters of protocol and civilized behavior."

If I had expected her ire at this public confinement to purdah, I was not to feel its weight. Raking Bocuse, the freeservant, Lorenza, and the onlookers one by one with glares of black disdain, Dominique rose shakily and slowly to her feet, not turning her attention to me until she was fully standing.

"Danke schoen, Captain," she said with an ironic gentility that seemed aimed at all but myself. "I would prefer your company to that of these shadows." She favored me with a bitter little smile. "Even if your preferred table talk be the behavior of their so-called civilization."

Naturellement, nothing she could have done would have achieved more in the way of inflicting upon me the raised brows and soured puckers of all present, nor could she have chosen a better method of preventing me from deflecting it. Though I had sought to remain neutral and impartial, her very graciousness toward me combined with her open contempt for the others to create in their eyes the illusion that the Captain had allied himself with the Pilot. Soon, no doubt, this would be transmuted into unsavory legend as the tale passed from ear to ear.

Although her gait was tottery and tentative as we walked together into the chamber of booths, I offered not my arm in support. Nor, mercifully, did she seek to secure it.

"So," Dominique said with some belligerence once we were seated across from each other in a curtained booth, "you wish to discuss protocol and civilized behavior." Now the black contempt she had publicly spared me was openly expressed in her bloodshot, rheumy, yet still darkly glaring eyes.

"Both of which you have egregiously violated."

"Indeed? And the refusal to serve an officer despite contractual droit—this is the observance of punctilious protocol, nicht wahr? My banishment from the sight of these apes humaine like some leprous beast—this, of course, is civilized behavior?"

"You are no starfaring novice," I told her. "You know full well that a Pilot doesn't . . . that a Pilot never—"

"Ventures from sick bay or her cabin to inflict reality noir upon the fantasy world of the Honored Passengers? Disturbs the social dynamics which enable these shadows to brave the void by denying its existence? Intrudes like the Ancient Mariner upon the feast?" She leaned forward on her elbows, crooked her sneer at me knowingly. "Speaks to her Captain?"

"All that," I said inanely, quite aware of my own lameness as I said it. But how *was* I to react? How does one speak of the necessities of shipboard dynamics to one whose proper role in the harmonic function of same is pariahhood? "I'm responsible not only for the safety and navigation of the ship but for maintaining the psychic tranquillity of the voyage."

"This is not the function of our so-beautiful Domo?"

"Not when an officer is involved."

"So now I am, after all, granted the status of an officer," she said slyly. "Therefore you cannot deny me the privileges of same."

"Damn it all, you know exactly what I'm talking about!"

"Vraiment, Captain," she said coldly. "Perhaps better than you do, or minimal, better than you are willing to say. I am Pilot; equipment, not crew. Thing, not human. An offense to the genteel eyes of the Honored Passengers. Voila, mon pauvre petit, I have said it for you."

"Well look at you!" I croaked. "You're . . . you're—"

"Indifferent to the appearance of my corpus material?" she suggested without rancor. "Verdad. You wish me to dress differently, I will do so in any mode you choose. Haute coiffeur, bijoux, lip paint, whatever, I do as you command in this regard with supreme indifference. Similarly, I shall take my nourishment in this closed booth and make your life the easier by intruding upon the reality of the Honored Passengers as little as possible. For that too I regard with supreme indifference."

The curtain parted before I could form any reaction to this perplexing tirade, and a sullen but carefully composed freeservant—a different one than before—placed Dominique's bizarre meal before her. On a silver salver lay a large wooden plate, a crystal wine goblet, and a silver pitcher of milk. On the plate Bocuse had arranged a huge seared slab of beef atop a bed of small boiled tan beans; this was frosted like a bare mountaintop with melted white cheese. Atop the cheese, he had placed the fried eggs to resemble a garish face—two gross yellow eyes, a bulbous nose consisting of the third egg nostriled with peppercorns, and a sprig of greens for a gaping mouth to make the whole effect plain.

Dominique seemed not to notice this at all, or if she did, it was one more nicety to which she at least feigned supreme indifference. She poured a goblet of milk, drained it in one unseemly gulp, refilled it, attacked the viand with knife and fork, thrust a large chunk of meat and cheese dripping with egg yolk into her mouth, and did not speak again until she had thoroughly devoured it.

"But where and how and what I eat, with this I will not countenance interference," she said, washing her words down with another full goblet of milk.

"A Pilot with a hearty appetite," I managed to say as she crammed another enormous dripping morsel into her methodically masticating mouth. "Will wonders never cease?"

"That depends on your state of being," she said. "All wonders protoplasmic cease. All matter eventually as well. Every energy proceeds toward extinction through ultimate entropy, nicht wahr? But one wonder never ceases, and if one's being could remain there, neither would you. But in the meantime—in this mean space-time—there is the necessity to preserve the corpus material as long as possible. Because while there *is* a wonder which never ceases, Captain Genro, that which perceives it is alas captive to the flesh."

No doubt my expression was a ludicrous sight as I goggled at her foolishly.

"I'm confusing you, Captain, ne?" she said, never pausing in her ingestion of protein and calcium. "A Pilot is a pale, deathly creature sans concern for bodily health, sans even the power of coherent speech let alone discourse in what you no doubt regard as the mode philosophique, no?" She favored me with a vulpine smile that for the first time seemed to betray some distant hint of human warmth.

"I must confess I've never encountered a Pilot like you," I admitted rather lamely. There was an intensity about her so close to coldness, an emotionless passion, an icy fire, that prevented me from forming a coherent conscious reaction. She was total paradox. Such a creature shouldn't be.

Now she actually laughed. "Nor are you likely to," she

said. "My name tale should have told you that, were you
capable of encompassing its inner meaning. My path has
been for my steps alone."

"Is that a quotation?"

She shrugged. "Words," she said, "they are all quota-
tions, no? Not one that has not been used over and over
again. A la the atoms of this food I eat, passing from it
into my body, then beyond. The universe of matter and
energy itself consists of endlessly requoted ultimate particles, nicht wahr?"

"While pattern itself is all that marches on?"

That made her actually stop eating for a moment. She
studied me as if she had never seen me before. "You are
not a stupid man," she said in a tone of discovery untinged with any irony that I could detect.

"Then why are you so hostile?"

"Am I?"

"Yes."

Slowly, as if lost in thought, she sipped down another
goblet of milk. "Between us there is a gulf, mon cher,"
she said in a new and softer tone. "But not, I think,
hostility. That would be a thing of personality—to which
I am indifferent. Vraiment, this tension is more impersonal and deeper, both. We do not inhabit the same
reality."

"We are sitting here in a booth on the cuisinary deck
of the *Dragon Zephyr*," I pointed out. "Surely that much
reality we share."

"So?" she said ironically, fixing me with her hard, deep
eyes. "Then, bitte, you will tell me the purpose of this
ship?"

"The purpose of the ship?" What did she mean by
that? "The *Dragon Zephyr*, as you must surely know, is a
combined freight and passenger configuration with—"

"*Your* purpose," she said. "Your reality, not mine.
Chez moi, the purpose of this ship is to contain a Jump
Circuit for me to be in, and your function and the crew

tambien is to send me forth into the Great and Only. And all else is shadow."

"And the purpose of the Jump itself—"

"The purpose of the Jump is to reach that state of being which is its own purpose," she said, washing down a final morsel with the last of the milk and rising shakily from the table. I could now see that she was in far frailer physical state than I had realized; the intensity of the inner fire had masked the full extent of her physiological exhaustion.

"So you see, liebe Genro, the purpose of nutritive ingestion is to preserve the corpus material as long as possible, and the purpose of corporeal preservation is to experience as many Jumps as possible until some day . . ."

She stared silently into my eyes, and for a moment I saw not the black circles under them, the pinkening of her whites, the wasted physiognomy. What I saw was what I had seen in that moment on the sky ferry—two empty opaque orbs in an archetypal mask, empty yet bottomless like the void itself.

I shuddered inwardly. "And my purpose in this cosmic scheme of yours—?" I muttered, saying anything to break the spell.

Humanity leaked back into her eyes. She cocked her head at me, and seemed to shake it imperceptibly, an ideogram of some unfathomable regret, a frisson of hesitant mercy.

"That," she said, touching a cold hand briefly to my cheek, "is not, I think, something you would be well served to know. Though in time—quien sabe?"

Between that strange and unsettling tete a tete and the time of the next Jump, I, like the *Dragon Zephyr* itself, ran on automatics. Which is not to say I stumbled about in a zombic trance, avoided human contact, or even neglected my Captainly duties chez the floating cultura.

Far from it—the altercation between Dominique and Bocuse, the necessary nature of my resolution of it, my sharing of the Pilot's table, had perturbed the harmonics already, and my duty clearly lay, not in exacerbating the situation by behaving bizarrely or refusing to demonstrate social behavior at all, but in soothing the roiled waters.

So I mounted a Captain's banquet for the entire complement of Honored Passengers, not without much stroking and praising of Bocuse while earnestly and artfully discoursing with him on our proposals for the menu. I explained to him the practical necessity of not antagonizing the Pilot, one exasperated professional to another, and I even praised the drollery with which he had arranged Dominique's fetid fare.

As a result of these ministrations, harmony was restored between the Captain and the great Chef Maestro, and Bocuse presented a series of dishes truly representative of his genius at the peak of its form.

This savory evidence of rapport between Captain and Chef Maestro did much to erase any lingering vibrations noir between myself and the Honored Passengers by the time the long meal ended, and the rest was washed away by my easy jocularity on the subject of the confrontation, Lorenza's professionally gracious praise of my Solomonic resolution of the matter, and many wines of noble vintage.

Yet throughout my performance at the banquet, I was aware of it as just that, the Captain playing out his archetypal role of bonhomie and raconteurship. Even as I feasted on the Peking Goose with Red Heldhime Fungi, the Delight Garden of the Ten Worlds, the Marfleish Stuffed with Sturgeon Pate in Sauce Haricot Noir, the Jalapeno and Palm Heart Salad, and the rest of it—even as my gustatory sense retained full intellectual awareness of the glories of the table, I could not rid my consciousness of Dominique's "supreme indifference" to the cuisinary arts, and part of me was watching all of us as protoplasmic mechanisms stuffing fuel into our input orifices.

"Shadows," she had called .them—*us?*—and shadows they all seemed, these Honored Passengers, these brightly plumed birds of passage twittering away in their gilded cage, which, carefully obscured from their conscious perception, floated precariously in the empty infinity of the void. A void which I myself was beginning to perceive as a shadow of something even greater and more absolute beneath the mask of what I had once considered the ultimate reality.

With such outre demons gnawing at my consciousness, it took a certain social heroism, or rather perhaps a certain psychosocial skill, to allow my persona to perform its accustomed functions without realtime connection to its animating being. I began to understand those moments in which Dominique's consciousness seemed to have vacated her eyes, and now and again in augenblicks of paranoia noir, I wondered if the same might be revealing itself on my own visage.

Maintaining this dichotomy between Captainly role and psychic malaise, while a smoothly running automatic process, proved quite fatiguing, and, once the banquet had lapsed into third cordials and psychoactive herbals, I pled torpor with no little justification and repaired alone to my cabin. There reality swiftly followed artifice, and I fell into a black, dreamless sleep which mercifully lasted until it was time to make ready for the next Jump.

"—checklist completed, and all systems ready for the Jump."

"Take your Jump position, Man Jack."

"Ship's position and vector verified and recorded . . . vector coordinate overlay computed and on your board, Captain—"

"Dumping vector coordinate overlay into Jump Circuit Computer . . . Jump Field aura erected. . . ."

The chimes announced the impending Jump, all my

ready points were amber, my finger was poised once more above the Jump command point—all was as it had been more times than I could count. Not an iota of the ritual had changed.

Only the subjectivity of he who perceived it. Naturellement, I had never been intellectually unaware that the Jump Circuit my fateful finger was about to activate contained more than inanimate machineries, that below me in the Pilot's module, floating in an ersatz amnion, breathing through the umbilical mask, electronically connected to the command point beneath my finger, was a human component. But previously that objective description had truly encompassed my total existential awareness of the act I was about to perform.

But now, unwanted and unbidden, awareness of another subjectivity in the Circuit had entered my cold equations. That human circuit module now had a name, personality, a connection to my spirit. I had eaten from the tree of knowledge, or rather, perhaps, had its bittersweet fruit thrust down my throat.

Now I was all too aware of another and alien sense of purpose alive in the Circuit, another subjectivity mated to my own by the mediating machineries, and with this awareness came a disconcerting sense of the relativity of my own objective reality. To me, the purpose of the Jump Circuit was to transport the *Dragon Zephyr* toward Estrella Bonita. In Dominique's reality, though, the purpose of the Jump Circuit, the ship, indeed of myself, was, as she had put it, "to reach that state of being which is its own purpose."

Her means was my end, my end was her means; there was a tension between our realities that was almost sexual, indeed—

"Captain Genro? Is something wrong?"

Argus had swiveled around in her seat to regard me with an expression of some concern.

"Wrong?" How long had my finger been poised above

the command points? Had I lost all sense of objective time?

"My board shows all amber. Do you have an anomaly?"

"No, all amber here. You are ready for the Jump?"

"Of course," she said, giving me a most peculiar look.

"Well then . . . *Jump!*" I said, and brought my finger down on the command point.

And as I did, the grotesque image that had been coalescing at the periphery of my consciousness sprang unbidden into full fetid flower.

Via the lightest touch of my finger upon the Jump command point, I was, in cold objective reality, quite literally inducing in Dominique an orgasm far beyond anything of which I would have been capable as her fleshly lover. As long as the Pilot had been a mere protoplasmic module in the Jump Circuit, this sexual connection between Captain and Pilot, this reality which went far beyond erotic metaphor, existed not in the sphere of my awareness. But now that awareness of her as a taled name, another subjectivity, a woman, had been thrust upon me, I was aware of myself as her cyborged demon lover, as electronic rapist, yet somehow also the victim of the act as I plunged into her with my phallus of psychesomic fire.

"Jump!"

One instant the stars were in one configuration, then in another. Did I imagine that I had experienced the impalpable interval between, that I could feel her being flash through its unknowable ultimate ecstasy? Did we silently sigh in unison or mutually shriek our mute violation?

One thing was certain as I sat there trembling—I now had a far deeper perception of why Captains did not want to know their Pilots, of the wisdom of the barriers our civilization had erected between.

And having been forced to that perception, I was forced to realize as well that I had unknowingly staggered across that psychic rubicon, that it was already too late to go back the way I had come. Any attempt at willful ignorance would now be futile or worse; the only talisman against excessive knowledge that might have puissance would be more knowledge.

So, once our new position had been computed, I too took another quantum leap along the geodesic toward my terminal destination.

In violation of all unstated protocol, I made my way down the spine of the ship to the Pilot's module, lingering in the passageway outside until the Med crew transferred Dominique to sick bay so as to simulate a chance meeting.

I did not have long to wait. In a few minutes, Lao and Bondi appeared, wheeling a gurney up the passageway where I stood along the route to sick bay, with Hiro himself trailing close behind.

"Captain?"

"What are *you* doing here?"

I froze, arms akimbo, living in a nightmare of what I must have looked like to the Med crew, the violator standing over the ravished in the presence of his accomplices.

"On my way to the generator room," I extemporized gruffly. "Something of a flicker in the output, but nothing serious, I think."

The three of them looked at me peculiarly; guiltily, I thought, perhaps perceiving yet another previously unexamined psychic reality, perhaps merely projecting my own angst upon them.

But the moment passed in silence, and then they were wheeling the gurney hastily past me. Not, however, before I got a good, full look at Dominique.

Her pale sweat-covered body was partially covered by a sheet. A red welt was fading across her forehead where the electrode band had been; there was a small plexiseal over the contused pit of her right arm; and bits of grayish electrode cement still clung to her forearms and exposed nipples. Her cheeks were a hideous blotchwork of flush and pallor, and there were great blackened hollows under her grit-sealed eyes.

And she was smiling beatifically.

VII

Naturellement, because I was Captain, there was no authority aboard to whom I could confide my mal d'esprit without undermining all confidence in my command. Thus far I had been able to pass off social intercourse with the Pilot, support of her right to limited officers' privileges, even the viewing of her ravaged corpus straight from the bed of the act, as random strokes of karma or the exigencies of command, but if I bared the nature of the consciousness behind my acts to officer or Honored Passenger, surely that person would question my fitness to fulfill my Captainly role and would hardly feel bound to social silence on my behalf.

Still, there was the ghost of a shipboard tradition far older than starfaring whereby captains of lonely command might seek a certain circumscribed counsel from the ship's physician, bound as that officer was by the ancient oath of Hippocrates to silence on anything that could be construed as a private medical matter. Of course this officer was not bound to silence in extremis, that is, in cases where the dementia of the Captain endangered the ship, but some semblance of this Hippocratic discretion still survived in the Second Starfaring Age as a sort of psychic safety valve.

On the *Dragon Zephyr*, the Healer was responsible for

correcting malfunctions of body and mind, but Maestro Hiro was First Medical Officer by dint of his overall responsibility for the passengers in electrocoma, and, more apropos in this case, by his responsibility for the functional maintenance of the Pilot.

Thus, using my "accidental" vision of the severely ravaged state of our Pilot as an excuse, and not without putting on a certain false innocence about such matters, I might use my legitimate Captainly concern for the safety of the ship to circumspectly approach Maestro Hiro on the matters that troubled my spirit.

While the customary social reserve between Captain and Med crew Maestro had not been breached, I had of course perused a summary of his name tale upon assuming command of the *Dragon Zephyr*.

Hiro Alin Nagy had been born on Earth. His father, Alin Mallory Fried, was an astrophysicist of some minor renown, specializing in mass-energy aspects of the Jump. His freenom, Alin, he had chosen upon acceptance of his thesis, homage a Alin Vladimir Khan, leader of the scientific team which had finally produced the first working Jump Drive. Hiro's mother, Nagy Toda Gala, was an exobiologist who had retired to a Terran university to pursue theoretical studies relating to the failure of the multiplicity of known biospheres to crown their creation with sapience. Her freenom, Nagy, she chose homage a Galen Nagy, a biologist of the early First Starfaring Age, the first scientist to study a complex extra-solar ecosphere.

Thus from his mother, Hiro had inherited a certain interest in starfaring as well as a bent for the biological sciences, while from his father he had received an interest in the physics of the Jump itself.

His freenom, Hiro, he had chosen somewhat bizarrely homage a Hiro Karim Abdullah, an involuntarily retired Void Ship Med Maestro he had encountered as a patient in a mental retreat.

A short, dark man of the reserve traditional to his calling, Maestro Hiro betrayed little overt emotion upon being summoned to my cabin, although surely he must have been bemused by this outre procedure, especially coming so soon after the unseemly confrontation outside the Pilot's module.

After a formal offer of liquid refreshment, which was just as formally refused, I decided to come immediately as close to the point of this peculiar seance as was politic.

"I realize this is a somewhat unusual occurrence, but then it is not usual for the Captain to view the Pilot, and especially not so soon after . . . ah . . ."

A mere raising of an eyebrow; I could sense a certain distaste, a total lack of forthcomingness hardly surprising under the circumstances.

"Quite frankly, I am concerned about the physical condition of our Pilot," I said. "She seemed, well, severely depleted . . ."

A brittle and entirely humorless laugh. "Trouble yourself not, mein Captain," Hiro said brusquely. "Of all the Void Pilots I have had under my care, Dominique Alia Wu has the strongest physique. Anomalously so, in fact."

"Indeed?"

"Vraiment. An amazing specimen. Most of these creatures remain in vegetative state between Jumps. This one exercises its musculature through perambulation—as you have had unfortunate occasion to observe. Most of them will not eat and must be nourished intravenously. This one not only cooperates fully with nutritional mandation but orders up viands on the cuisinary deck to the discomfort of all."

"But she looked so pale, so comatose, so near-moribund—"

Emotion for the first time—a derisory snort, a curl of the lip, a certain moue of unpleasant superior knowledge. "Au contraire, the physiological consequences of the Jump were minimal."

"Minimal? You call that *minimal?*"

"Minimal," Hiro said flatly. "You need parallax to comprehend this, mein Captain; you should observe what most of them look like afterward." He gave me a hard, speculative look, and for a moment I felt he was perceiving my inner being, that confusion of spirit which I both sought to bare and feared to reveal.

"I withdraw that, Captain Genro," he said. "Already you have seen more than you should have. That is the true reason for this meeting, nicht wahr?"

It was, I think, a certain act of courage for me merely to nod numbly.

A certain concern for my well-being seemed to steal into Maestro Hiro's features, albeit of a stern fatherly species. "There is a paradox noir about this Pilot," he said. "I have been favored with the most superior specimen of the breed that I have ever encountered, and one, moreover, who cooperates with the recovery regime to an unnatural degree; this should please a man of my profession. Alas, it does not. There is an aura of . . . unwholesomeness here, a blackness of das energei, a . . ." He threw up his hands in a gesture of verbal defeat. "She speaks, she examines her own physiological readouts, she treats us like . . . like . . ."

"Shadows?" I ventured. "Servants of her purpose rather than the accustomed reverse?"

Hiro's eyes widened; in surprise and perhaps a frisson of sudden self-discovery. "This is your perception, Captain, or . . . ?"

"Something she said to me," I admitted. "That the purpose of ship and crew, your purpose and mine, Maestro Hiro, is to send her forth into the Great and Only, and that all else is shadow. You are as versed in the lore of the Jump as any man may be. Can you elucidate the inner meaning?"

Hiro scowled, he shrugged, he threw up his hands—all an ideogram of philosophic dismissal that was less than entirely convincing. "These creatures, when they manage a coherent sprach, babble about naught but their Great and Only, aber semantic content, nil. . . ."

"It is a reference to Jump space itself, ne?" I persisted.

"There is no such thing as Jump space, Captain, as you well know; this is a contradiction in terms."

"Well then to the Jump itself, to psychesomic orgasm, to what happens between the time I touch the Jump command point and the time the ship—"

"This interval is also nonexistent," Hiro said testily.

"To psychesomic orgasm, then," I replied with congruent petulance. "Surely you will concede that *that* exists, being a verified expert on same."

"What is the point of all this, Captain Genro? You did not truly summon me here out of mere concern for the health of our Pilot, verdad?"

"Verdad," I admitted. "Dominique spoke to me of the sublimity of the experience, I have seen the baleful physiological results, and yet . . . You have never pondered these matters, Maestro Hiro?"

"What matters, Captain Genro?" he said with what seemed to be willfully, if not fearfully, crafted ignorance.

"The essence of it, Maestro. Of the Jump, psychesomic orgasm, the Great and Lonely, the mysterious nonexistent interval, that upon which starfaring and our entire civilization revolve, the center which is void."

"So . . ." Maestro Hiro said slowly. "This Pilot, she has projected her obsessions into your mindfield, nicht wahr? 'Dominique,' you have called her? You have been favored with the tale of this name perhaps as well?"

I could only nod. "You wish to hear it?"

"Nein!" Hiro snapped with unmistakable shrillness. "It is exactly what I do not want to hear!"

"You have no curiosity about the pedigree and freenom of your patient?"

Maestro Hiro inhaled slowly and deeply, held his

breath for a long moment, then exhaled fully; when he had completed this exercise, he seemed to have composed himself by an act of will. He now regarded me with an expression of sagely and perhaps slightly forlorn sympathy.

"I begin to encompass more fully what has compelled this consultation, mein Captain, though I fear you possess not full self-awareness of what moves you," he said softly and evenly. "I have observed this cafard before in members of my own profession, aber in a Void Captain, nimmer."

"Cafard of your profession . . . ?"

"Ja," Hiro said thickly. "Once have I observed the aftermath, twice the malaise in process, and other cases are enshrined in the literature. It is why it is a grave mistake to allow oneself to regard the Pilot as a 'patient.' Why also Med crews have Healers like Lao subordinate to the Maestro, even though, naturellement, all Maestros are versed in the Healing arts. If I may presume a philosophic digression . . . ?"

"By all means," I told him. I had shipped with many Med crew Maestros, of course, but all maintained reserve, as much, I think, by psychotypical inclination as by custom, and this was as close as any had come to revealing a bit of the inner lore.

"My duty absolute aboard this ship is to keep a functional Pilot in the Circuit, ne, just as yours is to command the actuation of same. Far better than you and in sehr grimmer detail do I ken the grave physiological consequences that each Jump inflicts on the protoplasmic module. Nevertheless, my duty requires the will to inflict same; thus I must divorce myself utterly from the connection empathetique of the Healer, for my duty is *not* to the well-being of any so-called 'patient,' which in cold biological fact it contradicts, but, like you, to the service of the Jump Circuit."

Hiro leaned back slightly, and his eyes seemed to glaze

with memory's haze. "Mal suerte to any Med crew Maestro who drifts from this perception and allows himself to become infected by psychic engrams from his Healer training! Twice as Man Jack have I observed the process of this cafard d'angst. In the primary phase, the Maestros delayed the voyage by insisting on longer and longer recuperation periods, their will sapped by angst and guilt. In the phase terminal, the Maestro develops an obsession mystique, a theory manque for relating the objective parameters of psychesomic orgasm to the inner subjectivity of the Jump, and in this dismal pursuit of the unknowable, attempts to draw the Pilot into endless arcane and demented discourse upon the subject."

Hiro's eyes came back into sharp focus; he regarded me with a strange mixture of distaste and sympathetic concern. "Not lightly do I reveal this secret shame of my guild, Captain Genro. I do this because I detect certain symptoms of the primary phase in yourself, and should a *Void Captain* degenerate into phase terminal . . ." He shrugged darkly. "Quien sabe? There is no precedent. Aber, do you not now detect this conundrum nibbling at the purity of your will? Is this not the inner reason for this meeting?"

"Your insight makes it appear so," I admitted, and in truth Maestro Hiro's discourse seemed to possess a puissance that cast a harsh white light into certain of my dark corners. Yet somehow a more subtle chiaroscuro of nuanced complexity seemed obscured by the very clinical clarity of his exposition. "What then," I asked, "do you prescribe as a prophylactic?"

"Summoning my counsel is a positive indication, a sign of your awareness of the problem; at this early stage, the elevation of this perception to the conscious level is a step toward cure. It now but remains to eschew any further intercourse with the Pilot, and, contra such impulses, I may offer the following inoculation. . . ."

Hiro's countenance took on a perhaps thespically

crafted visage of lofty irony. "Namely, that the victims of this cafard are universally loathed, detested, rebuffed, and shunned by the very objects of their obsessive concern. The circle of their futility is complete."

"By the Pilot? But why?"

Maestro Hiro threw up his hands in unfeigned exasperation. "Why? Because they are *Pilots*—psychically diseased creatures addicted to that which is destroying them! Would a man of sanity demand of a charge addict a logical explanation of his passion for the electronic ecstasy that is slowly erasing the personality from his cerebral hologram? La meme chose!"

Hiro studied my face expectantly, as if seeking to read the accepted cogency of his own weltanschauung thereon. With thespic deliberance, I arranged my features in the appropriate facial ideogram, sensing that I had reached a point of finality in his reality; a void, a paradox, which he both acknowledged and chose to deny, and upon which his own psychic equilibrium seemed to be precariously balanced. I dared not seek to press him beyond this self-defined limit.

"I thank you for your wise counsel, Maestro Hiro," I said formally, but not without a certain sincerity.

"My duty and my privilege, Captain Genro. You will now meditate upon it, nicht wahr, and free yourself from this mood malo?"

"Certainement," I told him, but in the end his words had brought me no peace. For as he had first admitted and then willfully forgotten, Dominique Alia Wu was an anomaly. Far from holding me in contempt for pressing up against the interface between our realities, she seemed possessed of the will to erode it. Already she had cozened me into the queasy perception of the absolute relativity of our subjective realities, and by so doing had destroyed my unexamined conviction in the absolute objective reality of the mass-energy universe itself.

And from somewhere in the depths of that Void be-

yond the void came the seductive and fearsome conviction that, for ultimate unknown purposes of her own, she
sought to dragoon me across that abyss to the other side.

Trepidations notwithstanding and psychic equilibrium
not exactly restored, I nevertheless threw myself into
the vie of the floating cultura until the time for the next
Jump by entirely conscious act of will, determined that I
would follow Maestro Hiro's prescription at least to the
extent of avoiding all contact with Dominique Alia Wu.
Minimal, total concentration on the duties of my Captainly role would remove the temporal opportunity to
succumb to any such temptation, and there was always
the hope that right actions well and properly performed
would cleanse my consciousness of its inner perturba-
tions, just as evil deeds even helplessly committed under
karmic duress so often engrave themselves upon the
soul.

Thus I arranged luncheon with Argus and Mori and
allowed each of them in turn to invite an Honored Passenger of her own choosing to this little fete, which was
held in the Han-style dining room. As my own guest, I
chose our Domo, so that the two of us might preside over
the meal as patrons of the voyage, a gesture of respect to
my bridge officers, and a statement of harmonious shipboard dynamics in petit.

Argus Edison Gandhi was born in the rings of Saturn.
Her mother, Edison Siddi Yakov, was a mining engineer
working in the Saturnian rings aboard one of the floating stations. Her freenom, Edison, she chose homage a
Thomas Alva Edison, a legendary engineering mage of
the pre-starfaring era. Argus' father, Gandhi Rasta
Krasnya, was a starfaring commodity speculator from
Jah. His freenom, Gandhi, he chose, perhaps ironically,
homage a Mohandas Gandhi, an ancient mythic figure
devoted to altruism and celibacy.

The two met while both were on holiday in the Vale of

Kashmir, a lavish pleasureland on Earth. Having little congruence save in the realm of pheromonic feedback, they nevertheless decided to incarnate their passion out of genetic idealism. The result, Argus, was brought up in the technically demanding environment of a mining complex floating in the void close by one of the scenic wonders of the human worlds, and after a wanderjahr spent by choice as a volunteer on an exploratory expedition, inevitably chose to enter the Academy. Her freenom, Argus, she chose upon graduation, homage a the ancient archetype of exploratory adventure.

The Passenger she Honored with her invitation was apparently chosen not as a romantic favor but as a gesture of conversational amusement. Maddhi Boddhi Clear was a bizarre pilot fish in the tropical aquarium of the floating cultura. A thespic white-haired dandy of unknown pedigree, he had chosen not merely a freenom but an ersatz pedigree homage a his own vision of himself as prophet. For decades he had savored the vie of the floating cultura through the patronage of its abundance of wealthy acolytes, or those who could afford the jocularity of harboring a man who claimed to be in spiritual contact with We Who Have Gone Before.

Mori Lao Chaka was born on Zule, a thinly populated planet maintained as an unmodified primal biosphere. Her father, Lao Michel Bote, was a freehold botanical farmer on Zule. His freenom, Lao, he chose homage a Lao-tze, sage of the Tao, whose Way he sought to follow. Her mother, Chaka Kali Moon, was a botanical scientist whom her father met while she was conducting a prolonged study of certain interactions of Zule and human molecular biochemistry. Her freenom, Chaka, she chose homage a Chaka Zulu, a Terran tribal leader of the prestarfaring era.

Mori was raised on Zule, passed through a short but apparently intense wanderjahr as a random charge addict, from which she emerged with a desire to go starfaring. Her freenom, Mori, she chose homage a Mori Masu Kelly, a terminal charge addict, who had sagely deflected her vector from his own chosen path on his way to ecstatic self-extinction.

The Passenger whom Mori Honored was Rumi Jellah Cohn, a merchant artiste, a speculator in the arts of others, and creator of his own environmental holosims, the combined income from which enabled him to join the floating cultura. An urbane, handsome man, he had been seen in Mori's company on the dream chamber deck on more than one occasion, according to Lorenza.

Our chosen luncheon mode was that of the communal feast. Each communicant chose a dish in turn, seeking to harmonize its idiosyncrasy into the whole, and we all ate in the Han mode, reclining on cushions around a low table and sampling the dishes with sticks and bowls.

Mori chose first and selected Tea-Perfumed Duck in Black Morel Gravy. Rumi countered with the Twenty Garden Delights, a more austere salad form. Argus selected Fire Prawns and Phoenix Peppers, a dry-flashed curry. The prophet of We Who Have Gone Before ordered up Poached Coho Salmon Stuffed with Grand Cru Caviar in Saffron Sauce. Lorenza added balance with Ariel Vaco Steaks simply seared to succulence and served sliced with smoked mushrooms, leaving me to complete the pattern, toward which end I assayed a Puffed Omelet with Fromage et Charcuterie Beaucoup Varie.

This sort of multimode cuisinary fugue was the pinnacle of the fame of Bocuse Dante Ho, and such was the puissance of his art that even *my* consciousness was drawn from its dark musings metaphysique into the gustatory realm of the senses. Until, that is, semi-sated dining gave way to increasingly animated conversation.

The post-prandial discourse began naturally enough with appreciation of the art of Bocuse and the vintages Lorenza had stocked to complement it. Thence to a discussion of the merits of the Grand Palais of the *Dragon*

Zephyr, laudatory to our Domo. Lorenza described previous Grand Palais of her design, and I recounted my other voyages with Bocuse Dante Ho and the cuisinary marvels thereof and went on to describe Grand Palais modules from a selection of my former commands.

Only when Argus in her turn told us of her wanderjahr on the explorer *Divine Eagle* did we begin to drift into less entirely esthetic waters.

The *Divine Eagle* had spent a year extending the boundaries of the human worlds. Five habitable planets had they discovered, three with thriving biospheres. Yet of course the dream of young Argus Edison Gandhi and her gallant companions had not been realized.

"Of course the dream of all on board was to discover other sentient life. I suppose all novice starfarers are driven into their careers by that dream—to sail our little canoe into the harbor of a great celestial city, wouldn't you say so, Captain Genro?"

"For my part, the far-flung worlds of men were sufficient romance," I said lightly. "Though needless to say, I would have been pleased to make the acquaintance of advanced sapients of another breed, or even to have happened upon another set of suitably melancholy ruins."

There was laughter at this of a somewhat more nervous sort than I had intended when I used myself as a crusty salt to deflect Argus from passionate speculation on the paucity of brother sapients in our corner of the universe. In all the centuries of our human starfaring, we have encountered so little in the way of circumstantial evidence that we are not alone in a cursed creation that even a puckish attempt to deflect genteel conversation from the subject only served to fasten attention upon it.

And of course it was Maddhi Boddhi Clear who seized upon my unfortunate opening to segue artfully into the exposition of his own obsession.

"I find not what was left behind by We Who Have

Gone Before melancholy, gut Captain, nor could you call their civilization a ruin," Maddhi said earnestly. "True, our other examples of the cosmic fate of sapience are limited to two planetary ruins and three dim ancient data packets transmitted from across the galaxy millions of years ago, but We Who Have Gone Before have left us a legacy of triumph, not tragedy."

"Mon cher Maddhi," Lorenza said indulgently, "they are by their own admission *gone*, ne, and we by our own admission are here. Racial seppuku may be an esthetically pleasing fini, but does it not take a peculiar esthetic indeed to take it as triumph?"

"It is true," said Rumi, "that the world they left behind was arranged as an artistically pleasing whole, not a ruin."

"And they left us the secret of the Jump," Mori said with bright innocence. But that part of me which had been carefully and willfully removed from my Captainly persona suddenly came alive with attention. What karma moved the voyage of the *Dragon Zephyr*?

"Hardly," Argus said loftily. "They left an analog of the device which merely stimulated our own research. It still isn't even clear whether they realized they had developed a true stardrive."

"But they called themselves We Who Have Gone Before, didn't they?" Mori insisted. "So they must have *gone* somewhere. I mean, they put their planet in order, left us the secret of how to follow, and went off exploring the galaxy, didn't they? I mean, I always thought—"

"Sheer supposition. The alternate theory has equal cogency: that they played with the fire of psychesomic orgasm in a demented and degenerate religious fervor, and far from using their discovery to go starfaring, destroyed themselves with it in a racial trance state."

"But—"

Maddhi Boddhi Clear, who had indirectly catalyzed this conflict between Mori and Argus, now sought to ameliorate it, and bend it to his own rhetorical end in the process. "Both and neither, gute madchen," he said smoothly. "The evidence is contradictory only when we insist on imposing limited human matrices. It is true that from a device of We Who Have Gone Before human science derived its stardrive. True also that they conceived it not as a mere propulsive mundacity. True too that they used it as an instrument of ecstatic racial seppuku. All true and all false. For this was no suicidal religious mania but the ultimate rational act. Having extended their weltanschauung beyond the maya of mass and energy, they committed their beings to the higher reality. They have Gone Before. They have gone voyaging, but not among the stars."

"Where then?" scoffed Rumi.

"Beyond our human concept of where," Maddhi said grandiosely, but there was a sincere vision behind his eyes. "Beyond our human concept of when."

"Into Jump space itself?" I blurted.

Argus gave me a superior look. "Jump space is a mathematical contradiction in terms," she said.

"Vraiment, meine kleine," Maddhi said indulgently. "They have gone into a contradiction of our terms, a black hole through our reality construct, into the Great and Only."

"Now you're babbling like a Pilot," Argus said. There was a hush of offense around the table, and an augenblick of Dominique's presence darkened my spirit, but she pressed on. "If I understand your theory correctly, We Who Have Gone Before were in effect a race of Pilots who all together decided to Blind Jump into nowhere one fine day!"

"As a phenomenological concept, it describes the objective phenomenon," Maddhi agreed amiably. "But like all such concepts, it touches not the essence."

I was seized by an arcane sort of deja vu, not of phenomena but, like the satoric puissance of the words that had triggered it, of the spirit. In that moment, I perceived my consciousness as being in the same psychesomic state that I had experienced when I first looked into Dominique's alienated eyes on the sky ferry, when the naked stars had ripped away the sunset veil of illusion in the vivarium, as I imagined the Circuit as an electronic phallus with which I had pierced her at the moment of the last Jump. I felt myself whirling in a cold, sweaty vortex.

"But surely such a surrendering of existence for the sake of a transitory moment of ineffability is itself a sign of racial dementia," I insisted. "Our own Pilots are rare specimens of obsessive and pathological psyches."

"Certainement, mon cher," Lorenza agreed lightly. "Imagine an entire species of such creatures! Impossible! They would have famished themselves into extinction before they were fairly down from their ancestral trees!" The laughter that greeted this from all save Maddhi and myself fairly slapped me across the face with the cold hand of guilt, with the sense that I had committed treason against I knew not what.

"The moment that We Who Have Gone Before sought was not transitory, nor are they in their own reality extinct," Maddhi said testily. "They still speak to those who have ears to listen."

"Such as yourself?" Lorenza said in a tone of high amusement. "And what do they tell you, these spirits from the great beyond? What sprach of Lingo do they speak?"

"They speak not Lingo at all. I perceive them in dreams, at the hypnogogic edge of sleep, under the influence of certain molecules and charges, and what they tell me is beyond my mental constructs, beyond the present perceptions of our species, beyond linear time. . . ." He shrugged. "Where they have gone, they have Gone Before, and our time to follow them is not yet. What they tell me is something we are not yet ready to know. What they tell me is to prepare the way we too will someday walk."

"Perhaps you miss your calling," Argus suggested dryly. "Why not enter the module as Pilot?"

The visage of Maddhi Boddhi Clear darkened, his eyes seemed to cringe, and for a moment he seemed a much older and forsaken man. This ideogram of despair he then seemed to slowly erase by conscious act of will. "As you know, among our species, that high privilege is alas reserved for your own fair sex," he said dryly. "However, in certain moments of sexual cusp, We Who Have Gone Before do speak to me. Lacking the physiology to utilize the Jump Circuit, I must make do with fleshly sub- stitutes. Would you care to assist my researches in a dream chamber of your choosing?"

At this, all tension was released in ribald laughter; even Argus had to smile at the thought of sexual con- gress with her bizarre Honored guest, at her own unin- tentional jocularity in mirroring Mori's favor d'amour to Rumi with this outre choice.

"You, perhaps, ma belle Domo?" Maddhi japed, leering exaggeratedly at Lorenza. "The other possibility seems entirely occupied." This with a knowing patronly glance from Mori to Rumi.

The luncheon fete was thus allowed to exhaust itself in sexual japes and thespic play at assignations; indeed, I openly arranged dinner a deux with Lorenza as an ap- propriate gesture with which to close the festivities.

But as we retired from the dining chamber, I sought and seized the opportunity to study the face of Maddhi Boddhi Clear in unguarded repose. What I saw then was not a mountebank rogue of self-possession but an old man suffering some ineffable fatigue d'esprit, some in- ner unfulfilled longing, an anguished pilgrim behind the prophet's thespic mask.

What I perceived then was that he had deliberately and in retrospect rather crudely diverted the discourse into ribaldry when something had penetrated that facade. As if Argus' suggestion had been taken seriously by his spirit, as if her jape that he become a Pilot had chanced to touch some inner wound. Chance that his escape from this slip of the mask had been into sexuality verbal? Or something darker and deeper which was becoming increasingly more difficult for me to evade?

That part of me which had rushed to view the supine body of Dominique Alia Wu fresh from congress with the mystery of the Jump yearned to draw him aside and slake some unwholesome thirst with the loathsome semblance of a kindred spirit.

Fortunately, however, Void Captain Genro Kane Gupta was still in command, and I forswore this empathetic temptation, retiring alone behind the mask of my own persona to brood upon my all too un-Captainly thoughts.

I spent the interval between luncheon and my intimate dinner with Lorenza seeking to escape true psychic contact with my fellow beings by chatting aimlessly with as many of them as possible and seeking to escape true psychic contact with my own chaotic inner being by overloading my sensorium and thus drawing my attention outward. Most of all, of course, I was seeking to escape from the true focus of my spirit's attention, a feat of psychic gymnastics problematical even for perfect masters.

I can code those words onto crystal now, sitting here in my cabin in the doom glow of hindsight with all the deeds that were then to come already done, but at the time I had no such ironic insight. Vraiment, insight was what I both fled and sought. I certainly knew on some unadmitted level that this was true, and I knew all too well that there was only one way to lay that paradox away—exactly the path I sought to avoid. The path to where I sit now, a moral monster screwing up his courage to face crew and Honored Passengers with his own bizarre version of the standard tactic of final desperation.

Yet even now there is an ambiguity to this tale as I recite it to my own spirit in the full knowledge of the enormity I have committed. Great is the sin I have committed against those entrusted to my stewardship, great the sin that Dominique Alia Wu committed against me. Yet in some way is this not also a tragic triumph of love? Even now, I cannot decide whether I was foolish dupe or noble and tragic lover. Or whether the two are one and the same.

With Lorenza, however, no such arcanities pertained. If Dominique was the invisible focus of the inner void, Lorenza was certainly the ubiquitously visible focus of the outer reality, the fete-mistress of the floating cultura into which I sought to flee. As her amour, my social patterns were programmed by my Captainly role, needing no true attention from my troubled spirit, and our dinner a deux in the chamber of booths proceeded smoothly toward its inevitable conclusion like the oft-danced pavane that it was.

No doubt this was in great part why I had made this assignation; by throwing myself into my Captainly role, I was in some measure able to bring about an inner state of relative thoughtlessness. Moreover, Lorenza Kareen Patali as a self-created work of art was a sexual offering of great pouvoir, our pheromones were relatively congruent, and I could look forward to erotic exercises in which performance was everything and psychic connections were nothing.

We dined with the curtain drawn open, to delectate the Honored Passengers and also, at Lorenza's insistence, to delectate ourselves with the knowledge of their titillated and approving observance. We feasted lightly on Fruit de Mer Cru Galatique, turning the consumption of the iced tray of assorted raw mollusks into a game d'amour as old as time, forking bits into each other's mouths, accepting them with overdramatic flourishes of tongue and lips, caressing the raw flesh lasciviously as we devoured it. All with foot play under the table, lidded glances above, and a liter of Ariel blanque.

As I played my role with a certain psychic detachment but growing somic involvement, I began, in an involuted way, to appreciate Lorenza Kareen Patali, and to comprehend her eminence as Domo supreme. Lorenza was a sincere citizen of the floating cultura, which is to say her social persona and her inner psychic structure were in congruence; her spirit clearly believed in the esthetic merit of the way she had chosen; there was no tension between role and reality.

If this gave her a certain flattening of inner ambiguity and hence of fascination, it also allowed one to meet surface with surface without qualms of insincerity. After a period noir of inner turmoil and half a liter of wine, I welcomed this refreshment.

"So, mon cher, your dinner has sweetened the taste of your luncheon, ne? You must teach your Second Officer the subtleties of table drollery, so as not to provoke such inartistic conversation. This foolish Maddhi of hers became a bore at her provocation. Do they no longer teach such arts at the Academy?"

"They teach the craft, Lorenza, but who can teach the art?" I said gallantly. "Genius such as yours is a genetic gift."

"So I have heard from my parents," she said lightly, playfully forking a final oyster into my mouth.

She was wearing transparent red pantaloons and blouson; beneath these, brazen latticework jewelry curled like vines and serpents about her breasts and pubes. A headdress of similar brass filigree secured her red hair into a flowing helmet, this actually done up in animal and vegetative forms, sapphire- and emerald-eyed serpents peering out from the forest of her coiffure. Red, brass, and black, mist over metal pressing skin; the whole was a sensual image of self-created erotic art. How could a natural man fail to respond?

She leaned forward and watched my mouth with those ice-blue eyes as I slowly ate the last morsel for her benefit, tasting, and smoothing, and licking my lips. "Now that we have tasted the appetizer, it is time for the piece de resistance, ne?" she said when I had finished, kissing my lips clean with gustatory exaggeration to the half-murmured attention of our fellow diners.

"I see no reason for resistance," I replied.

"You resist nothing, mon cher?"

"Nada," I said, "you are the Domo, are you not, the mistress of the fete?"

"I may choose a chamber of dreams and this time you will enter?"

"I will follow you anywhere," I said gaily, holding up her hand and giving it a courtly kiss. In truth, I did now welcome the synergy of erotic exercise and crafted fantasy which I had previously rejected. I was ready to follow our Domo into the playful netherworld of the floating cultura, to indulge myself in her reality and thus find respite from my own.

Boisterously and with much fondling did we descend to the dream chamber deck in the lowest part of the Grand Palais, and boisterously did Lorenza lead me through the serpentine rose passageway in search of the dream chamber that would pique her desire, deliberately yet in a curious sense unselfconsciously displaying the public flag of our romance and thereby fulfilling the archetype of our appointed roles.

After an artistically suitable movement of this social foreplay, Lorenza led me into her chosen chamber of dreams.

Lucent jungle-green walls of protoplasmic softness, heated to body temperature, enwombed us in emerald glory as we floated weightless in the thick, steamy, musk-scented air. No, we were not quite weightless; like leaves in a breeze, we drifted slowly to the floor, kicking ourselves off into flight again at the flick of a toe. Mantric fugues on stringed and electronic instruments vibrated the nearly palpable air with soaring energy.

We bounded and flew into a clean, perfumed sweat, intimately exploring the fleshly simulacrum in which we cavorted, its cunningly crafted mounds and folds, troughs and crevices, swellings and concavities, all somehow abstractly reminiscent of the textures of a lover's body.

Imperceptibly, Lorenza's diaphanous garments began to deliquesce into the air like vanishing tendrils of rose-colored fog evaporating into sunrise; as they evaporated, baring her gleaming black flesh restrained at breasts and mound by tight-fitting brass accents flashing emerald highlights with every movement of her body, the smoldering aroma of fire suffused into the musky air.

Slowly and languorously, she let her floating body find its rest not on the floor of the chamber but against the abstract erotiform wall, straddling a soft, saddlelike protuberance, supported on her pubes with her legs hanging free, arms thrown back into a long cushioned crevice between two mounds.

Surely this was as pure and artistic a sensual invitation as I had ever been presented.

I drew off my sweat-sodden clothes, let them slowly drift toward the floor where I stood, bounded lightly into the air, kicked high off the far wall, so that I soared slowly and languidly toward her from away and above, bellying in like a great swan upon the breast of a dark, still lake.

Arms outstretched, chest to chest, lip to lip, I landed softly in her embrace, and we hung by our mutual tantric junctures together on the skin-soft, flesh-warm erotiform perch.

Naturellement, like any other male of the species humaine, I had experienced upon occasion the inability to spring to erection when the situation warranted, either through fatigue or distraction or the triumph of inner esthetic judgment over situational expectation.

Now, however, I felt neither fatigue nor distraction, and esthetic judgment coincided gloriously with the expectations of both parties. There I hung, suspended pube a pube, mouths intertwined, in the embrace of a more than willing woman of dazzling beauty who had brought us together in this emerald garden of flying delights, light as feathers riding the mantras that fugued the erotically perfumed air.

Nevertheless, my natural man had deserted me.

There are, of course, certain exercises, techniques, and niceties that a man of civilized savoir faire has recourse to under such limp circumstances, and I employed a sequence of these before Lorenza could become offended by my lack of phallic homage to her undeniable charms.

I stretched out supine upon the erotiform divan and lavished upon her yoni such skillful and prolonged caresses as to transport her repeatedly into moaning peaks of distraction while I applied will and physiology to the problem at hand. Certain meditative yogics will more often than not harmonize the state of the soma with the desire of the psyche, and when these proved somewhat ineffective, simple venus manipulation achieved at least the desired physiological effect.

In fact in point of pure tantric performance, I was indefatigable thereafter. The test of any performer is triumph over mal karma, and the proof of such triumph is the approval of the audience; in that regard, Lorenza's surfeited peaks of ecstasy validated this self-perception.

Nevertheless, it was performance in more than metaphor. The pleasure I was giving aroused no joy in me, and the transports of Lorenza brought me no closer to release. I performed my phallic variations in conscious fulfillment of my duty, not in a trance of mindless ecstasy.

Ultimately it was Lorenza, overwhelmed with orgasm, gasping raggedly for breath, glowing with perspiration, who admitted her fatigue and satiation.

"Beacoup, mon cher," she panted in my ear. "Seek your own fulfillment."

This I attempted one more time, not informing her that my prolonged priapism had been anything other than gallantry, before ruefully admitting defeat.

At this imbalance in the ecstasy of our pas de deux, Lorenza displayed a sincere concern and bent her neck and her energies to oral caresses designed to redress it.

While her skill at these erotic exercises was unimpeachable and her intent of the highest morality d'amour, by this time I knew that the attempt was futile, for in my psychic exhaustion and physical frustration, I had passed over to the stage where the only pleasure possible to me was rest. Though it was ungallant of me to do so, there was finally no alternative, and with rueful but firm gestures, I bade her cease.

"Que problem, mon cher?"

"Quien sabe?" I said soothingly. "Perhaps it was the wine. Or the overwhelming pleasure that I sought to prolong into eternity. Or some temporary infirmity. De nada."

She looked at me inquiringly, and now perhaps there was something more speculative behind her concern.

"Certainly there was nothing lacking in the pleasure of the chase," I told her, "and the true pleasure lies not in the goal but in the journey, nicht wahr."

With this and other similar verbal niceties, Lorenza was mollified, and the pas de deux ended not in overt tension between us. We both had too much civilized concern for each other for that, and our roles in the floating cultura needed not further perturbation. We boistered through the passageway and into the grand salon together as if buoyed on tantric energies and exchanged light pleasantries with a number of Honored Passengers over brandies before repairing to our respective private cabins.

But despite these appearances, I sensed that the void within me, that black hole of confusion which had somehow been bored through my weltanschauung, had finally begun to fracture the phenomenological realm precisely at its point of greatest ambiguity—the sexual interface where psyche and soma could no longer be dualized. I only hoped that the pattern would not spread to the sphere of social duty, that this most subtle of breaches with the Domo of the Honored Passengers could be healed before its vibrations disharmonized the social dynamics of my ship.

I passed the period until the third Jump in a fitful melange of dream-haunted sleep and hypnogogic half-wakefulness, erotic ideograms of ever-increasing extremity filling my sensorium in hormonal frustration while my somic indicator lay unresponsive to the demands of release.

VIII

Hollow-eyed and haggard as I was from lack of any but haunted sleep, my condition was taken with unvoiced jocularity as the nobly earned aftermath of heroic indulgence by Argus and Mori when I arrived on the bridge. I was mercifully glad that neither of them sought to banter bon mots concerning events chez Grand Palais; surfeited of erotic imagery in word, deed, and thought, I was relieved to detumesce through duty's mantra into the professional performance of my absolute rather than social Captainly role.

Or so I thought as we began the countdown ritual, sitting on my throne of power gazing into the starry sea from the bow of my vessel.

"Jump Drive generator activated . . . parameters nominal. . . . Harmonizer circuits activated. . . . Jump Circuit electronics on standby. . . ."

But with every amber ready point that winked on in sequence, another quantum of energy seemed to surge into the strange tension building within me, a twisting wind in the viscera, an unbidden flow of prana from psyche into soma. . . .

"Primer circuit activated . . . parameters nominal. . . ."

Far from escaping the center of my malaise, I found myself whirling right into it. Far from detumescing through the Jump ritual, I was confronted in the most inescapable way possible with the fact that my libido had been magnetized by the sexual ideogram of the Jump. For as the moment approached, the treacherous schlange kundalini uncoiled into attention. All that had been missing in the dream chamber with Lorenza was activated now, and with it the realization that an engrammic dybbuk foreign to my will had seized control of my libidinal lance.

"Pilot in the Circuit . . . ," Mori chanted.

Pilot in the Circuit indeed! I satoried as the image contacted my sensorium. I understood with dreadful new clarity why Captains did not want to meet their Pilots. Why Captains *feared* meeting their Pilots, though they knew it not. Once this relationship was personified, it became eroticized, and once it became eroticized, it captured the imagination of the unnatural man. In the ancient literal sense, I had been bewitched by my Pilot; Dominique Alia Wu had secreted a succubus into my consciousness.

"Checklist completed, and all systems ready for the Jump."

As I gave my first command, I determined to take a more active role in the rite in more ways than one; I surrendered to the pattern moving through me in a therapeutic spirit. I would selfconsciously allow this enigma I had discovered within me to play out its scenario through me under observation of my intellection and thus leach it of its programmatic power.

"Take your position, Man Jack."

"Vector coordinate overlay computed and on your board. . . ."

"Dumping vector coordinate overlay into Jump Circuit computer," I found myself chanting with an unholy anticipation, and as I actually touched my first command point, I felt a momentary metaphorical if not electronic feedback from the Circuit, from the ship, and the sparkling stars, and the energies moving through my command.

"Jump Field aura . . . erected." Even random words of the ritual now seemed to synchronize into the building rhythm pulsing through me, driving me forward into a cyborged embrace.

My body seemed to crackle with unreleased energy as my finger paused above the ultimate command point and the chimes sounded, as if that digit were pressed as tight against the fabric of the universe as my nether pole against my trousers. I stared out into the bright, hard glory of the void as into the eyes of a lover.

"Jump!" I shouted, not, so it seemed, to Argus or Mori or to the ship's annunciators, but to the one person aboard my voice could not reach; she whose ecstasy lay at the touch of my hand, she whose ultimate purpose I now served as I touched the command point.

It was over. In an augenblick, the stars had changed configuration, Dominique had passed through ecstasy into coma, and the *Dragon Zephyr* had Jumped closer to Estrella Bonita.

And I, once more, was left in a state of hormonic and psychic frustration. During that imperceptible insertion through the fabric of space-time, did I seek to experience the subjective eternity of the Great and Lonely through which my machineries had propelled my cyborged demon lover through feedback with the Circuit? Had I imagined I had succeeded? Meaningless conjecture. The climactic moment came and went in an instant quite literally too short to leave a memory trace.

In my reality, nothing had happened, save the translation of the ship 3.8 light-years toward our destination; even the starfield shift, as always, had gone unperceived in the quotidian timestream.

So I departed the bridge in an extenuated amplification of the state in which I had arrived; my unfullfilled priapism wilting in the aftermath of yet one more dream of ideogrammically abstracted sexuality.

Yet now, minimal, I had achieved knowledge of that which had seized my spirit; by confronting the dybbuk I had beheld the face of that from which I fled. Since that exchange of name tales on the sky ferry, I had become a man obsessed; I was obsessed still, but now knowledge gave me both the courage and the anger to perceive the nature of that obsession and do what duty demanded.

Vraiment, I judged myself contaminated in spirit, impaired in the functioning of my Captainly role, sexually disharmonized, and in danger of losing my will to command the Jump. In these circumstances, I could conceive of only two honorable alternatives. I could remove myself from command for psychic disequilibrium and no doubt be rightly found unfit for another berth as Void Captain, or I could seek the knowledge necessary to free myself from this karmic quagmire from the source of the mal d'esprit herself.

Thus formulated, the proposition was a tautology. Great risk might there be in disregarding the prescription of Maestro Hiro and interviewing Dominique Alia Wu again, both to my authority as Captain and my own psychic destiny, but all this would in any event be lost if I surrendered my command.

Once breached, my innocence was gone forever, and the only path back to the Captaincy of my own soul was that of inner knowledge, that very knowledge which we are taught at the Academy not to seek.

During the first three hours of the recovery period, the Pilot remains in coma in sick bay as intravenous infusions and charge inducers bring her life readings into stabilized equilibrium and restore her to a semblance of consciousness. She is then transferred to her cabin, where, custom dictates, she remains to recuperate for the next Jump. Thus the recovery routine for that abstraction "the Pilot"; Dominique Alia Wu might be "exercising her musculature" and taking nourishment on the cuisinary deck within five hours of the Jump for all I knew or dared to ask concerning the generality of her unprecedented habits.

This interval I passed alone in my cabin, unwilling to submit myself to further social stimuli, uncertain of my ability to function within my role, and searching unsuccessfully for a mode of encounter with my Pilot which would not arouse the disapproving interest of Maestro Hiro or further project the disharmony of my being into the social dynamics of the ship.

But there was no socially benign path to further congress with Dominique Alia Wu, no channel of command or Captainly duty which I might invoke; even were I to arrange to encounter her by chance on the cuisinary deck, to engage her in conversation there once again would be a publicly proclaimed act of will.

Lacking any pretext that would have borne public or officerly scrutiny, I at last lapsed into the sad and tragicomic stratagem of stealth.

Thus could the Captain of the *Dragon Zephyr* be found slinking guiltily up the spinal corridor toward the Pilot's cabin like a buffoon in some farce d'amour, starting at sounds, and detouring up side passages at approaching footfalls, until at last the coast of his assignation was clear of observers and he could slide like a shadow through a half-opened door.

Dominique was propped up on pillows in a bed whose headboard displayed a full array of physiological parameters a glance at which told me that her inner resources were already recovering from her ordeal. A few welts and blotches were still fading from her face, and her eyes were still deeply pinkened and hollowed in greenish black shadows. She started at my clandestine entry, but what surprise she displayed in the afterknowledge of my identity seemed mere thespic display; perhaps it was my projection, but she appeared rather to be stifling some wry moue of amused confirmation.

"Mon Captain?" she said. "Que pasa? You look terrible.

Do sit down." Though there were two chairs in the cabin, she patted the bedclothes with a somewhat shaky hand, and I seated myself at the foot of the bed, wondering how I was going to begin. And what.

"Are you all right?" I muttered inanely.

"Nominal for this timeframe," she said, nodding in the direction of the headboard monitors. "Aber for small talk and salutations the Void Captain of the *Dragon Zephyr* does not secretly steal into the boudoir of the Pilot. Grand scandal were you to be seen in such an act. I shun not your company, liebchen, but your duty requires you to shun mine. So . . . ?"

"Very well, Dominique," I said sternly, donning my Captainly persona as best I could under the circumstances. "I have reason to believe . . ."

What? What could I say to her? I have reason to believe you have bewitched me? I accuse you of planting a sexual ideogram in my consciousness? Truth be told, in that augenblick I was confronted with my own perception of how demented any verbal rendering of the state of my consciousness would sound. What was I doing here? Should I not remove myself as Captain at once as unfit for command?

"Well?" Dominique snapped. "Can you not speak?" Then she leaned forward slightly, squinted her bloodshot eyes as if truly seeing me by active choice for the first time, and when she spoke again, it was in another voice from another place. "Perhaps I understand, Genro. There is something troubling you, ne, something that must not be revealed to another person, aber something that must be voiced for the sake of your psychic equilibrium, nicht wahr?"

"Yes," I gasped in simple amazement. Did she know? Was it written so plainly in my body language that all could see it? Or did she know because she had done it to me deliberately?

"So," she said in a strange, ironic, almost darkly gay

tone, "you have come to me, the Pilot, demi-person, a sympathetic ear sans transmitting mouth, a psyche in social purdah."

"I didn't mean to suggest I deny your humanity—"

"No, no, no, cher liebchen," she said, actually smiling upon me. "You are right. Any secret is secure with me. No hay falta. You deny not my essence humaine, merely my social existence, a lack of shadow role to which I could not be more indifferent. Speak, cher Genro, your dark secrets are as safe with me as if you were proclaiming them into the void." Her hands seemed to creep unconsciously toward mine over the bedclothes. Her words seemed to ambiguify their meanings. Her eyes, reddened and shadowed though they were, suddenly had the power to capture my gaze and then hurl it back like silvered mirrors.

I felt that we had passed over into another level of discourse. In truth, the knowledge of my malaise d'esprit *was* safe with she who was its focus; in truth, confronting her with it *would* be proclaiming it into the void in the center of the vortex. Somehow I had been given new energy by this frail creature newly returned from comatose exhaustion.

"Have you done this to me for the sake of revenge?" I demanded softly.

"Revenge?" she said ingenuously. "For what? Por que? What is it that you conceive I have done?"

"Since I unwittingly exchanged name tales with you on the sky ferry, my consciousness has been invaded by uncertainties, obsessions noir, matters that impair my . . . my . . ."

"Ach so," she cooed, rising from her pillows to regard me from a greater height. "Adam has nibbled little green apples from the tree of knowledge and now he has indigestion cosmique."

"And did not Eve hand the fateful fruit to him by act of will?"

"Blame the serpent of circumstance," she said. "A random meeting on the ferry, an altercation which required your intercession—from this I am accused of conspiring to seduce mein bon Captain from his faithful duty?"

"An altercation you knew would require my attention," I said more uncertainly, for is the essence of paranoia not the projection of willed patterns into random event?

Dominique laughed. She disentangled her body from the bedclothes and crawled prone across the bed toward me, then propped her head in her hands and stared at me with some dark amusement. "So smitten was I by your manly charms in our chance encounter that I fomented a cause celebre in order to be with you, vraiment, and then with this fleshly envelope I captured your imagination erotique, so as to seduce you into invading my boudoir with amorous intent, where I now hold you at my sensual mercy?"

She laughed again, colder this time. "You have no low opinion of your charisma d'amour, mi caballero," she said with a decidedly sharp edge to the jape.

"A Void Captain is an archetypal figure of romance; is it impossible for such an aura to have affected a Pilot who offered up her name tale unbidden in its presence? Particularly in view of our . . . functional relationship."

Dominique drew herself shakily up into a yogic squat, visibly feeble at first, but seeming to extract strength from the completed posture, facing me now eye to eye on a shared level.

"Precisely in view of our functional relationship, such infatuation is impossible," she said. "Not through any paucity of your manly potency or conscience sympathetique, liebchen, for I sense in you a hidden fellow being. Aber, chez moi, the fulfillment of the flesh stands revealed as a pale shadow of the Greater Glory, beyond the power of any tantric hero to grant."

"Then it *is* revenge! First you ensorcel me and then

you declare me the erotic inferior of a concatenation of electronic circuitry."

"But why would I do such a thing?"

"Is it not the ancient sexual technique of the femme fatale, the capture of the erotic impulse and its channelization toward a goal unobtainable? Is this not the classic feminine mode of vengeance?"

"Moi, femme fatale? Genro, Genro, can you not comprehend that erotic games interest me not, whether of the body or the mind? Least of all the pettiness of vengeance. Why vengeance? Por que?"

"The natural hostility between Pilot and Captain . . ." I muttered uncertainly as she regarded me as if I were some pauvre petit. Nevertheless, I pressed on. "After the last Jump, I . . . I chanced to see you being wheeled out of the Pilot's module. For the first time, I comprehended the full price the Jump exacts, and after all, it is in a very real sense I who . . . who . . ."

I realized as I spoke that I was dissembling, and not only to Dominique but to myself. Indeed I had a perception of this whole conversation as a pavane of dissembling, a careful tiptoe dance about the void at its center. I knew that she sought not vengeance. She knew that I was not consumed with fleshly lust for her body. We both knew that the Jump involved no rape of her will.

Nevertheless, I danced out the figure. "I fear my enhanced perception is weakening my will to command the Jump," I recited, repairing in guile to Maestro Hiro's assessment of my cafard.

Her eyes flared in alarm, then hardened into a frightening coldness. "I know what you are doing," they said.

"If it be my absolution you seek, take it gladly and truly, mon cher dummkopf," she said. "You know that any price I pay as fare to the Great and Only is a bargain I willingly make."

"Then it truly is worth everything to you—your health, your life, your spirit humaine?"

Dominique leaned closer to me. I could smell the acetone on her breath, the biochemical signature of the price she paid for the ecstasy of the Jump. Somehow this excited my pheromonic receptors, somehow I was aroused, somehow the smell of her words was the odor of truth.

"Truly, liebchen," she said softly. Her tired eyes seemed as human as I had seen them, and she smiled assuringly as she touched a tremulous hand to my cheek. "If you insist on metaphor erotique, bitte do not choose to imagine our transaction as the rape brutal. You ravish not my spirit."

"I think I believe you," I said, sexually aroused by her presence in my body space, the odor of dark mystery tainting her breath, all the hidden subtexts of our discourse. In that moment, I recognized through somic memory's congruence that my erotic vision of the Jump, the dreams that had haunted my sleep, my sexual dysfunction chez Lorenza, were all metaphorical dybbuks of the same erotic engram, the one that rose to the surface now, coded into my very hormonic metabolism. Even the lust I now allowed myself to feel for Dominique might be merely another somic metaphor for this psychic ideogram.

"I believe, but I don't understand," I breathed softly, aware that I too was leaning closer, that her hand was now pressed firmly and warmly against my cheek. "The enormity of the price you pay is all too apparent; explain to me then this glory for which you forsake all else gladly."

"No words can tell, poor creature," she said with sad finality, and I knew we had at last danced our way through to the heart of the matter. To the void at the heart of the matter, the mystery to which I found my phallic pulse beating.

"I don't know whether I can command another Jump without knowing," I said, half cruelly, and half provocatively.

"But you must!" she hissed in cat-sudden fury, clutching at my shoulders with both hands.

Startled by the angry passion I had aroused, I made sure my eyes gave the lie to my words, and she subsided almost immediately. A succession of expressions passed across her face in such rapid perfusion that the process of transformation was beyond my gestalting, but somehow, in the next moment, she was regarding me tenderly and holding me with a lover's touch.

"Ach, mein pauvre Genro," she said lornly. "Words there are not. You seek truly, but you know not what. You seek what I have found, but where I go, you cannot."

"Try," I implored simply.

"Try?" she said strangely. "You wish me to try in the only way I know how?"

I stared silently without waver into those hollowed, bloodshot, feverish eyes, smelled the odor of flesh pushed far beyond its natural limits on her breath, and my phallus pressed against the fabric of my pants as my spirit pressed against the interface of her secret knowledge, and the kundalini fire that ran along this circuit I somehow finally perceived as envy.

"Bon," she said, and without romantic preamble or false formalities, she freed that tormented serpent from its civilized restraints and exposed its declaration to the open light of day. "Surrender to the moment, imagine it forever, and quien sabe, maybe it is not impossible you begin to understand."

So saying, she arched her neck gracefully, swallowing the blind serpent of my forbidden desire down a long, warm, silky passage that both eased the pain of thwarted passion and inflamed it into a nerve trunk that drew my spirit down it into a place beyond thought.

Waves of ecstatic energy pulsed through me, mirrored in the moire light flashes that formed fantastically complex visual ragas behind my rolling eyes. My flesh seemed to ripple as knots of sour tension passed up and through me to discharge themselves through my finally activated tantric focus.

Faster and faster and ever more freely, these waves of pranic energy surged through me as I became a transparent medium for their transmission. Crest to crest they came now, compressing through linear time into a clear shaft of white light on all psychic and protoplasmic wavebands that lanced through me, a bolt of total discharge which left me shouting wordlessly in some time without space.

Slowly, the fragments of my consciousness reformed into an awareness of place and time, into the kinesthetic awareness of my back against the softness of the bed, into the sight of Dominique Alia Wu looking down at me, her features calmly composed, her eyes mirrored windows over what lay within.

"A shadow," she said. "Just a pale shadow."

That interior-focused moment passed and humanity returned to her tired, hollowed eyes. "So, mon cher liebchen," she said, "You will remember *that* should your will waver at the time of the Jump, nicht wahr, and you will at least know it is no rape you do."

And so it began. So it truly began.

———— *IX*

How can an act of social madness tranquillify the spirit? How can a breach of one's bound duty lead to the more proper performance of same?

No doubt our Healer could have supplied some theoretical abstraction to account for the generality of such paradoxical abreaction, but I was hardly about to consult Lao or Maestro Hiro concerning the alchemical sexuality of the specific release.

Suffice it to say that once I had made my secret exit from Dominique's cabin and returned to the environs of the floating cultura, I found myself somewhat more comfortable within my Captainly persona, more able to function in the phenomenological realm on a phenomenological level.

Naturellement, one did not have to be a Healer to know that release from the hormonic torture of the most prolonged and convoluted act of coitus interruptus that I could have conceived of had a good deal to do with restoring my psychic and hence social functionality. From the first faint stirrings at the time of the second Jump to the long-delayed release in Dominique's cabin, my metabolism had been flushed with adrenal and gonadal imperatives the continual arousal and frustration of which could hardly have been said to be conducive to psychic clarity.

Now, at least, the somic component of my "cafard" had been removed by the ministrations of Dominique Alia Wu and my psychic dialectic could at least proceed from a base of biochemical equilibrium.

The ancient volkwisdom that an erect phallus knows no morality is meant as an ironic jocularity, but it contains an approximation of the truth; when your libidinal energy is captured by a sexual engram, the logic of further action is that not of your will but of the engram itself until that energy is discharged.

Moreover, surrender to my passion noir had at least granted me a truer image of its essence; I had confronted the void at its coeur and passed through into knowledge however partial of my true position in the sexual equation of the Jump.

Primitive man evolved many cultural techniques for the sexual subjugation of the femme of the species, as crude as clitoral excision and as subtle as denying spiritual equality. Even in enlightened ages, this was perceived as economically motivated behavior or possessive greed, the transformation of feminine favors into a commodity of trade in the commerce of the masculine ego.

Actually, this is just one more transformation of the deeper motivation to a more palatable rationalization, albeit a self-admittedly unsavory one. What I had learned in the embrace of my Pilot was something well established in the annals of biology and even a truism of Jump technology: the orgasmic potential of the female of our species transcends that of the male.

Thus the sociosexual subjugation of femme by homme, far from being an aggressive act of phallic aggrandizement, is actually a defense mechanism, a flight from confrontation with this cosmic injustice. The whole cultural labyrinth of male courtship of feminine favors is actually a shrill denial of the true nature of the transaction, namely, that the erotically sophisticated male grants higher favors than any he can receive. Women of course collude in this deception, since masculine perception of the true situation would not only subject them to naked and unwholesome envy but reverse the polarity of the archetypal duality to their strategic disfavor.

The wall of purdah between Captain and Pilot was perhaps the ultimate expression of this denial, as the mechanism of the Jump Circuit was the ultimate extension of that which was denied. Here the imbalance reached beyond biology, beyond the realm of mass-energy phenomena, into the Great and Lonely itself; so named by those few female initiates who rode alone on the masculine machineries into its hidden ecstatic heart.

In cold scientific fact, not mere metaphor, the Jump was half of a sexual act; the result of my touch on the Jump command point was as much the granting of sexual ecstasy as my performance for Lorenza in the dream chamber, and in both cases it was not my own purpose that I served.

To expose a Void Captain to the human reality of his Pilot is to expose him to the sexual core of his duty, to the one-sided sexual congress of the Jump, to his own envy—of feminine platform orgasm, of the true mistress of the ship's destiny, of that which his masculine spirit cannot touch.

Small wonder then that our starfaring culture has evolved this wall of purdah around the mystery at its heart. Small wonder that the floating cultura has elaborated itself around it in order to divert the Captain's erotic attention into his archetypal relationship with the Domo. Small wonder that this relationship stands at the center of harmonious shipboard dynamics. Small wonder that once Dominique had breached that wall, my libido reverted its focus from the social to the psychic.

Naturellement, this logical analysis did not spring full-blown into my brow at the moment of Dominique's act of noblesse oblige; rather did it proceed to evolve to my present rueful understanding via contemplation, perusal of relevant word crystals, and further karmic lessons from that moment until this. Even now, as I code this ultimate justification onto word crystal, I am aware that I am still somehow dissembling, or rather failing to render a logical memory of that satori in a mode comprehensible to my quotidian mind.

Nevertheless, it is just to state that now I was aware that I was in the grip of a futile passion, not for the body or even the spirit of Dominique Alia Wu, but for that which I could only taste as a pale shadow through her mediation. The very ludicrity of such a fixation served to render it less puissant as a poisoner of my psyche, or so it seemed at the time. For this was no pheromonic infatuation or passion for psychoerotic communion, but a mere malfunction of my psychic processes, a mutation on the chromosome caused by a chance cosmic bolide. Like all such maladaptive mutations, would it not be self-extinguishing through the passage of evolutionary time?

Or so I seemed to have persuaded myself after a short period of untrammeled sleep, and judiciously distant participation in the niceties of the Grand Palais.

Upon stealing from Dominique's cabin, I had repaired to my own, where I almost immediately sank into dreamless slumber; upon awakening, I practiced several yogic asanas and a long, contemplative ablution, at the conclusion of which I had sufficiently reformulated my rationale to continue my digestion of inner events in the artificial outer world of the vivarium.

Here, amid the lush foliage, the groaking frogs, the insectile motes, the twittering rainbow flocks of finches, and parties of no less lavishly plumaged Honored Passengers, did I perceive the evolutionary imperatives at work. Frogs yearned not to fly, birds yearned not to swim, and the floating cultura that bridged the stars yearned not to encompass the region between. For a bird to swim the deeps is to die out of air; for a frog to fly it must cease to be a frog; for men to leap naked into the void is similarly proscribed by our genes. Of the three, however, only men had the power to transcend their species programming, to encapsulate themselves in technology and art and culture and invade the alien element in a bubble of their own self-created reality.

Thus, these human survival mechanisms, when functioning properly, represent not the triumph of determinism over the individual but the triumph of spirit over evolutionary determinism.

To be thrust by chance outside this reality humaine for a vision of what lay beyond and below was to achieve a more sympathetic perception of one's fellow travelers as they danced their part in the figure. I was sure that my mutant obsession had vanished in the cold clear evolutionary light of day.

Soon I was taking part in conversations, sipping wine from goblets, exchanging pleasantries once more with the Honored Passengers in my charge.

And was not the discourse of the floating cultura the highest to be found among the worlds of men? In a few hours of light banter, subjects of conversation included the outre ecospheres of two recently discovered habitable planets, a comparison of modern vintages with those of ancient Terrestrial tradition, the relative balance of yin and yang in our transtellar culture, speculations on the paucity of sapient life in our small region of the galaxy, trends in contemporary painting and sculpture, und so weiter, as well as the inevitable shipboard gossip.

If the floating cultura contained its fair share and then some of subsidized children of fortune, wealthy sybarites, refugees from ennui, and their attendant parasitic organisms, did these not serve as a communal matrix for the merchants, artists, scientists, esthetes, and pilgrims who traveled among the stars for higher purposes? In ancient days, the courts of monarchs served as similar distillations of the more rarefied essences of human culture; these too were gilded cages filled with self-pampered birds of paradise, but in their precincts were also to be found the philosophers, artists, and mages of the age.

Wealth of a primary order surrounds itself with choicest viands, vintages, art, and luxuriousness, but beyond these sensual indulgences of the rich lay the possibility of the ultimate patronly purchase—the company of the intellectual, artistic, scientific, and spiritual creme de la creme of human society. Surely in our Second Starfaring Age the floating cultura represented this heady distillation; churlish of me, nicht wahr, to look down my lofty nose at the pinnacle of my society from some haughty Olympus when in reality I too was the direct beneficiary of its patronage.

Thus had the secret violation of the central taboo of my social matrix somehow restored to me some semblance of harmony with same.

Only the inevitable confrontation with Lorenza Kareen Patali was to perturb this immersion in the social waters with the post- and fore-shadowing of the intrusive void; with intimations of the less social dynamics that nevertheless still surrounded and underlay both this golden bubble of human gaiety and my own presently integrated social persona.

I had made entrance into the grand salon in the company of Mori, her merchant artiste Rumi Jellah Cohn, Sar Medina Gondo, a ravishing golden-haired woman of great wealth and little intellect who had attached herself to my Captainly person, and Orvis Embri Rico, a somewhat threadbare light sculptor who seemed to be either her amour d'argent, under her patronage, or both.

Lorenza was reclining in a padded niche spotlighted in somber rose with a large muscular man in loose-flowing pantaloons and blouson of black silk; by their body postures, the pipe of herbal intoxicant they were sharing, the silver goblets of wine resting lip to lip on the tabouret before them, I surmised that they had but recently emerged from passage in a dream chamber.

Arcane, diverse, and unsettling were my reactions to

this perception. Lorenza was at her most enticing in this configuration of sated repose; her long red hair artfully disarrayed, her glowing ebon skin cleansed of all artifice, her body languid within a formless, translucent yellow boudoir robe. This vision, enhanced perhaps by the presence of her consort of the moment, aroused in me a certain glandular ardor of the sort that had been lacking in our recent pas de deux, a nostalgia for the pleasure in her embrace that had been denied me by my own psychic dysfunction, a desire to replay the episode to a more mutually satisfying conclusion.

At the same time, I felt a certain Captainly displeasure at this open proclamation of the fact of the matter, a frisson of atavistic male jealousy, but also a sense of disruption of subtle social harmonies of which I, not she, had been the true causal agent. While it is not unseemly for Domo and Captain to share dream chambers with all and sundry, the illusion, at least, of the meetness of discretion is better preserved in the public realm lest such liasons be perceived by the Honored Passengers as a statement of reproach, as deliberate violation of the archetypal fiction.

Which, I sensed, this tableau was meant to be; as if, somehow, on some subliminal level, Lorenza had been aware of my tryst with Dominique and sought to chide me with a public redress of the balance. Or so I surmised in my suddenly reactivated and guilt-ridden sexual malaise.

Hesitant as to whether to rise to the perhaps self-projected bait or to leave the pair to their own devices, I was relieved of this decision by Sar, who seized me possessively by the arm and paraded me toward them with the others in train.

"Ach, Lorenza," she said rather floridly, "I must to you give thanks for the enjoyment of a tres rare voyage! The cunningness of the vivarium, the glories of the table, the piquancy of the entertainment! The companionship sympathetique! The dream chambers so daring . . ."

The last with a thespic giggle, a rolling of eyes, and a drawing closer to me as subtle as the rest of it, which soured Orvis' expression and fairly caused Rumi to hide his amusement behind his hand.

Lorenza seemed oblivious to this repartee, or feigned indifference, or more likely perceived the nullity at its heart. "Merci, good Sar," she said languidly. "The appreciation of the connoisseur is the highest pleasure of the artiste." She was looking at the two of us as she said it, but the deliberate lidding of her eyes, the moist parting of her lips, gave me to understand that the inner meaning of the riposte was directed at me.

"And you, good sir, are you also a connoisseur of the pleasures of the Grand Palais, or do you travel in a more functional mode?" I said, addressing the black-garbed fellow.

"Neither, or perhaps both," he answered mildly, drawing on the herbal pipe. "Like yourself, Captain Genro, I provide service for Honored Passengers. Aga Henri Koram, servidor de usted, freeservant in the employ of our fair Domo."

"Indeed," said Sar with some raising of her brow. "And what manner of services do you provide?"

Aga smiled blandly at her with his calm brown eyes. "I am skilled in the serving of wines and cuisine in the classic manner as well as the composition and performance of musical odes," he said. "In addition, I have mastered the tantric arts, for the successful freeservant must be versatile in many modes of pleasure."

"A pleasure to make your acquaintance," Sar said silkily. "Perhaps before this voyage is completed I shall commission your services—"

"If so, I trust you will find my rates just and my performances appealing, as most have in the past," Aga said without either false modesty or boastful pride. "Domo Lorenza can attest to that; we have voyaged together on a number of occasions."

Lorenza, who had been regarding this byplay with a

carefully crafted air of detached amusement, inclined her head in Aga's direction with a slow toss of her hair, her icy-blue eyes fixed all the while upon mine, or so it seemed. "Vraiment, Aga's performances are of the highest caliber," she said feyly.

A moment of uneasy silence reigned; had it not been for this, it might have been possible for me to dismiss my perception of the inner dialog aimed at me as delusion of paranoid reference. As it was, the expression on the observatory faces confirmed my weltanschauung; Lorenza had deliberately fashioned this tableau so as to externalize the subtle disharmony between us into an only slightly less subtle social rebuke.

If the piquing of my manly and Captainly attention had been the ultimate goal of this charade, the ploy had met with no little success; after a seemly period of further niceties, I drew Lorenza aside on the pretext of discussing certain aspects of our duties. Though in truth, the harmonious performance of our duties was not exactly beside my point.

"You are angry with me because of what happened in the dream chamber; that is the raison d'etre for this public display of gamesmanship, nicht wahr?"

Lorenza regarded me from behind a facade of ingenuous innocence. "Gamesmanship? Public display? Que pasa, mon cher Genro?"

"Surely you do not deny sharing a dream chamber with this freeservant Aga?"

"Surely I do not indeed," she said mildly. "For what reason should I?"

I stared intently into her icy eyes, realizing that this mode of discourse could overtly communicate nothing without the collaboration empathetique which she was deliberately withholding. Paradoxically, however, true messages were being passed back and forth here below the primary verbal surface; obliquely, she was telling me she marked indeed my meaning. Which, after all, was only that her own previous oblique communique had found its mark.

"No reason at all, Lorenza," I said. "But it would be better if such rebukes were delivered less publicly."

"Rebuke, mon cher?" she said evenly. "Why would you imagine I wished to rebuke you?" But she favored me with a smile that reversed the polarity of her meaning.

"No doubt it is I who rebuke myself by projecting my own self-judgment upon your acts of innocence," I said, ironically nuancing my words with facial commentary in turn.

"Tres gallant," Lorenza said dryly.

To my own surprise, though perhaps not to hers, I was beginning to find this subtle duel erotically arousing. "I am not without such graces," I said evenly. "Though I do not profess the skills of the professional."

Her eyes warmed somewhat toward me and she delivered the next words with a small smile. "Pero for an amateur tantrique, your performance lacks little. Except, perhaps, the true sincerity."

"Perhaps that may be remedied with sufficient practice."

"Quien sabe?" she said with a little laugh. "Vraiment, I am willing to continue this dialog in more intimate detail after a suitable period of reflection."

"After the next Jump?" I suggested. "In another dream chamber of your choosing?"

"No, cher Genro. This time, the choice of venue should be yours, ne, since my previous choice did not entirely fulfill your satisfaction."

"You too are not without gallantry, Lorenza," I said, sealing the assignation with a kiss of her hand, although in truth we both knew that I was being challenged.

Thus was the veneer of civilization maintained and defended, thus did Captain and Domo preserve the rhythm of their public pavane from unseemly disharmony. Lorenza took my hand as we returned to the milieu of social interaction; and by eye contacts and touches, shared wine and duets of jocularity, did we proclaim that our personas had returned to the proper fulfillment of our expected roles.

No doubt those unfamiliar with the rarefied atmosphere of the floating cultura may protest that such obliqueness represents not so much the niceties of gentility as a certain anomie, a spiritless charade, a decadent concern with surface over substance.

Perhaps this subjective truth has its validity, just as the converse proposition is not without its own puissance—namely, that true civilization consists precisely of conventions, rituals, and modes of oblique communication whereby the chaos within and the void without may be expressed and contained within the harmonious consensus of shared social objectivity, thus maintaining our bubble of crafted reality, the necessary illusion. Indeed, there are those who define the essential nature of all artistic forms in just this manner.

Be that as it may, the transaction between Captain and Domo, sincere or not in terms of Genro and Lorenza, served not only to reharmonize the social surface but to submerge my inner chaos beneath the social dialectic of the dance. For the next few hours, I do believe that I was entirely concerned with the duties and niceties of my Captainly role, my interior musings given over to considerations of an appropriate choice of dream chamber, to the esthetique d'amour, rather than arcane metaphysic, to style rather than substance.

Only as I made my way to the bridge for the fourth Jump did this comforting mantle of illusion begin to unravel.

As I walked briskly toward the bridge up the ship's spinal corridor, awareness of a by-now-familiar tension began to creep into the forefront of my consciousness with every marching step. For the first time, I believe, I noticed how few Honored Passengers that I chanced to meet saluted me, nor did I acknowledge their existence; as if by unstated, indeed by until-now-unperceived, agreement this transition from the inner illusion of the floating cultura to the outer reality of my true command was a solemn rite to be conducted in social isolation.

Indeed, as I emerged onto the bridge, I felt my persona dissolving under the cold black vault of the starry void; vast impersonal energies seemed to pour in upon me from those millions of unwinking stellar eyes; a hard-edged and entirely indifferent reality enfolded me in its chill yet somehow darkly sensual embrace. Clearly the armor of psychic construct, the cultural surface of the persona, was entirely inadequate to confront the naked countenance of the void; how vain seemed such illusion in the face of this pitiless reality.

Yet what greater grandeur could the true spirit within encompass than to sit here on the throne of the Captaincy, naked before this ultimate unveiled, and dare to challenge it with the mere machineries of men?

As the familiar countdown ritual began, I perceived it as if for the first time as solemn rite in more than metaphor, as the mantra whereby we few initiates who faced the visage beyond maya's veil, here on this ersatz mountaintop above the inner world of men, might shield ourselves from the true sight of chaos in our functional dance of duty.

Thus did we exchange one illusion for another; thus did we avert our gaze from the ultimate challenge to our spirits.

"Jump Circuit electronics on standby. . . . Primer parameters normal. . . ."

As Mori went through her checklist, I found myself reversing the polarity of the ritual; rather than focus my gaze and attention on the amber ready points winking into incandescence on my board, I stared upward and outward at the naked void itself, letting the rhythm of the words carry my consciousness not into the rite but beyond it, into awareness of all that it sought to deny.

"Pilot in the Circuit . . ."

A cold wind seemed to move through me as the ritual reminded me that deep within the enveloping machinery, enwombed and sightless in the Pilot's module, Dominique, of all aboard, alone confronted the true reality, the true unreality, the faceless and formless Great and Lonely before which even the universal void was but illusion's final veil.

". . . checklist completed and all systems ready for the Jump. . . ."

"Take your position, Man Jack."

"Vector coordinate overlay computed and on your board. . . ."

"Dumping vector coordinate overlay into Jump Circuit computer," I chanted, touching the command point through kinesthetic memory, the starry blackness still flooding my sensorium. As I did so, I was aware of this action as the umbilical connection to quotidian reality, the projection of human will into the impending mass-energy discontinuity of the Jump, the bread-crumb trail through the forest, the way through to the hearth of home.

"Jump Field aura . . . erected. . . ."

In truth, once more I felt erotic stirrings, but now these were overlayed with empathy humaine; if eros is the sharing of psychic communion through translation into the sprach of the flesh, then dare call it love that I felt as envy of the voyage fused with admiration for the voyager.

Slowly I moved my finger toward the Jump command point as if through the thick crystalline syrup of time; the interval seemed to expand as my consciousness poured satori into it.

The first note of the Jump signal sounded, reverberating through the bridge, the ship, my body; everywhere but the center, the Pilot's module, the hub which was void.

With it came the memory of Dominique—leaning into my body space, the acetone smell of her breath, the odor of the void and the courage to dare it; and with that olfactory memory-trace, the congruent memory of my sexual arousal, called forth now in realtime.

The second note sounded, releasing the words she had spoken. "If you insist on metaphor erotique, bitte do not choose to imagine our transaction as the rape brutal. You ravish not my spirit."

But now the music of those words seemed to be a tune of new meaning. "You ravish not my spirit," sang the melody. *Au contraire, au contraire!* whispered the after-beat.

The final note sounded.

My memory track looped back upon itself, compressing her lips gliding down the nerve-trunk of my phallic ec-stasy into temporal congruence with her last words ut-tered in the afterglow, her eyes glazed like mirrors over the beyond within: "So, mon cher liebchen, you will re-member *that* should your will waver at the time of the Jump, nicht wahr, and you will at least know it is no rape you do." *Au contraire, au contraire!*

And as I stared out into the starry blackness as into a lover's eyes, her eyes, with my finger paused in erect attention over the point of ultimate penetration, I un-derstood.

"Jump," I said, my mouth seeming to form the word with infinite slowness, rolling it, tasting it, and blowing it into the void like a kiss. Neither rape nor cold mechan-ics nor ideogram of psychic malfunction, I perceived my touch upon the command point as act of love; true, ulti-mate, and beyond the realm of selfish satisfaction.

In that durationless augenblick, I seemed to feel an electric channel open; from my mouth surrounding our single shared word of love and the tip of my finger upon the electronic quick of her center, through memory's orgasmic trace, to Dominique, up there in the Great and Lonely, down there in the Pilot's module, and a great soundless sigh of airy energy exploded from my inner being.

The stars had shifted. The moment had passed. In fleshly realtime, my body hummed once more with the jagged energy of unreleased fulfillment.

Not without enormous psychic effort and duty-bound act of will did I remove myself from the seat of that fast-fading satori. It seemed as if I might somehow recapture that which was dissolving from the forefront of my realtime mind into the depths whence it came by contemplation of that starry mandala we take for all that is, or failing that, to complete the circuit by congress with the only soul aboard whose spirit had touched mine in the moment that had passed.

But Argus had announced our new position, my crew awaited orders to secure the bridge, Dominique lay comatose, and my assignation with Lorenza awaited. Once more must Genro Kane Gupta don the mask of role and duty; once more must my disharmonized spirit serve the harmony of my ship. Already, Argus and Mori were regarding their Captain peculiarly as he slumped there staring into space.

It was a thing of some small mercy that I had arranged to meet Lorenza in the deck of dream chambers itself rather than in the grand salon or other social venue; for as I made my way through the corridors and lifts, I was sorely pressed indeed to return the salutations of those I passed along the way. Shadows, poor, pale shadows, and I an unwilling player in this quotidian charade.

Was I then aware of the slippage of my persona; did I

perceive in the mirror of passing faces my own gathering social anomie?

As the lift deposited my corpus in the nether reaches of the Grand Palais, Lorenza was there to greet me. Wrapped in flowing gauzy veils whose rosy hue matched to perfection the uterine walls of the corridor coiled about the dream chambers, her long red hair trailing off into the subtle currents of perfumed mist, she seemed a concatenation of the atmosphere itself, an apparition, a dryad of this lust-pink forest.

Nevertheless, it took a certain act of will, a blinking back of darker spirits, to rouse my natural man from his bubble of fugue, even in the face of this vision of fleshly delights.

"Ah cher Genro, what dream shall we now share?" she said, gripping my hands lightly like a small child anticipating a trip to a fete.

"Nada beside the vision which now is mine," I replied, summoning up the ghost of gallantry while avoiding a specific response, for in truth such considerations of venue had not passed through my attention since I had last entered the bridge, and indeed even my previous musings upon these erotic esthetics had fled down memory's abyss.

With a show of some gaiety, I led her through the maze by the hand, peering teasingly into this chamber and that as if sure of my destination but spicing what was to come with playful mock indecision; naturellement, the reverse was true, as I sought a chamber that might pique not only her desire but the flagging spirit of my own.

Was it karma working through random motion, the subtle sense that the charade was wearing thin, or was it outer congruence with my inner tropism that finally made the choice? In truth perhaps all three, for the venue presented itself just as Lorenza's hand in mine was tightening with a certain questioning impatience;

and certainement, the dream chamber that presented itself at that very moment mirrored that which called to me from within.

The dream of this chamber was space itself: an illusory infinity of jewel-pierced blackness into which we floated free from gravity's turgid embrace. Naturellement, not the cold, deadly void beyond the hull of the *Dragon Zephyr* but a stylized abstraction of same. Not a frozen vacuum but lambent, humid air heated to the temperature of the blood's desire. Nor were the stars fixed like eternal vertices in a crystal lattice; rather did they perform a complex and stately interweaving waltz to the music of some celestial orchestra. The void, yes, but denatured and molded closer to the human heart's desire.

"Que drole, mon Captain," Lorenza said, her amusement perhaps shaded with a certain dubious restraint as she drifted slowly in the swirling mists of her garments. "The Void Ship Captain chooses the void, ne?"

No bon mot sprang to my mind; indeed, for an augenblick of paranoia noir, it seemed as if those ice-blue eyes had seen to the very core of my transfleshly desire. And in truth a strange energy began to uncoil down the chakras of my spine to raise my phallic lance to rigid, somehow metallic awareness; not the sensual unfurling of prana humaine but the sudden cold flashing of bright-blue electricity along the circuitry of my wires.

I unpeeled myself from my clothing with mechanical efficiency, scarcely noticing the slow disrobing dance of veils which Lorenza performed for my delight. As if some hidden sensors had marked this opening movement of our pavane, the music's tempo began to quicken, and the stars whirled faster in their interweaving orbits.

Ebon skin naked against the deeper darkness, Lorenza's body seemed to melt into the void, becoming a mounding, curving, palpitating extension of the atmosphere itself, an esprit de la nuit emerging from the clinging black waters in a foam of stars; blue eyes, white smile, red nebula of hair incarnating the ineffable itself.

Stars whirled faster, music quickened, and I drifted open-armed toward her, down, down, down the vortex of memory's desire—into the Circuit, into the void, into the Captain's throne, my finger erect over the command point as I stared out into the countenance of the great beyond.

My spine was an arc of cold electric fire, my phallus was engorged with painful charge; my sense of who, and where, and what, like the vortex of stars drawing me down into their center, like the face of the incarnated void itself, seemed to dissolve and fragment into chaos sans form, sans interface between.

As we touched, as our arms enfolded, as flesh rippled into flesh, as lips and tongues coalesced and intertwined, as the music rose into an ongoing crescendo and the whirling stars became a black hole vortex around our central void, there was naught but a searing succession of lightning bolts sparking down my spine and into the tortured lance of my phallus, twitching and throbbing in the throes of the heterodyning charge.

Groaning, my finger touched the command point; with a single swordstroke thrust, I penetrated to the core quick of the darkness—

Jump!

—and exploded in a sharp-sharded shower of electric glass, bolt after bolt of searing cold ecstasy surging through my galvanic flesh into the vulva of the void.

Like the Jump itself, it was over in an augenblick, leaving me spent, fragmented, and rapidly detumescing, hanging limp and panting in the darkness.

Lorenza floated before me, eyes like cold blue marbles, lips curled into a violent sneer. *"Animal!"* she snarled roughly. "This is for you the art tantrique?"

I floated there for a long, silent moment under the withering contempt of her gaze; absorbing it, encompassing it, making its judgment my own. Wretched with shame, squamous with vile and unvoiceable secret knowledge, shivering in my own guilty sweat, how could I reply?

And yet . . . and yet . . .

Slowly, my psychic focus began to coalesce back into my quotidian Captainly persona; I became all too aware now of the enormity I had wrought, the unseemly breach between Captain and Domo, and all which it might portend in the social realm. Hesitantly, I swam toward her, my conscience politique aroused to some reptilian notion of redressment via the willful but juiceless application of the oral tantric arts.

"No!" Lorenza shouted, holding up a fending hand, arching her body away from me in an ideogram of reflexive disgust. Then, regarding me through narrower and more thoughtful eyes, more softly: "No . . ."

"I'm sorry, Lorenza, I—"

"Vraiment!" she snapped. "You are sorry indeed!" Then, once again, a softer echo: "Vraiment, mon pauvre petit." She sighed, her shoulders relaxed, and slowly she came to regard me more in sorrow than anger. "Truly, you are possessed by some malaise, Genro. First the priapic frustration for you, then this . . . this loss of civilized control."

I nodded my mute agreement, grateful for her sympathy on this level, but knowing full well that a true connection empathetique between us was impossible on a higher one.

Aware now of my shameful discomfort, she moved somewhat closer, brought her hand up as if considering a touch of my cheek. "De nada, cher Genro," she said. "I have experienced the maladroit performance sexual before. Surely Healer Lao will cure you of this malady."

"I think not," I told her, shaking my head. For I knew full well that no cure for my affliction could be found within the sphere of the Healer's art, if indeed that which had infected my spirit could rightly be called disease.

"Por que no?" she said with some renewed pique. "To fail in the pas d'amour through some malaise, this I can pity, but to refuse to seek a cure out of foolish masculine pride, this is conscious act of ego!"

"Call it what you will," I said with the stubbornness born of secret knowledge which I could not reveal. "But you will, bitte, speak of it not to passengers or crew. We must not infect the social realm with our . . . with our—"

"*You* presume to hector *me* with the canards of duty?" she snapped. "You, who refuse to properly perform your own? I am Domo of the Grand Palais of the *Dragon Zephyr*! I will disturb not the harmony of my own domain with personal pique! We will, naturellement, maintain the facade civil."

"I appreciate your discretion, Lorenza."

"Discretion, pah!" she declared with loftly coldness. "I maintain the facade civil for the sake of my duty, my wretched Captain, and that is all!"

I nodded, I sighed, I retreated behind the wall that now lay between us, a barrier of my own creation, willful or not. But as I drew my clothes over my cold, detumescent flesh, I was possessed by a perverse sense of bitter freedom. I knew now that the focus of my consciousness had been released from the performance of my Captainly role into a self-imposed purdah d'esprit. Like Dominique, the purpose that my spirit served was now its own.

Or so in my malaise did I believe.

—— X

Mal d'esprit, sexual malaise, cafard, obsession noir; thus might masters of the healing arts have taxonomized my mental state as Lorenza and I went our separate ways. Those of less therapeutic but more moral bent not without the justice of the tribe might deem me a rogue bull, a sociopath, a monster of anomie faustian.

Chez moi, I would no doubt have pled my guilt to all these things, then as now. The turning away from succor's hope into the darkest heart of the obsession itself was surely a willful act of my own choosing.

And yet, now as then, at the baleful end-point of this self-chosen geodesic curve of fate, I still cannot deny a certain secret pride in having chosen the vision absolute over the quotidian vie humaine.

Voila, I have at last allowed this awful truth to pass from my self-occluded coeur onto the word crystal of this account where all may confront it, even if the only soul ever to read this naked truth will be my own!

Think of me what you will, regard me as did Lorenza as a prideful fool in love with my malaise; as I left that chamber of voidly dream, I longed not for the status quo ante, for the lost innocence of my Captainly role, but for she who had led me into the dark depths of this cafard—indeed, for the orgasmic countenance of the void itself.

But though an age had turned in the augenblick of the dream chamber, in the realm of flesh and time barely an hour had passed since the Jump, and Dominique lay in sick-bay coma still, leaving me to wander the ship like the Fliegende Hollander of ancient operatic lore, a lorn ghost-Captain in a shadow realm.

Hours passed in a fugal fog. Lorenza had departed for the environs of the grand salon; I therefore repaired to the entertainment deck, where we would not meet, where congress with Honored Passengers and crew might meetly be confined to the silent communal passivity of the spectatoral mode. Here I attended the performance of a string and electronic septet, a holocine in the kabuki mode, a dance of sword and fire, an erotic triplet, a concert of spontaneous musical odes.

Or rather did I drift from one to the other, sipping at this and that but never drinking deep; notes and movements, costumes and gestures, words and vistas, melanging into a fragmented abstraction of the arts humaine, the frenzied dance of captive spirit through maya's forms, or so it seemed to me in my timebound daze.

Flaming torches arching from hand to hand, the silken rolling of flesh on flesh, tautened wire vibrating to the human word, ideogrammic gestures of fear, love, and rage, the mathematical grace of bodies moving through space—all seemed revealed as shadows on the void, the pauvre panoply of man's attempt to transcend the universe of space and time through the transmaterial purity of abstract form.

Yet beyond this noble dance of human art, the highest expression of our spirit's striving to transcend the realm of time and form, lay that which could not be encompassed by the artifice of man. From nothing are we born, to nothing do we go; the universe we know is but the void looped back upon itself, and form is but illusion's final veil.

We touch that which lies beyond only in those fleet-

ing rare moments when the reality of form dissolves—
through molecule and charge, the perfection of the
meditative trance, orgasmic ego-loss, transcendent peaks
of art, mayhap the instant of our death.

Vraiment, is not the history of man from pigments
smeared on the walls of caves to our present starflung
age, our sciences and arts, our religions and our philosophies, our cultures and our noble dreams, our heroics and
our darkest deeds, but the dance of spirit round this central void, the striving to transcend, and the deadly fear
of same?

Only now, in the machineries of the Jump, via the ultimate expression of our mastery of the matrix to which
our spirit is bound, have we at last thrust our will beyond
the boundaries of mass-energy's maya into that formless
realm.

Only then, as I drifted from shadow play to shadow
play, each a striving to transcend and an illusion with
which to deny, did I begin to perceive the meetness of
the Pilots' name for the unnamable—the Great and Only,
that which lay beyond even our quotidian void.

Cafard? Obsession? Anomie? Or the vision absolute
from which our spirits shrink? Cannot they be the same?

After a time, I wandered from this venue of the arts
to the vivarium, where previously my spirit had been
drawn in such fits of existential angst. Here, in the company of the mindless trees, the free-flying birds, the
bugs and frogs that passed from stimulus directly to response without the interval of consciousness between,
did I hope to lose myself in the living mandala of evolution's less self-tortured forms.

Instead, as fate would have it, I encountered that most
exotic denizen of the *Dragon Zephyr*'s aviary humaine,
Maddhi Boddhi Clear, the one man aboard whose obsession matched my own, a kindred caricature of my spirit.

He was sitting alone on a crumbling stone bench staring into the artificial sunset now deepening the illusory
rose and purple sky toward the impending appearance of

the starry void, as if to capture the moment when the illusion dissolved into the true vision of stellar night. This most thespically social of Honored Passengers, this white-maned pilot fish of the floating cultura, seemed lost in the private contemplation of his own secret realm; I felt both a reluctance to intrude upon his solemn meditation and a magnetic attraction to the very inwardness his face now seemed to declare.

It was he who spoke awareness of my ambivalent approach.

"Ah, Captain Genro, seek you also the sight of the naked stars?"

I started somewhat at this manner of greeting, so close to the core of my secret mood, so distant from the mode of discourse between Honored Passenger and Captain. "Quelle chose!" I dissembled. "In the course of my duties on the bridge, I view them to surfeit. It is Honored Passengers such as yourself who might find the sight outre or picturesque, not to say daunting."

He stared up at me with even dark eyes. "They daunt me not," he said, "though admittedly my fellow voyagers tend to vacate these premises when the illusion at last gives way to less occluded vision. In that respect, at least, I sense in you a fellow creature."

Indeed, as the shadows lengthened and the disappearing rim of the sun sent flickering umber and carmine shafts through the foliage, I now perceived parties of passengers scurrying for the exit with a certain uneasy haste, even as the birds of day retreated into their treetop perches. There went Mori, arm in arm with Rumi, glancing in our direction with a certain widening of eyes at our congress as they made their way along a nearby path.

"Will you not sit here beside me and watch the stars come out?" Maddhi invited.

I hesitated for a moment. Certainement, the public sight of the *Dragon Zephyr*'s Captain seated together with this outre personage, this mystical mountebank, would no doubt become a topic of some bemusement, not to say jocularity, in the gossip of the floating cultura; yet I could not deny that I sensed a certain desire in myself to seek his counsel on matters which otherwise need go unvoiced.

As I stood there frozen in stasis between my true desire and the social bounds of my Captainly role, I spied Lorenza walking round the far shore of the nearby pond, brightly plumed admirers clustered about her. She chanced to glance in our direction, and a quick moue of distaste puckered her lips, her eyes narrowed, her eyebrows raised; then she turned and said something to her companions which elicited a twittering of mirth, a covert flicker of glances in our direction, no doubt at my expense.

"Por que no?" I said to Maddhi, speaking also to Lorenza and her party in my heart of hearts. I seated myself beside him, flourishing my indifference in the sight of all; if I was Captain of this ship, was I not also the Captain of my own soul?

"May I speak to you frankly?" I asked somewhat foolishly.

"It can hardly be prevented."

We both laughed good-naturedly, albeit perhaps not without a certain reserve.

"Jocularities aside, Captain, I do believe I already know what you wish to ask, and the difficulty of framing it within the bounds of politesse and taste. Con su permiso, allow me to relieve your burden. Is this so floridly named fellow fraud or seer, mountebank or pilgrim? Do We Who Have Gone Before truly speak to him in dream and trance and sexual cusp, or is this a ploy to cozen otherwise unwilling lovelies into his somewhat overripe embrace?"

I laughed again, this time a discharge of uneasy tension. "I would not have quite framed it thusly. . . ."

"But you would have it answered, nicht wahr?" Maddhi said, the humor vanished from his eyes.

I nodded silently. The last oblique rays of artificial sunset glazed his eyes with blood-red highlights and chiseled his features with chiaroscuro shadows; a trick of lighting, a change of voice, and all at once a deeper spirit seemed to speak through this thespic shell.

"If you will indulge, I will answer you with the tale of my name, though I warn you it is no less outre than my cognomen's form. . . ."

"Por favor. . . ."

Maddhi stared up into the near blackness as he spoke as if unwilling to miss the moment when the planetary illusion gave way to the tele view of the naked void itself. Perhaps with thespic intent as well.

"My name is Maddhi Boddhi Clear, and as you have no doubt surmised, I have chosen all three as freenoms, leaving my pedigree in the mists of the long-forgotten past. Tambien have I chosen them not in homage to some personages I admire but as ensign of my chosen path, homage a the satoric moment that set my feet upon it, and admittedly with declarative intent as well.

"I was born a considerable time ago on a planet I choose not to name for reasons that also leave my pedigree best unsaid. Suffice it to say that poverty was my birthright and knavery my means of escape therefrom; in my youth and indeed far into mature manhood my physical charms were held in high repute by femme and homme alike and I did utilize them sans merci or shame for the pecuniary advantage of the moment.

"Thus did I find myself on the nameless planet of We Who Have Gone Before as courtesan companion to a woman of great wealth and great age, whose name I will not defile in this outre tale. Suffice it to say that though her corpus had long since decayed beyond my body's desire, her spirit was such that each performance of the tantric arts which I was compelled to give might fairly be said to have been an act of love, if such sentiments may be granted to a plyer of that trade.

"I knew not what she sought, there on that world of

ancient mysteries in the twilight of her life, save that I knew her to be a far-traveling seeker of those ineffabilities whose essence I was then far too jejune to comprehend; indeed, I had surmised that her connoisseurship of outre molecules and charges, of sexual excess, was a famine not of the spirit but the flesh.

"When at last her true goal was revealed, scandalized, horrified, I at first refused. Until with tears and blandishments and discourse which hovered just beyond my powers to understand, mayhap through subtle influence of the venue itself, I was persuaded to relent.

"Scattered about that planet, clustered here, in isolation there, are the ultimate machineries of We Who Have Gone Before; deceptively simple black cubic slabs, or couches, or altars, within which lay the devices from which our scientists have derived the stardrive of the Jump. Most have long since ceased to function; the few that remain active are closely guarded by the curators of that planetary museum.

"But wealth in the service of true obsession may purchase all, and so we secured a period alone, high on a mountain crag under the all-knowing night sky, in the presence of a still functional altar. And there the deed was done.

"Naked beneath the stars, we ingested some arcane brew of molecules of her devising, and, when the air seemed pregnant with the ghostly spirits of that discorporate race, when the blood beneath our skins seemed to boil, and the stellar concourse seemed to whirl about us in a cosmic dance, she laid herself out on that altar of the unknown.

"As is known, these devices are not precisely tuned to the nervous system of our species; sin embargo, when I laid myself upon her and began to apply my erotic skills, almost at once was she transported into orgasmic ecstasy's embrace. Not once, not twice, nor any discretely numerable amount of times did she achieve her orgasmic peaks; rather did her cries and spasms meld into a single, endless, fiery plateau of ecstasy too extreme to bear pleasure's name.

"At the moment when I could prolong this state no more, as my being sought to pour itself through my phallic connection to her state of masculinely unknowable transfleshly grace, she bit upon a poison cap, and in that instant, she was Gone Before. Leaving me behind to tell this tale."

Somewhere in the darkness of the deserted vivarium, a single frog croaked its forlorn song. Dreaming birds rustled the leaves in their sleep. Above us glowered the million pinpoint eyes of the stellar abyss, each an oasis of pale, frail light in that black sea of nonbeing, a random speckling of matter thrown across the void. Maddhi Boddhi Clear turned from that countenance of the infinite deeps to stare, human to human, man to man, into my own.

"What did I feel in that moment of her blissful death? Did something then speak to me from the great beyond? The drug? My own orgasmic peak? A final farewell kiss of thanks? Quien sabe? Memory would not bind."

He sighed, a sad, longing, regretful sound. "But one thing I will never forget—in the moment of her death, as my body poured forth its measly manly essence into that which she was leaving behind, I gazed upon the last instant of animating life moving through her face. Never, before or since, have I seen such perfect, tranquil, utter bliss."

He shrugged, he smiled ruefully, he seemed to don his quotidian persona by conscious act of will. "Thus, mein Captain, was my life transformed. Pilgrim? Seer? Mountebank? All that and more. From that day until this, my entire life has been the effort to taste that which left me behind. Seer have I become in hope of attracting greater seers. Mountebank to the rich and seeking so as to finance my pilgrim's travels—"

"But do voices from the Great and Only truly speak to you in dreams and at the peak of sexual embrace?" I asked, regarding him now with sympathetic eyes.

Chilled with this confirmation that my obsession had touched another's heart through darker deed than any I had done, I was yet moved by his courage to speak its black name clear. For was his quest not that which in less naked guise had seized my spirit as I ejaculated into the void of Dominique's releasing lips Lorenza's abstracted flesh, pierced to my own quick by the mystery's black and fiery lance?

"Do We Who Have Gone Before truly speak in dreams or orgasmic cusp to my poor mannlichen ears?" Maddhi said, throwing up his hands in a gesture of self-reflexive irony. "Quien sabe? Long have I studied all the available lore, long have I dreamt in waking hours of the fulfillment of my denied desire, long have I lusted after such communion beyond and within the flesh. Does something truly speak to me from beyond the void or is it merely my own desire? Do I use this vision to entice women into my embrace or is the reverse the truth? After all these years, am I sincere, or is all this but a ploy to gain largesse?"

"You yourself do not know?"

Maddhi Boddhi Clear seemed to shrink in upon himself then, beneath the pitiless eyes of the all-seeing yet occluded void; yet a third persona seemed to emerge, this an aged, weary man facing the end of his long unfulfilled quest.

"One thing in truth I know quite well, mein Captain of the Void," he said in undissembling tone. "I seek a path I have not found. And I know it to be there."

"*Know?* Or merely believe?" I said without an interval of reflective thought. And immediately was chastened by the frisson of pain that passed across his face and then was gone.

"I *know* that We Who Have Gone Before . . . have

Gone Before. I *know* that she followed through aid perhaps of their instrumentality and my own phallic grace. And I sense in you, Genro, a fellow creature, a man who has looked through the window of the Jump itself and seen what lies beyond, if only in the mirror of some woman's eyes, nicht wahr. . . ?"

I started in guiltily unmasked surprise. Our eyes locked, gaze to gaze, homme to homme; fellow creatures beneath it all, and that I could not deny.

"Beyond that, are we not reduced to logical belief, you and I?" said Maddhi Boddhi Clear. "We Who Have Gone Before appear not to have been a race divided into genders of femme and homme. Where they went, their species went entire. And this prison of mass and energy in which we find ourselves confined teems not with halfling remnant races left behind, though all our science declares that sapient spirit should arise as the crown of every biosphere. Vraiment, justice is more than we can expect from evolution's random chance, but does not logic itself declare that we poor human males be not the only poor benighted sapients doomed to be forever left behind?"

"You truly believe that it is possible for us to . . . to . . . ?"

The concept could scarcely form itself within my mind, let alone frame itself in words upon my lips. In what manner were his quest and my obsession one? Only in that place sans words or form. But as I stared into Maddhi's haunted eyes, there I saw the mirror of my own as down some contracting warp of time, old with years, freighted with knowledge, yet still peering longingly at that final mystery beyond the voidly veil.

"The path must be there for us as well," said Maddhi Boddhi Clear. "Otherwise . . ."

Otherwise, are we not lost? I thought, and sensed the congruent frisson of doubt pass through his anguished heart.

"Otherwise, we overpride ourselves on our unique wretchedness in the universal scheme, nicht wahr?" he said, breaking the intensity of the chilling moment with dryly delivered jocularity noir.

He shrugged, he looked away, far away, up into the eternal, endless night. "In fifteen billion years did spirit out of less than dust evolve," he said. "In fifteen billion more will not this universe of stars to less than dust return? Whence did it come? What is there when it is gone? Surely, mein gut Captain, we are not paranoiac enough to believe that such paradoxes are posed solely for the chastisement of the sons of Earth? That would be reference delusions on a cosmic scale! If the path exists for spirit to transcend this sorry scheme of things entire, vraiment, it must exist for all."

Or for none at all, I thought, but deigned not to voice.

And so we sat there for a time in silence: two sentient creatures hunkered on a slab of stone beneath the leafy trees by a tranquil pond, moving in our bubble-world through the great abyss. Wrapped around us, the vision of the seemingly all-embracing void, the womb of time which gave us birth. Was that too but sentience' veil of dreams, a bubble of illusion in a greater beyond?

In such a state did my spirit confront the self-appointed hour come at last, and so once more I found myself stealing up the *Dragon Zephyr*'s spinal corridor, not like a lover in some farce d'amour, but like a somnambulist in a fever dream. I started not at the sound of approaching footfalls, nor did I scuttle crablike up cul-de-sacs to avoid the sight of Honored Passengers or crew.

Was it clarity of vision that made all else seem a shadow play, or had my obsession clouded my perceptions of the puissance of the quotidian realm? Even now, as this other Genro sits here at the terminus of his spirit's path through time, I cannot say. My ship seems doomed, my duty betrayed, my honor gone, and yet, gifted or cursed with foreknowledge of its end, would I have stepped away from this path? If clarity be madness, then must we not make the most of it or be doomed to make the least?

As fortune and custom's use would have it, few were the witnesses to my zombic march, and none to see this gaunt-eyed ghost slip inside his Pilot's cabin, though not through any worldly care of mine.

Dominique feigned not surprise at my apparition; indeed she awaited me, propped up alertly on pillows in her bed with her hair combed neatly, as if this were an assignation long since planned and I a tardy swain.

Vision seemed to sharpen, fog to dissolve; in this innermost of all forbidden venues, the charade was over, for the game of persona, having never begun, could neither be won nor lost.

"So, cher liebchen, we tryst once more," she said, a thin smile creasing her bluish lips.

"As we both knew we would. . . ."

"Vraiment, am I not your fated femme fatale?" she said dryly. "You will sit here beside me, no, and fear not, mein pauvre petit, la belle dame in an outre sense perhaps, aber nicht sans merci."

Without verbal riposte, I found myself reclining on the bed beside her, close enough to smell the sour perfume of metabolic malaise, close enough to see the capillary red marbling the whites of her fevered eyes, the bits of whitish crust at the corners of her lips. Was *this* my fated femme fatale? I was seized by a protoplasmic revulsion for that which drew my spirit near. What manner of man was I to eschew the arms of the fair Lorenza to seek such unwholesome embrace? And yet . . .

And yet . . .

And yet I felt my treacherous phallus on the rise as a cold and nauseous serpent oozed down the chakras of my hollow spine.

"Do you know what you've done?" I finally said.

For a moment, her rheumy eyes seemed to peer deep down into my soul, and then, as if rebounding off nether truths, glazed for an augenblick into mirrors of my own internal void, her pale and blotchy face stylizing into a lifeless mask through which peered some dark spirit which animated us both.

"I have awakened that which might better for you have slept," she said in a clear voice devoid of all remorse. In this same emotionless, unromantic spirit did she lay a cold and clammy hand upon the undeniable proof. My reflex was to shrink at this all-knowing touch, a chill went through my protesting flesh, but it was all a foolish psychesomic lie. The serpent uncoiled into her pitiless hand, its kundalinic body engulfing my spine, an electric connection between my phallus and my mind.

She gripped my cold-blooded erection in a demanding fist. "What do you feel now, mein Captain? This is not the amour, nicht wahr?" I groaned as she deliberately kneaded my flesh just this side of pain. Her eyes showed not passion, nor would they let mine alone.

"Fear not the truth, Genro," she said. "I know that this burns not with passion for the beauteous Dominique Alia Wu. Nor do I feel fleshly lust for my Captain of the Void. Aber we both seek consummation of the selfsame desire, liebchen, and in that, our spirits touch."

"A consummation which only you have found."

A tremor of some momentary irony humaine flickered beneath the mirrors of her eyes; her mouth quivered with a hint of unknown fear or loss which, though occluded, failed not to touch what remained of my human heart. For a moment, it seemed as if there were something more than congruent desire that we shared.

"A consummation which you have not found, vraiment," she said. "And which you wish to understand."

"Which in my madness I seek to contain," I said, and felt the serpent's mouth engulf my brain as my soul at last admitted all.

Dominique touched my cheek with a trembling hand. "I have awakened that which better should be left asleep, poor creature," she said again.

"Such was not your intent?"

"I serve that purpose which is its own intent," she said. "Toward you, mon cher, I had no intent at all."

"And now?"

"And now, perhaps, I am infected with the conscience humaine. Quien sabe? But we are fellow seekers now, travelers together, though we are each alone."

"Mad creatures both, beyond the social pale," I said, and in so doing felt a tension part, a crossing over to another realm, where figure had reversed with ground, and the dancer dared to step beyond the dance.

As she had exposed my true karmic state to its own self-aware perception not without my own collusion, so did she now free its priapic proclamation from the camouflage of social concealment not without my own inevitable aid.

"Shall I give you the ghost of what you desire as best I can?" she said, gripping my heated flesh with a hard, unsensuous hand. "Ah, liebchen, if I could give you more . . . ," she said with a sigh, palpating waves of sensation up my central core to batter at the portals of my final pride.

"When I'm on the bridge now," I whispered, "when my finger is poised above the Jump command point, it feels like this, Dominique, it feels as if . . ." I shuddered in a spasm of self-revulsion, unable to go on.

But my Pilot eased away this clotted moment with a suddenly tender hand, a finger placed upon my lips, and words that balmed and cozened. "Ach, mein Genro, do not imagine that this is the perverse passion to one who understands! You wish to be with me in the Great and Only now, do you not? So, mein pauvre petit, I take you there in the only way I can. Imagine I do for you what you do for me and be not ashamed. Who are the shadows of this ship to say that what we do is not the act of love, verdad?"

I felt my flesh surrender to her ministering hand, my spirit surrender to my flesh, and both surrender to the moment itself—the timeless, mindless now, beyond the moral realm of future deeds or judgments past. Who indeed could say that what we did was not an act of love? Through this inadequate flesh did not Dominique in selfless mode seek to repay my own altruistic role for its service of her spirit in the Circuit of the Jump? Was it not a mere cruel trick of time that our completions could not in temporal congruence merge? Was it not a grace to transcend our timebound fate through mutual act of selfless will? If this is not love, the word has no meaning; I believed it then, and I believe it yet.

I closed my eyes and gave over my mind's eye to her words: "It is velvet dark in the Pilot's module, liebchen; there is neither light nor sound nor pain. You float as if in the womb, sans gravity, sans temperature exchange, sans tout. There is neither a you nor an it, for you have melted into the perfect, formless, featureless darkness. . . ."

Waves of stately energy moved in tranquil grace up the kundalinic connection between our fleshly nexus and the darkness behind my eyes. Under her tantric ministrations, I practiced the yoga of sensual disconnection, cleansing my eyes of vision and focusing my sensorium on the sound of her words and the electricity of her touch. Slowly but steadily, the tempo increased, bringing me to the quivering brink of orgasm and holding me there on the sweet razor edge as I floated in the timeless and formless blackness.

"And then, at once, you are there! From nothing into All, from darkness into the endless white light!"

Spasm bolts of lightning seared up my spine to explode in brilliant shards behind my eyes, piercing the pleasure centers of my brain, galvanizing my nervous system with a white-hot charge—

"Ah, the moment, liebchen, when the blackness explodes into the light and you are all, and you are not, and it is Great, and it is the Only, and it is forever, beyond the veil containing space and time . . ."

—the fibers of my body contracting in a coldly glorious final tsunami of formless, modeless, emotionless ecstasy pouring my spirit through my phallus into the vulval void!

". . . soon, alas, to end, as webs of darkness fracture the light into form, into the vortex of maya drawing you down into the dance of space and time. . . ."

Slowly my eyes opened to the vision of Dominique, staring down at me with a thin but not entirely cruel little smile, a knowing communion of the unknowableness of the unknowable, a moue of empathetic loss.

"Tu sabes, liebchen?" she said softly. "For you, it is to know but the shadow that poor words and flesh can give you; for me, it is to taste the Great and Only vraiment, and then to be cast out once more into the shadow world."

I lay there in supine and detumescent lassitude on the soiled and rumpled sheets of our transaction, feeling in truth soiled and rumpled myself, aware now of the fluids and sweats that are the quotidian aftermath of the highest psychesomic cusp.

And yet, even in this most extreme of revulsive post-coital depths, I understood that the bargain was worth the price, that to touch the heights one must indeed wager all, that the spirit's purpose truly was indeed to serve no purpose lower than its own.

"To awake here slowly in agony and pain to pay the price . . . ," I said, clasping her hand to me and stroking her ragged hair.

"The aches and agues of the body our Healer soothes with drugs," she said. "Aber, to be returned from the Great and Only, that, my friend, is the pain for which there is no balm."

"And so our spirits touch in exile in this shadow

realm," I said. "And comfort each other as best they can."

She kissed me lightly on the lips. Her pale, sickly face was transfigured by the first smile thereon that had truly touched my heart. "Ah, mein liebe Genro," she said. "Your Pilot meets a Captain whose spirit understands."

Like this word crystal being replayed, the period confined within the temporal bounds of the next three Jumps seems a subjective nonlinearity measured by event rather than duration; it all seems to exist simultaneously before memory's unreeling eye.

Naturellement, I fed my body, eased its fatigue with sleep, abluted and relieved myself when necessary, and performed my duty's rounds. Perforce did I also hold congress with Honored Passengers and crew like a socially conscious man.

But these concessions to mundane imperatives existed in a timestream alien to the causal skein of meaningful events whereby the spirit measures time; as heartbeat and breathing are given over to cerebral centers beneath the cortical crown, so were the biological and social niceties given over to the peripheral systems of my mind.

For in truth those events which mattered were warps through linear time, compressions of experience whereby temporal distancing was overcome, at least within the illusion of subjective desire.

How convoluted and arcane does that apologia sound as I play it back with its true meaning hovering just beyond my own comprehension! Vraiment, I am dissembling still, or perhaps any craft is insufficient to render a coherent image of vision or madness from memory's other side.

The unembellished truth is that my full attention came alive only at the moment of the Jump and at the time-warped completion of the act in Dominique's boudoir; the interval between was the realm of shadows through which my true spirit slept.

How this puppet Captain must have appeared to the other actors on the stage is something which even now I can but dimly recollect as data shorn of all affect.

Seven meals were taken, or mayhap eight; six of these were social events spiced with discourse in which I no doubt took part. There are sense memories of many noble dishes artfully prepared and vintages of appropriate savor. There was a grand banquet given by Lorenza, where I was the object of a certain jocular contempt for my congress with Maddhi, as well as thinly veiled japes from our Domo of a more unseemly erotic nature. There was a meal with Argus and Mori passed in formal discussion of the ship's duties and events. Other repasts were taken in various cuisinary venues with names and faces that blend into a babble of sprachs.

A customary status report on the human cargo stored in electrocoma was made to me by Maestro Hiro; this impressed itself upon my memory owing to his expressed concern for the status of my health. Erotic overtures were made to me by a somewhat unusual plenitude of Honored Passengers whom I repulsed with as little personalization as possible, feigning weariness or malaise or pleading duty elsewhere.

On a number of occasions, I was entrapped in conversations of hermetic intensity which in another state might have piqued my curiosity or attention, but from that period my memory can extract only intellectual shards. A discourse by Rumi Jellah Cohn on the dialectic between the universality of the artistic impulse and the diversity of cultural forms. A woman who spoke of faint messages now perhaps being received from the galaxy of Andromeda, millions of years in our nonrelativistic past. A scurrilous tale about a Domo who conceived an infatuation for her ship's Second Officer and sought to undermine the Captain's authority in the service of her inamorata's ambition.

It all seems an automaton's dance to me now as did it then, a shadow play in which I slept through the playing of my own part. Only one imperative seems to have left the memory trace of the exercise of my will: not without consciously applied skill and guile did I seek to avoid Lorenza, Maestro Hiro, and Maddhi Boddhi Clear—the only humans on board who, through divers instrumentalities, might have penetrated the perfection of my fugue.

If analytic perception may be granted to a being in such a state, it seemed to me then that only by abstracting my being from the intervals between could I endure the temporal gaps between the Jumps and the discontinuity between Dominique's fulfillment and the shadow of my own. Indeed, the universe of space and time itself had become reduced to an unseemly intrusion between those augenblick perceptions of that which lay beyond.

As for those brief bright moments themselves and her with whom I shared them, if Dominique and I were lovers, it was by no classic definition of the dramaturge's art. We stared not limpidly into each other's eyes, we shared not romantic meals a deux, no soulful solitary strolls, and of dream chambers we knew only one, and that the product of no human craft. Certainement, all the loverly sentimentality and sacraments of the quotidian realm sullied not the purity of the passion transhumaine that we shared.

There are certain tantric dyadic asanas in which erect lingam penetrates yoni immobilely for the duration of the mutual meditative trance. If such partners in the solitary inward quest may be said to perform an act d'amour, then mayhap Dominique and I were lovers, for although our tantric configuration was different, its goal and spirit were the same. If such exercises be informed with mutual caritas, are they not a rarefied act of love?

Certainement in the linear timestream our discontinuous performances were unselfish acts of love; on the bridge, I served her spirit, in her bed, she served my flesh, and never in this time-warped transaction did yoni and lingam meld to give as they received.

Was this not a human bond between us, this leap of trust through time? Were we not two souls in our isolation magnetized by the same pole?

She was the Pilot of my kundalinic circuit, as I was the Captain of her own. But in the chord of our mutual vibration, I was the minor note. What the Captain bought was not half so precious as what he sold, and I now perceive that even then the baser note of envy was a throbbing undertone.

Thus while our time-transcending congresses had merged into a seamless generality where event was subsumed into the archetypal now, as I replay that memory's worldless crystal, I see the fault lines of its eventual shattering marbling the whole.

I sit on my throne of power beneath the canopy of stars as it seems I have always done, and as the familiar Jump ritual proceeds, the now-familiar electric current begins to flow along my spine, deja-vued by memories and anticipations coiled round the illusory now.

I gaze into the starry void, into Dominique's eyes, into the blackness behind my own sealed eyelids as her lips envelop my lingam, and I feel a feedback channel opening between this creature of obsession and the dormant natural man.

"Pilot in the Circuit. . . ."

Even as my spirit perceives our cycle as a time-warped act of love, phallic logic goads me with its egobound primal throb; now she would ride the whirlwind and I would be her steed, through the electronic Jump Circuitry my will would serve the purpose for which my flesh was disdained. . . .

". . . checklist completed and all systems ready for the Jump. . . ."

In the Jump, I was the master of her ecstasy, and in the flesh Dominique the mistress of my surcease; au contraire, was she then not the servant of my flesh and I now her spirit's slave?

"Captain? *Captain Genro?* The checklist is completed."

"Well then, take your position, Man Jack," I say with serene distraction, and Mori repairs to her chaise with an expression of bemusement that seems to be eternally there.

"Ship's position and vector verified and recorded," Argus declares, her voice shrill and peremptory as it seems to have always been. "Vector coordinate overlay computed, Captain, and on your board."

Was this erotic equation not truly the ideogram in which we were bound, and was it not an injustice, an imbalance in the universal scale? Had not Maddhi—

"Captain Genro, the vector coordinate overlay is on your board and ready to be dumped!" Argus fairly snapped; the slap of her voice, the keen edge of contempt in her eyes as she turned to regard me shattering the crystalline temporal generality into the unseemly and all-too-specific now.

"Are you all right, Captain?" Argus demanded with little show of sympathy. "Are you suffering from some malaise?"

"Attend your console, Interface," I snapped with an ersatz Captainly peckishness. "Dumping vector coordinate overlay into the Jump computer now. Please activate the final two command points."

Sullenly, Argus returned to her duties, and the last two command points reddened on my board. "Jump Field aura erected," I announced with a deliberate reduction of curtness, although I jabbed the command point with a vehemence I was hard put to understand.

Like a reveler awakening the morning after a multi-molecule binge and wondering what enormities the gap in his memory track conceals, I found myself surveying the traces of the past three ship-days in the timebound causal world. Had this disharmony on my bridge been building while my attention was vanished from my Captainly role? Had I sleepwalked through my duty as I had through the floating cultura in a somnambulistic haze?

Even then I knew that my fellow officers were no just objects for my ire, nor in hindsight's clarity was it Dominique against whom my passion raged. Nevertheless, as my finger curled toward the Jump command point like a tautening steel spring, slowly did the unselfish tantric figure reverse with the angry thwarted ground, did impotent envy come to inform the impending act.

The Jump warning notes sounded, reverberating down my spine, and my digit stiffened into a vengeful phallic lance. My lips twisted into a soundless sneer as I confronted my rider in the void, serene in the crystal blackness beyond my manly powers.

"Jump," I growled gutturally, "Jump, damn you, Jump." And as I thrust at the red quick of the Jump command point, I longed to feel that orgasmic moment impaled on my own exploding flesh.

In an augenblick the moment came and went. Outside the ship, the stars were different, and on the bridge, I sat there foolishly, regarded with discomfort by the widened eyes of my crew.

Mori's startlement seemed innocent of knowledge or judgmental tone, but Argus studied me narrowly as if I sat there naked, sweating, and tumescent on my Captain's throne.

"Captain Genro, are you sure you're all right?" she said. "Would not a consultation with our Healer be—"

"I am in perfect health and in command of my faculties," I replied coldly. "Though I appreciate your concern."

"I only meant—"

"It is of no importance, Interface; I will let the matter pass," I said with as much authoritatively Captainly finality as I could feign. I locked eyes with my feminine Second Officer, willing her accession to the authority of my command, to the potency I longed to feel.

After a moment, Argus looked away from what she saw, and in that moment perhaps I might delude myself that some sense of my manly power had been regained. But this was the pouvoir of the Captain only, not the puissance of the man.

I departed the bridge with my consciousness in a somewhat less fugal state—not that my spirit had been deflected from its inner focus; rather that quotidian events of sufficient import had intruded themselves upon my attention to the point of forcing me to act. For the first time in three ship-days, I had truly donned my Captainly role and dealt with a psychic exigency of command beyond the mechanical round of automatic duties.

True, I had done this only when my Captainly authority had been frontally threatened; true tambien that my own prolonged disattention had been the causal agent of Argus' challenge. Nevertheless, the event *had* occurred, and it opened my void-glazed eyes to the effects left in the wake of my somnabulary trajectory.

In retrospect, I then began to see that while my spirit had been traveling other realms, its animating absence from my persona had perhaps not gone entirely unnoticed by those who encountered the resulting creature in the course of duty or social discourse. My Second Officer had perceived it well enough to challenge my authority not so much as Captain but as a properly functioning man, and even my young Man Jack had not been oblivious to the bizarre nature of my behavior. Truth be told, I feared a seance with Maestro Hiro or Healer Lao, for my confidence in my ability to pass the muster of their profession was not exactly great.

Yet even as I left the bridge with a certain determination to restore the potency of my persona as Captain in command, even as I admitted to the practical cunning of avoiding the close perusal of the Med crew, I doubted not the absolute reality beyond the worldly veil, nor did it seem to me insanity to pursue it.

Rather were the realms in which I found myself in disjunction with the ideal spiritual state. The bubble-world of human culture was but a shadow parade through timebound space, and that which lay beyond it lay also just beyond my grasp, floating mockingly before me in the tender ministrations of Dominique. Once more I empathized with that first lunged fish to crawl out of the englobing ocean into the open unknown air; I was gasping on the interface between the lower and the most high, unable to go on, unwilling to return.

But unlike that first self-tortured amphibian, I was possessed of the dualities of mind and the reflectiveness of spirit to realize that in order to evolve, an organism must first survive. Chez moi, that meant survival as Captain of my ship, and as I tentatively entered the grand salon, I wondered what I would find. How far had the erosion of my social persona drifted while its essential spirit was gone?

The grand salon was well attended as is customary during the Jump. Like gaily colored tropical fish habiting a convoluted coral reef, Honored Passengers of every species and hue were floating about the levels, nooks, and cubbies of the great sculpturefied room in hovering schools and shoals. Trays of dainties were everywhere, carafes and goblets of spirits, essences, and wines, herbal pipes, and braziers of intoxicating incense.

As I stood there on the entrance landing in the high-lighted sight of all surveying this generality as if from a mountain peak, a certain psychic odor seemed to waft to the back reaches of my brain: the ripeness of overrichness, the proclaimed artifice of superabundant perfume, the ozone of circuitry sizzling near overload. Private islands of variously tinted light picked out archetypal floating cultura scenes as if some classic painter had laid out a vast genre canvas of the fete. Here were lovers bent together on a pinkly chiaroscuroed chaise, there a scene of Maddhi Boddhi Clear amid feminine acolytes in a hazy golden glow, a slim woman playing a sandovar silhouetted in bright white, drinkers, diners, amorous adventurers, and the quite intoxicated all incarnating this dramatic baroque tableau.

Here was the vida real of the starfaring floating cultura, the distilled and heady essence of this greatest age of man; here were wealth and art and beauty, science, curiosity, and intrigue; why then was I reluctant to be the Captain of its ship of fate, to play my leading role? Why then did I stand there until I had once more made myself a strange-eyed spectacle to these brightly accoutered shadows?

Indeed, Sar Medina Gondo, with great thespic flourishes of her flowing white, gold-embroidered robes, ascended from the fete to fetch me like a great maternal bird.

"Ach, gut Captain, you have been quite an illusive figure," she said, capturing my arm in hers and leading me like a prize down the stairs before all.

She clung to me assertively as she guided us through the swellings and thinnings of the throng, never ceasing all the while to prattle of this and that in a grand, projecting voice. "I see that Rumi and your little Third Officer are still keeping to themselves, pero from other voyages with that bravo, I tell you it will not last, of course we sophisticated voyagers know what rogues d'amour you Void Ship officers are, and nicht wahr, mi mannlein, you can say the same; why even you apparently have become indifferent to the great Lorenza's charms, leaving other hearts to hope. . . ."

She stole a glance d'amour in my direction as she offered me a goblet of wine from a tabouret, her long blond hair combed into golden waves, her shining green eyes clear and empty as fine crystal.

When this was not returned, she continued apace, squiring me about the grand salon and simulating our rapt conversation with an endless monolog of public bon mots.

"Ah, mon cher, there is Ali Barka Baraka, surely the richest creature aboard, they say he owns an unreported planetary system in the outer fringes where the economic overlords of creation gather to engage in unspeakable vice, though alas I've never been invited, but I did once share a dream chamber with one of his lovers who had the most amazing tales, speaking of which, I'll wager you've heard some droll ones from our Maddhi over here. . . ."

By design or fortune, she had thrust me into the center of a group gathered about Maddhi Boddhi Clear, with her own person attached and little reluctance to assume responsibility for the intrusion.

"Why everyone is talking about your little tete a tete up there in the darkness together, my dears, have you finally made a convert out of a comrade of your own foolish gender, Maddhi, pero surely, nicht wahr, not through the usual means . . . ?"

Maddhi, not to be nonplussed in his own venue, shot a brotherly glance in my direction and replied in fine, florid style. "My heterosexuality is a legendary scourge of the galaxy, cher Sar, as you have had occasion to know; it goes beyond the fleshly tastes to regions alas beyond your ken. As for the Captain of the *Dragon Zephyr*, I judge him a similar spirit, a fellow pilgrim of the way."

At this there was jocular and at the same time befuddled laughter from those gathered about us, whose numbers now seemed to have spread.

"So this is the cause of our Captain's distraction," some unseen sly voice said. "Like Maddhi Boddhi Clear, he listens to voices in his head."

The laughter at this was raucous and prolonged, and to his own considerable discomfort Maddhi was unable to sail a jape above it, which is not to say he did not try. "Like Maddhi Boddhi Clear, he has not stoppers in his ears."

But this riposte sounded lame to his clearly critical ear even as he launched it, and it was in any event shouted into a whirlwind of jocularity, in which it vanished without a trace.

"So does it happen to those who stare into space too long!"

"Better men than we have gone before!"

I found myself within a flock of bright-plumed and riotous parrots, squawking their laughter at their own birdbrained sallies, shrill life-denying cackles flung round my smarting head. No riposte presented itself to my blushing mind, nor could I flee except in even more unseemly disarray, and so I was reduced to standing there like a comic foil till the japery finally died away.

Yet though I clearly stood there as the victim of their jests, still did it seem to me that there was a higher joke of which they were the butt, the cosmic conundrum which their laughter sought to veil. Was this japery not their means of trivializing the unconfrontable profound? Was not the laughter longer and louder than such banalities should command?

Mayhap such analysis is the rationalization of the public buffoon, and certainement I itched with the burning rash of same, and verdad it took the mercy of the good-hearted Mori to effect my extraction by leading me away with my ears still ringing on the pretext of some nonexistent technical question.

But even as I released my rescuer back into the dyadic company of her inamorato and attempted to melt away into the anonymous generality of the fete, I smelled even more strongly a shrill, overripe odor in the psychic air, of hidden and unbidden alchemies smoldering beneath the scenery. Beneath all this gaiety and baroque complexity lay the simple and so carefully denied: beyond the thin metal surrounding us was the endless humorless void. Hollow rings the laughter of orphans in the night.

The embarrassing and unsettling scene chez Maddhi was not, at least, without its practical compensation: in the process of being rescued from my discomfort by Mori, I had been extracted as well from the clutches of Sar. I resolved to make myself the center of no more attention than was unavoidable and certainement to eschew the company of anyone whose style or intent was likely to propel me into bold relief.

Indeed, I contemplated leaving the fete for some more solitary venue, there to pass the time until my hour with Dominique away from this madding throng. But in a peculiar fashion, my very unease in the grand salon made it both psychically and practically difficult to depart. Of what unseemly and perhaps less humorous gossip would I become the object if I retreated from the venue of my jocular disgrace into solitary broodings? Might not my comings and goings become a subject of closer public scrutiny, endangering the secrecy of the ultimate enormity of my assignations with the ship's Pilot?

Certainement as Captain I could ill afford to appear unwilling to face the discourse of my own Honored Passengers, and as a man I refused to slink off like a creature of no consequence from the bemusement of these shrill buffoons.

So, like a nectar-dipping butterfly, I fluttered from bloom to bloom, tasting this conversation and that, sipping wine, inhaling incenses, nibbling dainties, never securing a static perch but hovering at the peripheries while sampling the garden's questionable delights.

Nevertheless, I was the object of no little attention and not merely the accustomed flutter attending the Captain on his social rounds. I was constantly aware of covert glances behind my back of the sort conducive to a self-diagnosis of paranoia, had I not occasions to trap unwary watchers with a sudden shift of my gaze. While I encountered no more verbal assassins lurking in the shadows, my mental state seemed the subject of subtle probing scrutiny assayed through the idle discourse. Particularly were my difficulties with Lorenza an object of prying gossip.

"Quelle chose, my dear Captain, why was our Domo not in attendance at our lunch?"

"It was a rare meal Lorenza conjured, Genro, peculiar you weren't there."

"She seemed more than willing to share dream chambers with us all."

"Ah, my roguish Captain, you have the secret amour, ne? For surely poor Lorenza's behavior reveals the claws of a woman scorned."

"Or is it you, pauvre Genro, who have lost Lorenza's favors? Is that the cause of your malaise? If so, allow me to suggest a stratagem d'amour which I've never known to fail. . . ."

"Certainement, mon cher, there are others more than willing to cast away your gloom. You need only look about you—or into my own eyes."

Und so weiter ad infinitum, as I wandered in a growing discomfort which began to take on an edge of anger as the proceedings evolved. For as they all assayed me, I passed over into judging them, and in my vision they were no less haunted figures than the Captain whom they regarded as such an object of psychic speculation.

Indeed, while my admitted distraction might have

wrapped me in enigma, and the disharmony between
Captain and Domo might be ample cause for this social
concern, the true meaning was beyond their courage to
attempt to comprehend. Thus, while their perceptions
were clouded by self-willed ignorance, mine were honed
by the all-too-puissant clarity of the inner eye.

From which vantage did all this gaiety seem somewhat overheated and thin, like a phantom oasis city
shimmering in the desert eye. Like wasteland travelers,
did they not dwell in their own mirage, wrapping their
illusion round them in the empty awful night? So fragile
was the structure of their reality that a single unsub-
sumed consciousness, a solitary ripple in their little pond,
was enough to roil the social waters into a frothing, bur-
bling foam.

"Ach, the wandering spirit returns!"

I was in the act of pouring wine into my goblet from
a flagon, standing for the moment alone in a blue-
illumined concavity, rather like a tiny sea-cliff grotto
carved into the overhanging rock, a bubble of relative
solitude, or so I had thought.

But there Lorenza found me, and not without her entourage. Two of them were supporting her, or, rather,
she lounged luxuriantly in their arms. Aga Henri Koram,
the freeservant master of erotic entertainments, done
up in bare chest and mail of brass, held her about the
waist like a sack of plunder while she draped her arm
around the neck of a thin blond fellow dressed in wine-
red silks artfully arranged to simulate noble rags. Lorenza herself wore but a short white sarong clasped with
a wooden brooch and slit to expose her inner thighs and a
wreath of bejeweled golden flowers choked tight about
her throat. Sweat glistened on her body or mayhap some
unguent gel, and her ice-blue eyes were glazed with intoxicants and the reddened haze of voluptuary intent.

Behind them, like the background in some erotic
frieze, were half a dozen Honored Passengers similarly

dressed for festishistic fantasy of diverse styles and modes, leaning against each other and regarding me with lidded eyes.

"Greetings, Lorenza," I said stiffly. "I see you are enjoying the spirit of the fete."

At this, there was tipsy laughter from the followers in her train; no few of them were charged or moleculed, and sans doubt all of them were drunk.

"And you, pauvre Genro, are your pleasures being met?" Lorenza said somewhat thickly. "Or would you care to join our troupe?"

I stared evenly into her bleary eyes. "You seem quite well escorted at the moment," I said. "What need do you have of me?"

"What indeed!" she said with a sudden ice-hard coldness that provoked intakes of breath. The moment hung there suspended like a thundercloud of storm. Blue daggers of lightning seemed to flicker in her eyes. All within range seemed locked in unwholesome attention.

"Ah, but surely, mon cher, there is always room for one more," Aga said with naive good-naturedness despite his chosen persona of naked flesh and chains.

With that, the tension burst into erotically overtoned laughter, in which all save Lorenza joined.

"Yes, do come along, we have more than enough of everything to go around."

"Come let me stroke away your gloom."

"Let us all repair to a dream chamber and invent an erotic figure no one has seen before."

"What do you say, my gallant Captain, is this not an occasion to which you can rise?" Lorenza said in a slurry yet piercing tone that silenced the sycophantic rustlings like the cracking of a whip.

"The question is, mon cher," I snapped, "whether *you* can remain erect much longer."

There was a collective inhalation at my bluntly pointed rejoinder, a whiff of the ancient arena of our most time-

less gladiator game; the onlookers observed this contretemps with a naked hungry glee.

"Supinity will suffice for my part, ne, is not the other
yours?"

My ears fairly burned crimson and my groin grew
damp and cold. The audience laughed uneasily in a
squirm of sympathetically crawling flesh.

"I fear our fair Domo has passed beyond the realm of
nicety," Aga said distastefully, loosening his grip upon
her waist.

"Oh, the niceties and gallantries have long since passed
between the Captain and myself," Lorenza pressed on,
hazy of countenance but crystal cold of eye. "Verdad,
Genro? No doubt there are numerous others who have
piqued your manly interest. As there are others, many
others, to be honored in your stead."

Now Aga disengaged himself with righteous manly indignation. But Lorenza barely noticed, merely flowing
closer against her other momentary swain. "Unless you
have become a sour celibate, as the all-knowing Sar
would have it."

"Or perhaps there is another whose charms exceed
your own," I snapped back cruelly, no longer prudent in
my shameful rage. "Is such an unlikely miracle beyond
your ego's power to imagine?"

"Name her, then, and tell us her tale!" Lorenza said
with serpent softness. "Produce this beauty for our delectation. Hide not treasures for yourself!"

"And if she conducts her amours not as theater as
some others I could name . . . ?"

Lorenza looked coldly into my eyes and I glared just as
coldly back. Though my mocked and outraged manhood
called for vengeance against her taunts, my higher cor-
tex abruptly clarified with the knowledge that this scene
had been played out much too far.

Lorenza too seemed to have attained this relative state
of cerebral civilization or at least had seen what was in

my eyes; she gave off staring with a thespic wobble of her head, feigning a sudden awareness of her own intoxicated state.

"I do believe I am not entirely within my powers, good playmates," she said in an exaggeratedly syncopated voice. "Let us find a place softly cushioned and leave our Captain to his ectoplasmic soul-mate."

So saying, she departed with her entourage in her wake, and I stood there for quite some time in my shadowed little niche, watching them reel and bob like flotsam through the wrack of faces, spreading the gossip of this latest unsavory addition to my unwholesome mystique like windblown foam.

─── *XII*

BY THE TIME I had screwed up my courage and screwed down my anger to the point where I might risk another immersion in the floating cultura, the effects of the contretemps were all too evident in the lidded and carefully neutral eyes that everywhere met my glance, in the murmuring and swift whispering that sprang into being wherever I turned my back.

Goaded into an unthinking reaction by intoxicated outrage to my manhood like some naive adolescent or detumescent aging roue, I had myself exacerbated exactly the perception that I had sought to prevent.

Now, sans doubt, Lorenza's accusation of impotent celibacy would contend as a theory for my bizarre mood with my own foolish proclamation of a hidden amour. My movements and actions would be subject to the prying scrutiny of all and sundry, my mental state would continue to be a prime topic of idle speculation—all of which, alas, being that which I had made my appearance at the fete in order to avoid arousing.

Under such circumstances, my continued subjection to this reality served no tactical purpose, and, feigning wooziness myself, I beat my rather disorderly retreat from the grand salon.

Out in the empty spinal corridor, I paused to catch my

psychic breath, clearing the fog of social banalities and games of persona from the center of my perceptions. And I must confess that, as I stood there with the long tubular corridor stretching away to vanishing points fore and aft like the geodesic of my own lifeline, reflection upon the state of my own sanity could not remain absent from my scrutiny.

I began walking slowly up the corridor through solitary, coupled, and grouped Honored Passengers crossing over from the grand salon to the stateroom module, drifting through this area of cross traffic like a wraith. Soon I had passed beyond this habited country into the long empty passage to the bridge at the *Dragon Zephyr*'s bow.

Behind me, the world of the floating cultura seemed to recede down a corridor of time, becoming a memory, a distant shadow play, a place I had left, and to which, in a certain sense, I now knew I could not return in the same karmic form. The figure of Void Captain Genro Kane Gupta was now irrevocably an object of unwholesome surmise; unarguable also that on this voyage Captain and Domo had become the polar foci of disharmony rather than the ritual leaders of the accustomed pavane.

Nor could I deny that the unwritten social contract had been nullified by an act of my own will. Just as I had donned the robes of pariahhood in the eyes of my charges, so had they become less than wholesome to my own inner eye. Between us lay a barrier of fractured expectation and shattered illusion, an intrusion of more puissant forces through the fabric of the reality we once had shared.

To those whose lives were seamlessly subsumed into the mass and energy of maya's realm, was not a consciousness such as now possessed me beyond their ken? Were not they sleepwalkers through a vain illusion from the vantage of this outre apparition in their midst? Verdad, if sanity is a social definition, then Genro Kane

Gupta was mad; aber if the spirit is the highest judge, then was I not the only sane person aboard?

Dominique and I.

Who served no lower purpose than our own.

I found myself approaching the Pilot's cabin just as our Healer, Lao Dant Arena, was shutting the door behind him. "Captain Genro?" he said from under raised eyebrows. "Why are you not in the Grand Palais?" Meaning, naturellement, *Why do I encounter you in this province?*

"I seek," I said spontaneously, "the solitude of the bridge."

"The bridge?"

"Indeed. I was just on my way there now."

"Is something amiss with the ship? Some anomaly or malfunction in the mechanism?"

"There is nothing to fear, Lao. I merely wish to . . . to commune, as it were, with the stars."

The Healer now regarded me with a certain professionally sympathetic concern. "I have observed in you a certain malaise of the aura of late, if you will forgive me, Captain," he said. "It is said that you have been lacking some subtle elan vital, that—you will pardon my concerned intrusion—that you reject all overtures to erotic exercise."

"I was not aware that the duties of a Healer included serving as a conduit for mendacious gossip," I said sharply but without fire, determined not to provoke any more suspicion than my appearance in these environs had already warranted.

Lao squirmed nervously and leaned closer, an expression of acknowledgment of his transgression of the bounds of nicety which I somehow found engaging. "I meant only to open a conduit between yourself and the exercise of my art," he said hesitantly.

I stared at him in unfeigned befuddlement. He drew even closer and lowered his voice to a tone of confidentiality even though there was not another person in sight.

"As a Healer, I do well know that the broaching of such matters presents certain difficulties of the ego. . . ."

"Difficulties of the ego?"

"Vraiment, alas. Foolish but true. If a man suffers from dysfunction of the stomach, or the heart, or the bowels, or discerns in himself a depressive metabolism, he suffers no qualms over seeking a Healer's aid. But let his phallic organ become the victim of somic or psychic malaise, and more often than not he will suffer in silence rather than forthrightly acknowledge his disease and be cured."

"Are you suggesting that I am suffering from . . . from a phallic dysfunction?" I said, feigning lofty amusement even as my scrotal sac contracted.

"Only you are presently aware of any such symptoms," Lao said nervously. "However, from the secondary data available to me, such a possibility does present itself. A certain anomic flattening of zestful social intercourse, solitary broodings, mystical studies, as it were—these are all peripheral effects not so much of the malady itself as of the secretive defensive reaction to it. Indeed, para-doxically, the lancing of the boil of secrecy is ofttimes sufficient to restore normal erotic function."

The touching yet also clinically detached mien he had fashioned, the rational placitude of his words, somehow made me wish that I could plead to a simple case of im-potence; indeed, had such been my state, I no doubt would have unburdened myself, for clearly Healer Lao knew his art well. How less taxing it would have been to quaff a few capsules, perform a prescribed series of special asanas, and be relieved of all psychesomic dis-harmonies!

Unfortunately, my tantric conundrum, if malady it in-deed was, would hardly prove susceptible to potions or exercises, being not a symptom of dysfunction in the psychesomic matrix but of the spirit's dialectic with the universal corpus in which it was bound.

Vraiment, all other supplicants might find me less than a natural man, but she who waited behind that closed door had the power to raise my priapic lust to be something more.

"I assure you, Healer, my lingam is in fine working order," I told him. "Rather, perhaps, has my taste been jaded by excessive indulgence in the pulchritude habitually available to a man of my station. Alas, it now takes a rare morsel to tempt my so thoroughly sated fancy."

"As you say, Captain Genro," Lao said neutrally. "Though such a complaint is rather rare in the annals of the amorous chase."

"But then we Void Captains are a rare breed, nicht wahr?"

"So I have noticed," Healer Lao said. "But should you have need of my services in future, do not hesitate to seek them out."

"Naturellement," I said ingenuously, and seeing that Lao was not likely to end this seance on his own, I turned and resumed my supposed journey toward the bridge, not daring to glance behind me to see if I was indeed being observed.

Thus did I deem it politic to actually enter the deserted bridge in order to fulfill my ruse in the sight of any watching eye. The chamber lay in darkness relieved only by the faint amber and green lights of the bank of monitors. The tele, of course, was deactivated, and its great overarching glassiness gleamed palely in the ghostly glow. How long had my destiny lain in this venue and where was it leading me now?

From the Interface console, I let in the cosmos, or the color-compensated simulacrum of same, activating the tele sans the orienting gridwork of man. A million stars and nothing more looked down on me as I stood there in the darkness—points of light that cast neither illumination nor shadow, like pinpricks in a black curtain lit from within.

Like a miserable microbe, I scuttled under this enigmatic cold scrutiny for the psychic shelter of my Captain's chaise. Like fabled King Canute did I sit there staring out into the dark ocean and commanding the waves to part; like that archetype of hubris, did I too fail to prevail.

Verdad, I was the victim of impotence, but alas not of the flesh. Did I not throb with desire as I performed here? Did I not achieve orgasmic completion at the hands of my Dominique? Was it not merely in the temporal discontinuity that I failed the test of a natural man?

Indeed, my phallus now ached with thwarted desire under the bleak and lonely stars. Soon it would be time to make my way down the corridor to Dominique's cabin, where this thirst would be slaked. Or would it? For while any thoughts of protoplasmic impotence were banished by the evidence within my own trousers, under the pitiless truth of the void, I could not deny that I suffered from an impotence of the spirit.

I could neither achieve the true completion that I sought through the masturbatory manipulations of Dominique nor transport her to that higher realm with my machismic puissance, though I served as the will for the demon lover of the Jump Circuit. Was this not a form of impotence, albeit of a species unknown to Healer Lao's art? My phallus quivered with the somic memory of the act it failed to perform here, with the transference of tantric function to a finger on a command point as Dominique rode my will, shunning my flesh.

Yet in the moment of time-warped reciprocation, when her lips or her fingers gripped my kundalinic nexus and released its fleshly constriction, did my consciousness not batter futilely against the ultimate, did I not also eschew her womanly reality for the fantasy of the genderless orgasm of the Great and Only? Were not her descriptions of it as she cozened my lingam the only sweet words she whispered in my ear?

All at once the bridge seemed to grow colder, as if the airless chill of the void itself were leaking through its very image on the tele screen, as if the concept alone were enough to shrivel my flesh.

I could bear this venue no longer, for here did the source of my frustrations lie, and only in the arms of Dominique might I at last complete the broken tantric cycle and release the true kundalinic charge in the only way open to a mortal and natural man. I burned with the passionate yet coldly desperate desire to master her now, in the flesh, as a man, to feel her ecstasy surround me in the moment of my own, to pierce the wall of time between us with my disdained phallic lance.

In short, perhaps through Lao's suggestion, my spiritual dilemma had found expression in the sprach of the flesh, and so too, I then believed, did its solution appear to be a simple, straightforward coital act.

Reasonably secure in the knowledge that no Honored Passenger or crew member would be lingering in these deserted environs, I strode boldly down the corridor, following the thrall of my determination through the door of Dominique's cabin and to her bedside without further rational considerations.

Dominique lay propped up on her pillows awaiting my arrival with the expectation of established custom; not long out of unconsciousness, her spirit shone brightly through eyes still reddened with the Jump's sickly afterglow.

But this time I perceived as her glance fell upon me that what were hours of coital interruption in my timestream passed in little more than an augenblick in hers. As her psyche swam back into consciousness, the Jump had occurred only a subjective moment before. One more convolution in the temporal maze between us, yet another point at which our realities did not touch—all the more reason to skewer this Gordian knot with my sword.

"So, cher Genro," she crooned, as I eased myself onto the bed beside her, following the ideogrammic pattern of what had become our frozen tantric form. Sans hesitation or truly passion, she slid her hand up my thigh with repetition-honed surety, enfolding the response she knew would be there.

"So, liebe Dominique, I have become an object of unwholesome surmise to the passengers and crew of my own ship; my manly potence is questioned by all and sundry, and all for the love of you. . . ."

I gazed into her eyes as I said it, or rather into a focal plane just short of her face, so that naught but ambiguity might be read from my intense stare, and I nuanced my voice with wry irony even as I made my face a mask of stone. As for me, I remained to myself unreadable as well, distant from whatever might have lain at the heart of my meaning of this phenomenological and social truth.

"You know not what you say," she said.

"Perhaps," I replied. "Certainement, I know not what I do."

"Mein pauvre petit," she said, stroking my cheek as if I were a lorn little child, a gesture I now perceived as having become a commonality in the ritual of our affair.

"My femme fatale," I said enigmatically, undertoning passion with irony as I grabbed her up in my arms, determined to proceed with my phallic intentions even though no psychic mode of amorous procedure seemed to present itself to the flesh with any conviction.

"Vraiment, Genro," she said as her body tensed into resistance, "you do indeed know not what you do."

"What I do now is the *only* thing I do with clear volition," I told her, speaking at last a plain, unambiguous truth.

So saying, I reached back into the memory track of a

thousand such moments and kissed her full on the lips, open-mouthed and with full labial honors.

Her pliant lips were unresistant to my own and nothing more, her breath metallic with chemical fatigue, and her body remained a fleshly statue under my touch. Yet somehow this very nonresponsiveness seemed to fuel the fires of my lust with the determination to shatter it into womanly passion.

I slid my hand under the bedclothes to seize her at the quick, even as her immobile hand remained fastened to my own tantric focus.

At this, she pulled her mouth away with a cool, calm lack of either startlement or distaste and looked me evenly in the eyes.

"You'd rather not," she said.

"You mean *you* would rather not. I assure you I know exactly what *I* want."

A thin smile creased her puffy, bruised lips, and the spirit seemed to vanish from the windows of her eyes, robbing her face of mere human expression. "Nein, liebchen," she said. *"I* know what you want. Do not make me cruel enough to tell you."

In response, as if to shout *"This* is what I want!" like some brutish lout, I tossed her on her back and fell upon her, tearing aside bedclothes and raiment with an unseemly haste, and not without her assistance. This accomplished, I moved my mouth toward hers as she reestablished her hold on my lingam.

But as my lips descended toward her, she rolled her head away, still without expressing any displeasure by releasing her grip on my manhood. She stared up at me with something short of defiance and something more than rejection's ice.

"You may do as you believe you desire without any ill will chez moi," she said softly. "Only then will you believe what you already know."

"Only then will you know what I believe!" I countered angrily, but not without a certain tender passion, and I prized her hand away from my phallus and penetrated at last to the core of the matter with the first heartfelt thrust.

There was no resistance to my penetration. Nor was there any discernible response. My rage engorged by this ultimate affront to my manly puissance, I threw into the fray all my frenzied vigor and all my not-inconsiderable tantric skill. Nevertheless, I was thrusting my kundalinic prana into a vacuum, I was delving a featureless void; I evoked not a sound or movement, not even as my control eroded after what seemed like an eternity of fiery calisthenics and my flesh was carried by its own momentum toward the edge of its solitary release.

Indeed at the ultimate moment, I looked full into Dominique's eyes, and what I beheld there staring back at me from some unfathomable distance was a mask of indifference, sans feeling or passion or even triumphant self-control; merely a nothingness so absolute that my orgasm became an ugly explosion of soul-chilling ice.

"It's not you, mein pauvre," she said as I lay upon her in exhaustion and no little despair. "You are the noble stallion of the tantra, but chez moi, it is no use."

"The first occasion is seldom representative of the full possibilities," I whined with a certain wounded pompous pride, "If you will allow others, I will prove it to you."

"I allow you all, Genro, provided you do not fail to allow me the One," she said with a strange passionless indifference. "But even should you be skilled enough to evoke your desired response, you will only learn that you have not gotten what you really want."

"And what is it that I really want?" I demanded, rolling off her into a squat, and glaring down at her supine form from above.

"You know it already, though alas, you must hear it from my lips," Dominique said, slowly rising to face me level to level. "What only I can have."

Chilled to the coeur, frozen in timeless amber, I looked

unwaveringly into her eyes, into the voidly visage of the Great and Only, into the opaque-mirrored black vision of my own impossible desire.

"Ach, Genro, you yearn to be my lover in the Jump, ne, to share the cusp of the spirit beyond the mere orgasm of the flesh. And would I not give you this gladly if it were mine to grant? But this is impossible, my poor creature. Unless. . . ."

"Unless?" I hissed sharply as I felt my blood beat in my suddenly echoing brain.

"Unless, like me, you are willing to forsake all else; unless you are truly mad or sane enough to travel the path to its ultimate end."

"There is a way?" I said, aware now that this moment had been preordained on the sky ferry, and mayhap by her will. I sensed with the cold certainty of hindsight's logic that all had been a prelude to this, that despite her protestations to the contrary, she had sought to bring me here from the start, and for purpose of her own as she herself had declared. If a sympathy of sorts had evolved between us in the process, it was no doubt incidental to her true quest, the object of which she had now made my own. Yet despite this satoric knowledge of her guileful manipulations, I hung breathless on her words, although I feared what I was to hear.

Dominique, somewhat shakily, eased her body back into her nest of pillows for support; I remained squatting where I was, but our eye contact never wavered.

"You have never seen the face of a Pilot who has died in the Jump," she began. "Aber, mon cher, I have, on the *Feather Serpent,* the face of the Pilot who died on that voyage, Dominique Noda Benares, whose destiny and freenom I took upon viewing it."

She shivered. For a moment her eyes became shimmers of mirrored opacity, but then I began to glimpse something forming out of my own inner chaos beginning to be reflected back.

"Tres drole, no, sehr macabre, I look into the face of a corpse, and I know that I can be a Pilot, and I know tambien that I *must*. Had you seen it, Genro, perhaps you would understand. The face of a soul that had died transformed."

In her eyes, in the memory of her own mask of comatose bliss glimpsed on the gurney, in the congruence of her words with Maddhi Boddhi Clear's description of the dying moment of his lover who had sought this apotheosis on the altar of We Who Have Gone Before ecstatically impaled on his lance, I could almost see the dead Pilot's face.

"Perhaps I am beginning to understand," I said. "You sought that blissful moment of final release, you were seduced by ecstatic death."

Dominique shrugged, breaking the intensity of the moment, perhaps through breathless choice. "Could I truly know *what* I was seeking before my first Jump?" she said. "I knew not what I sought, only where it was to be found. It took me many Jumps to begin to understand."

She paused, breaking eye contact and leaning back against the pillows as if to inform me that this discourse had a distance to go before it reached the answer I both sought and dreaded.

"Dominique Noda Benares must have been gifted by fate with the death of the body in the moment of the Jump. Somehow, the *Feather Serpent* passed through, and she went on."

"Went on?"

"On. On and on and on. Forever."

"I don't understand."

"Poor creature, of course you do not!" she said ruefully. "To you, the Jump is an augenblick too brief to register on your instruments, nicht wahr, aber within it lies eternity. There is no time in the Great and Only; therefore, within it, there is all time. There is no space, and so there is all space. Nothing is contained, and so the spirit contains all. . . ." She shrugged, she squirmed, her face twisted and twitched, as if her whole corpus were frustrated by the impossibility of speaking the unwordable.

"The antique human religions, nicht wahr," she finally said, "with their cravings for nirvana, Atman, life everlasting in the heavens above—these must have been dim perceptions of that which underlies and transcends this temporal illusion, where spirit grows from flesh, only to depart into the nothingness from which it came."

She sighed. She smiled at me, a smile not without human warmth but not without something else too.

"We swim in deep waters, liebchen," she said softly. "Con su permiso, we go deeper still. I hold back nothing; I tell you my dream that I have never dared to reveal to another soul. The dream that makes me a sport even among Pilots, the hope that has caused me to preserve my flesh with nutriment and exercise so that it may maintain my spirit in this realm as long as possible. I have told you I do this so as to experience as many Jumps as possible in my life span. But now that I have found you, I reveal the truth of which that is the shadow. . . ."

She stared into my eyes, uncertainly it seemed, as if trying to verify some conclusion written therein. I stared back at her shorn of all artifice or manipulative intent, opening my windows to reveal whatever unknown essence she sought to perceive within.

"My dream, cher Genro, is to find a Captain who will help me to make one last Jump into the Great and Only, who will let me go on and not come back. And I believe I have found him in you."

"WHAT?"

"You have heard of the Blind Jump, nicht wahr," she said in a strange, distant tone that seemed to echo down the corridors of my mind. Without conscious awareness of the process until it was completed, I found myself sinking silently into the pillows beside her as if my body were no longer willing to bear its own weight.

"No one here knows what happens to a ship that Jumps Blind except that it vanishes from the here and now," she went on. "Science has its limited surmises as to how. A malfunction of the electronic instrumentality. Biological failure as the overlay guides the Pilot through the cusp. Some mad test of a Pilotless Jump Circuit. This much you are taught at your Academy, verdad?"

I nodded numbly, reduced to silent absorption of what I already sensed was about to be revealed.

"But there is that of which the scientists dare not speak," she said. "The Blind Jump achieved by the will humaine. Aber not by the will of the Pilot. What I have sought is a Captain of the Void with the vision and the understanding to do it for me. And you, mein Genro, are you that man?"

"What is it you expect me to do?" I whispered.

"In technical terms, a trivial act. It is the vector coordinate overlay which guides the Pilot and through her the ship through the Great and Lonely back into this pale realm, nicht wahr, which *forces* her spirit to return. When next we Jump, neglect to feed the vector coordinate overlay into the Jump Circuit computer, let me Jump free, up and out and on into the Great and Only. Set me free, liebe Genro, set me free!"

"Set you free!" I shouted. "Kill myself and destroy my ship for the sake of your cosmic unnamable! What ego! What arrogance! What madness! What demonic gall! How can you believe that I would even consider such a thing? What kind of monster do you think I am?"

Dominique looked back into my outrage with eyes of black ice. "You were told that to achieve what fleshly destiny has decreed you can never have you must forsake all else, mannlein. You were told that you must be mad or sane enough to follow the path to its ultimate end. Now you have arrived."

Her voice had become distant and hard and cosmically

cold, sans emotion humaine, sans pity, sans morality, and yet, somehow, informed by a quality that seemed to transcend all of these.

"What happens to a ship that Jumps Blind, Genro?" she asked in that same even and unyielding voice.

"No one knows," I said softly. "No one can." But already my visceral precognition was oozing forward within my bowels toward the awful inevitable, toward the ultimate and monstrous bargain offered up to my soul.

"If Pilot and ship Jump free into the Great and Only, if there is no vector coordinate overlay to dragoon us back, will we not go on together eternally in the time-lessness beyond the void, and will that untimebound moment not last forever for our spirits? Free me, Genro. Free me and I'll take you with me."

"And everyone else on this ship."

"Yes," she said coldly, without a flicker of regret or guilt.

"That's mass murder . . . ," I declared righteously. "That's evil beyond all rationalization. . . ."

"Only if you also believe it is suicide," she said evenly. "Aber chez moi, if you believe as I believe, as you cannot help yourself from believing, is it not the bestowing of the ultimate good?"

"No man has the right to make such a choice for an-other," I said firmly. In that, at least, my conviction was not feigned.

"Forsaking . . . all . . . else . . . ," she said slowly and harshly, emphasizing every syllable as if to express the whole as a single, terrible, indivisible truth. "You were told that was the price. *All* else, mannlein. *All* considera-tions of this shadow realm."

My heart seemed to stop in my chest as I saw my own depths mirrored in her eyes. As I looked through those windows into the eternity within, time froze, perspective reversed itself, and all that I saw seemed a reflection of myself.

"I'd never do such a thing," I said bloodlessly. "Surely you must realize that." Was the waver only in my voice, or had it already come to express a tremor in my resolve? Was it the thin, knowing smile on her lips that made my own words ring hollow in my ears, or was it already the shadow of the inevitable emerging like leviathan from my own depths?

"There are many Jumps between here and Estrella Bonita," Dominique said calmly, dismissing my protestations from her discourse as if their finality had never been uttered. "And never is not so long a time as forever, verdad?"

Our eyes locked in a long, silent contest of wills.

"Never," I finally said, crawling from that bed of unspeakable temptation to stand as my own man. "And never will I allow you to tempt me so again. I put all this behind me! It's time we said goodbye."

She looked up at me evenly as I backed toward the door. "Say what you will, mon cher," she said with ruthless knowingness, "this is only auf wiedersehen."

───── XIII

I WANDERED STERNWARD down the main corridor in a daze, or, mayhap, stunned by the clarity of too much truth. Past the entrances to the stateroom module and Grand Palais and through the cross traffic as if on rails, oblivious to anything outside the compass of my own inner universe. If indeed anything could be said to exist outside the parameters of the conundrum which had now become my own inner demon.

I had exited Dominique's cabin in a burst of righteous indignation, but this emotional clarity felt fraudulent even as I allowed it to move me; and once I was outside, other, more serpentine voices became insinuated in my inner ear, and all I knew at that moment was that I had to escape the chaos inside my own mind before I could even begin to center a focus.

In previous bouts of what the ship's gossip was no doubt calling my cafard, I had sought out either the solitude of my cabin or the pseudo-natural realm of the vivarium as refuge from the storm, but now the company of my own four walls offered anything but the promise of escape, and the vivarium, with its simulated biosphere and false sky seemed but the quintessence of the floating cultura of maya. As for social roles and niceties with my fellow denizens, I hardly trusted my ability to maintain a coherent persona.

My feet propelled me ever sternward, beyond the habited area of the ship, into the sections of corridor to which the various freight modules were secured; regularly spaced hatches leading to inspection passageways lined this seldom-traveled section of the *Dragon*'s spine on both sides. As this pattern became a featureless generality my footsteps slowed, my mind began to ruminate on what my spirit had swallowed, and I began to understand why I had brought myself here.

The true ambivalence of my connection empathetique to Dominique Alia Wu could not for long be subsumed under the rubric of moral outrage, which is not to say that in a moral matrix her small suggestion was less that outrageous. But I could not deny that my spirit was amorally attracted to this ultimate temptation as my conscience was morally repelled by it.

As for emotions of a human level, here too, repulsion and attraction were locked in stasis around the central void.

Had this utterly ruthless creature not seduced me step by step into this ultimate confrontation with my own spirit for her own self-proclaimed higher purpose which brooked of no tender feelings for me as a man? Or had something in her sensed a kindred something in me which drew us together in our outre tantric pattern like the more fleshly but no less unwilled tropism of mutual pheromonic lust?

Certainement, there was truth betweeen us, in abundant surfeit. Truth absolute, truth noir, but truth without a moral dimension. My very state of being proclaimed that we were, alas, kindred spirits, although that to which we together were kin might be a less than romantic matter.

Against the will of self-esteem's desire, I could not fail to acknowledge that the true chasm between us lay both below and beyond the moral realm of ethical esthetics. Indeed, her ruthless dedication to her one true grail, proceeding as it did from a single absolute axiom to an entirely unwavering pursuit of this axiomatic higher good, might be said to be at least formally superior to my chaotic involutions.

Which is to say that I had become a creature of unresolved doubt while she never doubted her priorities for a single instant.

Did I not envy such terrible clarity of spirit even as I was repelled and outraged by its ultimate expression in the realm of action? For her certainty, her ghastly willingness to ignore all morality in the pursuit of the eternal Great and Only, was based upon the actual experience, whereas my morally superior outrage was that of a spirit in ignorance.

Each cargo module was connected to the central core of the *Dragon Zephyr* by an inspection passageway. Each passageway had a tele monitor for inspecting the condition of its module via remotes. In case of emergency necessity, each passageway was also equipped with an egress and a rack of voidbubble belts.

Excursions out onto the exterior of a Void Ship faring between the stars at relativistic high velocity are not common, which is to say that, uncommon as they are, Void Ship crews would prefer that they be less common still. Indeed I had attained to my Captain's rank and served in that capacity for many years without ever experiencing the unmediated reality of the interstellar void.

The bridge tele and lesser viewers scattered all over the ship were all equipped with compensation circuits which rendered outside reality not as it would have appeared to the naked senses but as the eye would have perceived the galactic abyss from some abstract point of rest. Thus, the starry seas I surveyed from my throne on the bridge were at once another illusion and recreated reality in its untimedistorted incarnation.

Those whom emergency has constrained to work outside a ship declare the experience most unsettling. At these relativistic speeds, the spectrum is dopplered blue toward the bow, red toward the stern, and the shockwave f the ship as its shield deflects the velocity-compacted interstellar medium paints a rainbow aura before it; these effects, however, are said to be mere outre visual curiosities. But the bending of space itself does things to the human visual sensorium that are described as akin to staring into the foveal blind spot in effect, if not in content.

Despite the queasy and arcane repute of this experience, in another sense because of it, I found myself opening a hatch and entering an inspection passageway, moved by the perverse determination to match Dominique's experiential knowledge of the naked void with as close an encounter as I could conjure this side of sharing her Blind Jump.

Quien sabe? Somehow I felt I owed such a direct confrontation to her and to myself; somehow I perhaps believed that the most absolute morality demanded that I look as deeply into the ultimate as my nature would permit before I could in true conscience put it behind me. Only by facing that reality could I in true clarity renounce it.

The inspection passageway was a simple flextube connection between the *Dragon*'s spine and the freight module, about fifty meters long and atmosphere-sealed at either end so as to do double duty as a roughhewn airlock. Immediately upon entering, I confronted the rack of voidbubble belts, donning one and sealing the hatch behind me before proceeding up the tube to the simple egress hatch equidistant from both ends. This was equipped with a system for valving air in and out of the sealed passageway, and twin green-glowing ready points, which now indicated that the seal was complete.

The tele remote monitor was installed directly across the tube from the egress for convenience' sake, and before erecting my bubble, I paused before it to regard for the last time with virgin eyes the electronic simulacrum that had always been my least-indirect perception of the reality of the deep interstellar void.

The image on the tele screen was a snugly contained picture of what lay beyond the ship's skin, unlike the great firmament of illusion which overarched the bridge; the necessary distortion of representational scale served, in that moment, to render the still pointillist starscape obviously unreal.

Nevertheless, it was, in a sense, a truer image of the reality than my naked vision was about to experience in the reality itself. On the tele, the distortion was the product of craft and intellect striving to represent an image of the absolute from a theoretical point of detachment, whereas the relativistic distortions of the raw reality were the means by which random chaos hid behind its own veil.

Thus did that which lay beyond the egress insinuate its vibrations into my perceptual field by the mere fact of my decision to confront it. I erected my bubble of polarized force and began valving air out of the passageway, staring at the tele as the pressure came down as if to impress this human representation of the transhuman reality onto my brain before venturing forth.

All exterior surfaces of the *Dragon Zephyr* were charged with a quarter-gravity field perpendicular to their plane, so that when I opened the egress hatch and crawled out, I was immediately able to rise to my feet and stand at an unsettling angle to the curved exterior of the passageway without kinesthetic vertigo or backbrain fear of falling, like a fly upon a glowglobe.

When I allowed my visual focus to shift from the metal beneath my feet, however, my equilibrium was severely taxed.

I was standing on a thin branch of an enormous metal tree, the stem, as it were, of one of the dozens of huge metallic fruit depending from the trunk of the *Dragon's* spine, which towered up toward a rainbow sheen high above me. Attempts to look out into the depths around me were met by a sense of nauseous and formless constriction, as if reality itself were hiding in the blind spot of my visual field no matter where I tried to focus my gaze. Blue-and-red-streaked reflections in a black distorting mirror swirled around me at the edge of my peripheral vision, which itself seemed to iris in to a narrow perceptual tunnel warped at a bizarrely pitched angle.

Stomach heaving, I redirected my visual focus to the sight of my feet touching metal, and walked hastily and easily with my eyes downcast to the juncture of the passageway tube with the central core of the *Dragon*. Here I placed one foot on the "wall" before me, leaned backward as I completed the perpendicular step, and found myself standing on the ship's spine itself, looking forward along the mighty length of my vessel.

Like an immense metal javelin, the *Dragon*'s spine on which I stood seemed to pierce the fabric of space as it hurtled into the rainbow shield of the ship's deflectors, a giant needle whose prick maintained a prismatic meniscus of surface tension through the oil-slick surface of reality.

Streaming like a spiraling comet's corona from this central anomaly, space was a reversed whirlpool of darkling nothingness smeared with a cloud of blue motes, forever exploding into being before me as I rode ever onward into the eye of the storm. Behind, the universe was a red-misted vagueness drawing down a long tunnel to a vanishing point, and the tunnel itself, the reality of my visual perception, seemed to have neither length nor sides.

Unable to form this visual input into a coherent sensorium via quotidian parameters, my perceptual centers were forced to coalesce my consciousness around an altered matrix. This new spirit perceived itself as a viewpoint on the surface of its own sensorium, a second-order abstraction of the interface between sensory data flow and internal processing mechanism.

Thus, even the absolutism of physical objectivity was revealed as arbitrary itself from the point of view of this ultimate subjectivity.

From this altered perspective, I was riding through the cosmos in a bubble of time, which is to say that the only true reality was the great ship on which I stood and the viewpoint that stood upon it, for this was the only reality of which that viewpoint was equipped to form an image.

Vraiment, was not that reality sufficient to fill the soul? There I stood, a tiny mote upon the back of this mighty metal leviathan, this great silent silvery dragon burning its way through the fabric of the universe itself, the ultimate defiance of the process from which it arose. And was I not, despite all fathomable appearances, the master of the preternatural behemoth on which I rode?

Thus the warped and twisted reality radiating from the prow of the *Dragon Zephyr* became a mere artifact of the system, a phenomenon of the interface between a given input and the essential spirit within, which perceived it as through glass darkly.

I had ventured into this realm in order to confront the unmediated absolute directly, but the revelation which it had forced upon me was the paradoxical nature of the conundrum of absolute reality itself.

If this star-filled void had any objective reality, was it not that still, cold blackness of invariant crystal pinpointed with abstract points of light which was simulated by the ship's teles? Contrariwise, was that diorama not an illusion, and the present unmediated natural chaos the unmasked face of the ultimate?

Au contraire, was my present reality not an illusion generated by the relativistic motion of the ship?

Vraiment, they were both real and both illusion. For was not the arbitrary distinction between illusion and reality the ultimate illusion itself?

Cosmic physics informs us that our universe exploded into being from a single space-time point in the deep but finite past; particles, atoms, stars, planets, biospheres, sapience—all implied in that ancient eruption of existence into perfect void. Tambien do the cosmic physicists tell us that this hyperglobular shockwave of being is still expanding to fill the indefinable matrix in which it has occurred. But of that which surrounds this universal exploding mandala of space and time, even our greatest mages remain mute. Indeed, there is a theorem, proven unprovable by its own terms, that knowledge of what lies beyond the universal material matrix is by definition beyond the powers of an internal viewpoint to conceive.

But as I stood there overcome by the spectacle and by this ultimate perception of that most essential of voids, I realized as well that by one single instrumentality did consciousness thrust its tendril beyond the absolute theoretical shell of this universal egg—the Jump itself transcended the absolute rules which prevailed within.

And by so doing verified the possiblity of attaining a viewpoint beyond maya's veil.

I marveled at the clarity of this awesome satori. The absolute reality of the Jump was confirmed within our quotidian realm by the translation of the ship from locus to locus in defiance of our treasured universal laws of mass-energy phenomena. Thus did our technology produce an effect which transcended the weltanschauung of the very science that produced it, thus did the serpent of the cosmic paradox swallow its own tail, thus was chaos supreme reborn out of the ultimate order.

I was daunted by the implications in our shadow world of forms. Of all phenomena in the realm of maya, only the Jump itself allowed the spirit to transcend the mass-energy matrix which gave it birth, and in a manner which paradoxically allowed our very intruments to record this fact. Yet just as my sensory perceptors could form no coherent image of the relativistic whirlwind at whose subjective focus I stood, so was our entire rational starfaring civilization unable to gaze with clarity into the anomaly in its very concept of reality, upon which it was nevertheless centered.

Small wonder then that an intricate floating cultura

had evolved to insulate starfarers from this perception. Less wonder still that this social matrix had evolved a wall of purdah to separate the rational will of its Void Captain from the transcendent reality of its Pilot. No wonder at all that these cultural instrumentalities rang hollow in the spirit of one who had seen too far.

And if I, who even now still viewed the ultimate through distorted reflection from within the illusion, had become a rogue spirit within the human herd, what reality could a concept like social or even human morality have for Dominique, who had experienced the most intimate of congress with that which I apprehended only in tormented fantasy?

Vraiment was the Great and Only that which served no other purpose than its own. Great. And Only. And solipsistically Lonely.

The temporal duration of this satoric moment I perceived not; all this could have passed in an augenblick, or I might have stood there transfixed for an hour. Be that as it may, it was a moment that I passed through, not a state of being that my psyche could long coherently contain. And once I had passed through it, my vertigo returned redoubled, transformed from a confusion of the senses into a nausea of the spirit.

On trembling knees and with my eyes downcast to focus on the mechanics of perambulation alone, I retreated to the egress hatch, all too aware as I crawled through it and closed it behind me that I was scuttling like a blinded mole back into the comforting darkness out of a surfeit of light.

Reflexively, I activated the passageway's tele as I waited for it to fill with air, retreating behind the illusion crafted by the sensors of my bunker, striving to purge my consciousness of its vertiginous clarity.

When the atmospheric pressure had equalized, I folded my voidbubble, returned the belt to its rack, and shakily re-entered the reality of the ship.

There in the corridor to be confronted by my Second

Officer, Argus Edison Gandhi, regarding me with bemusement and no little concern as I emerged from the
hatch.

"Captain Genro? What *are* you doing here?"

"I might ask the same question, Interface," I rejoined
hollowly.

"There was an instrument reading to the effect that
someone was out on the hull in this area," she said. "Mori
picked it up on a routine scan. I couldn't find you, so I
came here to investigate myself." She peered at me narrowly. "Were you . . . outside?"

I nodded silently, unable to frame a coherent verbal
response.

"Is there something wrong with this module? Do we
have bolide damage? Did you detect an air leak?"

"External conditions are nominal," I managed to inform her authoritatively.

"Well then, why were you outside?" Argus demanded,
as if *she* were the senior officer.

My initial impulse was to dismiss her with a frost of
Captainly ire. My second thought was to invent a harm-
less anomaly which might have caused me to investigate.
But as I regarded this ambitious young officer, this future Void Ship Captain, with her expression of dutiful
earnestness, her air of self-conscious competence, and
her uncomprehending rational bright eyes, I decided for
once to be true to my own inner nature, and thereby,
perhaps, to the respect I owed her as an officer and a
fellow being.

"You have never been outside, Argus?" I said.

"In orbit, but never . . . never . . . *out here.* . . ."

"Well, neither had I before now. I thought it was
time."

"Time?" she inhaled, openly regarding me now as an
object of unwholesome speculation.

"Time to apprehend the reality through which I guide
my ship," I dissembled. "Has it never occurred to you
that we are in a sense traveling blind, that we perceive

the seas we sail, as it were, only through the mediation of our technical instrumentalities? Have you never
wished to experience the true void firsthand?"

Her eyes widened. "Everything I have heard of the
experience causes me to believe that it is unsettling in
the extreme," she said. "Is this not so?"

"Verdad. But such unsettlement might make one a
better officer, ne, certainement a more knowledgeable
one at any rate. I commend it to your consideration,
Interface."

"Are you *ordering* me to go outside, Captain Genro?"
Argus said in a challenging tone of some insolence. But
her expression belied this with a certain fearfulness.

"I merely grant you the option of the experience," I
told her. "As I have granted myself."

"Captain, are you sure you—"

"The matter is now closed," I snapped in Captainly
fashion, and I strode briskly up the corridor toward the
habited areas of the ship without looking back, either
upon the further reaction of my Second Officer or upon
the gateway between our shared reality and that which
lay beyond, through which I had perhaps even then irrevocably passed.

Much to my dismay, but in a certain sense to a higher
form of indifference, before many hours had passed, my
sojourn in the void had become common knowledge, not
to say obsessive gossip, within the floating cultura. No
doubt in the absence of any order to the contrary, Argus
had discussed the matter with Mori, who in turn could
not have kept the tale from Rumi Jellah Cohn, and
thence to the general diffusion via word of mouth. Perhaps Argus herself had also made the subject a matter of
public conjecture so that the tale quickly rippled through
the body politic from an ever-expanding multiplicity of
foci.

Whatever the vectors of diffusion, it soon became impossible for me to appear anywhere without my mental

state and unfathomable motivation for this outre behavior becoming the center of both obliquely inquiring attention and pointedly averted eyes.

Some, like Maddhi Boddhi Clear, Rumi, and a cosmological physicist named Einstein Shomi Ali, sought openly to engage me in discourse upon the subject of my questionable adventure. Einstein wished fervently to have a detailed description of the distortion effects; Rumi, seeking a somewhat deeper cut, wished me to repair to his cabin, where I could compare my sensory experience with certain paintings and objets d'art said to have been created by artists in various states of psyche-somic transport. Maddhi, naturellement, in his florid public style, probed me for evidence of the traces of We Who Have Gone Before written in the perception of the naked firmament, although I sensed beneath this posturing a deeper longing to apprehend the essence of the experience itself.

To this sort of interrogator I replied with candid truth, albeit of a careful narrowness defined by the parameters of the question. To the cosmologist, I described my sensory experience in terms of distortion, without divulging the psychic consequences. Rumi I put off with the generality that no art I had ever seen expressed this reality, although perhaps in future I would accept his invitation to peruse his collection of arcana. Chez Maddhi, I told him my experience had led me to believe in the ultimate sincerity of his ultimate quest, though I had detected no trace of alien sapience.

In truth I obtained a certain unwholesome satisfaction from speaking at last from my authentic spirit, be that essence as it may, rather than dissembling through my persona, though I retained enough self-consciousness of the necessities of my Captainly role to refrain from transcending the weltanschauung of my questioners.

As for those, who, like Sar, Argus, Mori, Aga, and most of all our Domo Lorenza, sought to diagnose my malaise with oblique inanities and loaded pleasantries, it was this insinuating interrogation which finally drove me to the solitude of my cabin somewhat against my will.

The vague inquiries as to my pattern of sleep, content of dreams, and physiological function were discomforting enough, but when Lorenza turned this process into a public inquisition, I could tolerate it no longer.

Although I had been scrupulously avoiding her company as best I could, the most socially conspicuous figure aboard could hardly expect to escape confrontation with the mistress of the Grand Palais indefinitely.

I was sitting in the refectory of the cuisinary deck where hunger had driven me when the inevitable occurred. Here, where the long white tables and bench seating created the communal ambiance of a barracks dining hall, one might assuage one's hunger without making of it a social event, at least to the extent that such a thing was possible to the Captain of the ship. Though the public refectory was crowded, here the social niceties required that one did not engage in conversation with one's neighbor unless the desire was mutual, and such solitary communion with one's meal was not looked at askance.

Thus, I had for the moment successfully retreated both from babbling tongues and from inner voices into the sensory universe of a platter of Pasta Goreng a la Fruit de Mer, a confection of noodles, vegetables, seafood, eggs, and spices of daunting complexity, when Lorenza made her grand entrance.

Bereft now of retinue, she was dressed in a simple white costume of pantaloons and blouson, and her long hair had been gathered behind her neck in a queue. Sans bijoux or pigments, she seemed a bit puffed and haggard, as if from a surfeit of pleasures perhaps too determinedly pursued. Nevertheless, it was impossible for Lorenza Kareen Patali to enter a room in a style not calculated to announce her presence, and not for our Domo the etiquette of privacy in a communal dining hall. She marched up to where I sat and seated herself beside me in a manner which brooked not of the possibility of suave dismissal.

"I'm sorry for my outburst in the grand salon, Genro," she said in a normal tone of voice which nonetheless carried to at least the nearest half-dozen Honored Passengers scattered the length of the table. "I had partaken of a considerable complexity of spirits, molecules, and charges and was in the throes of amorous intrigues as well."

"A trifling event," I said with a combination of gallantry, true indifference, and desire to keep the subject closed. "We all have such moments, ne?"

"But it was an act of cruelty to tax you for your erotic indifference when in fact you were suffering from some deeper malaise."

This remark sufficed to draw my attention up from my platter to regard her with raised brows. Tambien did the attention of all within earshot focus upon this confrontation, though their eyes were fixed all the more fully on the meals before them.

"Ach, pauvre Genro, it is known to one and all that you have been wandering all over the hull of the ship like a lost soul," she said with an expression of solicitude, although it was impossible not to detect a certain malicious edge to her voice. "How gauche of me to attribute your lack of ardor to indifference to feminine charms when in fact you were the victim of some psychesomic dysfunction."

"I am aware of no such malady," I said frostily, squirming under the covert but obvious scrutiny of our tablemates.

Lorenza leaned closer, as if into a sphere of confidentiality, but curbed not her verbal projection. "Ah, mon cher, that is the most disturbing symptom of all. You behave like an amateur erotique in the dream chamber with one who has already experienced your sophistication in the tantric arts, you engage in strange seances with the likes of Maddhi Boddhi Clear, you float silently about the ship like a ghost, you spend long periods in solitary brooding, and finalement, you wander . . . *outside* where no sane person would want to venture, and yet you cannot detect any dysfunction in your behavior!"

Diagonally across the table, a woman made tiny choking noises as if swallowing her laughter, and several pairs of eyes could not resist sidelong glances.

"I am not aware that my duties have not been performed properly," I said angrily. "As for the rest, there are philosophic concerns which may cause the attention to transcend the realms of social niceties and erotic interest, though mayhap these are beyond your comprehension."

Lorenza clicked her tongue and shook her head slowly in a ruefully maternal manner. "Mon pauvre petit," she crooned with poisonous sweetness, "I seek to aid your recovery, not chide your actions. It is likely your condition has some organic basis, I do believe. Have you trouble sleeping? Does your breath have a peculiar savor? Are you experiencing cerebral agues?"

I glared at her in something of an impotent rage. The attention of the surrounding Honored Passengers had now become forthrightly overt and titillation seemed to have been replaced in several cases by a certain fearful concern for the mental equilibrium of their Captainly steward.

"My sleep is undisturbed, my breath offends not my own senses, nor do I suffer head pains," I snapped.

"Is your appetite lethargic or outre?" she persisted. "Is your sense of smell perhaps preternaturally keen? Are your bowel movements regular?"

"I hardly believe my defecations or lack thereof are a fit subject of discourse between us in this or any other venue!" I shouted in dumbfounded outrage.

The murmurings of conversation lapsed into total silence throughout the entire dining room. All eyes were turned in my direction. Brows were raised, jaws hung agape, and I was suddenly surrounded by a mass perception of my own unwholesome exposure so naked and complete as to set my face burning.

"Poor Genro," Lorenza said into this thespic hush, touching a hand to my flaming cheek. "Do you now not think it wise to seek medical attention?"

I could hear the intake of breath at the voicing of this suggestion, and I could see a dozen glances exchanged with nearly imperceptible nods, as if Lorenza had spoken for them.

I bolted to my feet, flinging my chopsticks into my dish with disgust, and raked my gaze angrily around the room so as to compel a ripple of averted faces.

"I thank you for your solicitude," I snarled at Lorenza, "but I, not you, am still the ultimate authority on this ship! You would do well to keep your insinuations to yourself!"

So saying, and with the lack of any other recourse, I stalked out of the room in righteous outrage, but not quite swiftly enough to escape the sound of the pandemonium that erupted as soon as my back was fairly turned.

I could not have been sulking in my cabin for more than an hour when Healer Lao interrupted my broodings with a request via the annunciator to visit the sick bay for a medical perusal, which, he solicitously hoped, would restore the confidence of crew and Honored Passengers in the health of the Captain of their ship.

Nor could I say that such a summons had been entirely unexpected. While there was no authority aboard to supersede my own, in extreme instances a Captain might be placed under medical supervision of the Healer if that functionary was sufficiently convinced of his inability to perform his duties to risk his own career on such a diagnosis and if the Second Officer could be persuaded to assume command under the circumstances at even greater risk than his own.

Such involuntary transfers of command have been exceedingly rare, and instances in which the Healer and Second Officer involved were later held blameless are rarer still, to the point where the particulars of them all are known by all Academy graduates.

Therefore there remains a wise and practical ambiguity as to such procedures; the situation is recognized as one by definition so extreme that no regulation can define its parameters. Thus an extreme politesse is maintained in these matters between all parties. I could refuse Healer Lao's request with Captainly impunity, but to do so might incline him to draw conclusions therefrom which could expand speculation further and cause him to ponder more extreme measures. Whereas a cooperative attitude and a nominal chart, as it were, might do much to tranquillify the situation if it were made public knowledge.

I therefore readily agreed to proceed to the sick bay at once and made my passage thence as conspicuous as possible, rather than slinking like a miscreant to some shameful venue. Indeed, I took several conversational opportunities to inform the generality that I was on my way to the examination, a disclosure which was greeted with a mixture of relief and bemusement.

Only when I reached the Healer's lair was my composure fractured. For waiting for me there amidst the cabinets, chaises, and instruments was not a solitary Hippocratic monk, but a veritable conclave of inquisition: Lorenza, Argus, and Maestro Hiro himself, surrounding the obviously disquieted Lao with grim expressions.

"What is the meaning of this?" I snapped, donning my persona of command.

"This examination was suggested by our Domo," Lao said uneasily.

"And by myself as well," said Argus. "When Domo Lorenza told me of your bizarre behavior in the refectory, I agreed that such was prudent, coming so soon after our own encounter. I trust you will accept our initiative in the dutiful spirit in which it was intended."

"Under the circumstances, Healer Lao naturally thought it meet to have me present," Maestro Hiro said evenly.

I paused on the brink of asserting my power to dismiss these onlookers; to avoid the appearance of a conspiracy against me, they could hardly refuse to grant me privacy, and I was outraged by their unseemly presumption.

But upon reflection, I realized that I had much to gain and little to lose by their witness. In the unlikely event that Healer Lao was willing to opine that my functionality was impaired, they would be informed in any case, and when I was found fit to command, as I was certain I would be, what better vectors to spread the word of this outcome than my chastened accusers?

I met their eyes, one pair after the other, with a cold, unwavering gaze. "Very well," I said, "since you all consider yourselves sympathetically interested parties, I would be an ingrate and a churl not to allow you to remain. Let us proceed expeditiously; I wish to have my usual full untroubled sleep before the next Jump."

And so, under the nervous gaze of my Second Officer, the professional neutrality of Maestro Hiro, and the lidded stare of Lorenza, the Captain of the *Dragon Zephyr* gave his corpus up to the probings, readings, samplings, and palpations of the ship's Healer. Electrodes of all sorts were attached to various portions of my anatomy, samples of blood, skin, hair, saliva, and the like were collected and analyzed. Arcane instruments were passed over, around, upon, and into my nooks and crannies.

At length, vraiment at considerable length, these rituals were concluded, and the diverse data digested by a med computer, which shortly displayed a summary readout for the perusal of Healer Lao and Maestro Hiro.

The two medical officers studied this for a time together, whispered to each other briefly, nodded their agreement, shrugged, and turned to report their findings.

"Well?" I demanded. "Is there any evidence of dysfunction?"

"Your metabolic intake has a slight insufficiency of calcium, your brainwaves indicate an undesirable level of fatigue, and there is a noticeable deficiency of iron in your corpuscles," Healer Lao said owlishly. "I advise you to consume more cheeses, fresh green vegetables, and organ meats and to sleep more regularly."

"And you, Maestro Hiro, do you have anything to add to this calamitous diagnosis?"

"Only that such an examination reveals only the absence of any somic components of psychic malaise," he replied unhappily. "Without a detailed psychic audit of some duration, no further conclusions can be drawn, for only subjective analysis can detect purely psychic anomalies."

"But what of behavioral bizarrities?" Lorenza demanded. "Surely these are objective evidence of a malfunctioning mind?"

"Behavioral bizarrities?" I shouted. "I lust not after your favors, I choose not to make idle conversation, I exercise my Captainly prerogatives to inspect the exterior of my ship, and these are self-evident proofs of derangement?"

"There has been no talk of derangement," Lao said soothingly, clearly embarrassed at such unseemliness in his sanctum.

"Indeed?" I said with exaggerated evenness. "Then you are now willing to attest to my full possession of sapient sanity?"

"I have no cause to attest otherwise," he replied.

"Then as far as I am concerned, the matter is ended," I declared. "Be assured that I lodge no recriminations. My Med crew was merely performing its appointed duty, and my Second Officer can be accused of nothing worse than an excessive concern for the safety of the ship."

I shifted my attention to Lorenza, whom I had deliberately exempted from this profession of forgiveness. "As for you, cher Lorenza," I said cruelly, "while your comportment has been less than exemplary, who cannot forgive the folly of a woman scorned?"

With a wordless growl of outrage, Lorenza stormed from the room.

As Argus somewhat shamefacedly made to follow, I held her back. "A moment please, Interface, I have an order to give you before you are dismissed."

Argus turned to regard me with a neutral professional readiness which aroused my own professional admiration under the circumstances even though my ire against her could hardly be said to have completely cooled.

"I delegate to you the duty of reporting via the ship's annunciators the result of this inquiry," I said.

Her eyes widened. Lao and Hiro glanced at each other in bemusement.

"You . . . you wish me to report publicly to the Honored Passengers that the Captain is in full possession of his faculties?" she said incredulously.

"I *order* you to do so, Interface," I said. "Since you so rightly perceived it your duty to ask the question on behalf of the commonality, it is tambien your duty to announce the answer to same, nicht wahr?"

"Captain, do you think such a procedure is advisable?" Maestro Hiro said.

"If I did not, I would hardly issue the order."

"But—"

"Enough," I said roughly, but without losing control. "In medical matters, I defer to your judgment, as I have just proven. But as Captain of the *Dragon Zephyr*, I will brook no argumentation on the procedural orders I give on my ship."

And to spare both them and myself further confrontation, I let that caveat serve as my exit, assured that I had reestablished the rightful authority of my command.

——— *XIV*

THE TELLING OF this tale nears its end; soon, all too soon, I must put aside this word crystal encapsulating the past and face the ultimate consequences of my action in realtime. While I approach the moment when I must leave this cabin to confront my Honored Passengers and crew with something less than serenity, I believe that these confessions have lightened my burden, not so much through the hoary tradition of guilt-lancing self-flagellation as by enabling me to view past incarnations through hindsight's ruthless clarity and by so doing becoming at least no less than the integrated product of assimilated karma.

In such a state of clear untimebound composure, I can now comprehend the wisdom, or at the very least the low self-serving cunning, of what from a more merely rational perspective, such as that of Argus or Maestro Hiro, must have seemed self-defeating madness. For the Captain of the ship to order the Second Officer to publicly proclaim that he has been found not mad was, naturellement, to induce the opposite impression in the community at large to the detriment of his authority.

While such a bizarre pronunciamento from *any* quarter could hardly fail to exacerbate the paranoia of the floating cultura, by ordering Argus to make it instead of the Healer himself, I had served public notice that my ability to command had been challenged, that the ship's Healer had found me fit, and that therefore this question was now closed by order of the Captain and accepted as such by his Second Officer.

Thus, from the moment of that announcement to my present command of this Pilotless marooned ship, no further challenge to my authority has presumed to appear, despite the growing conviction that I was possessed by dark demons. Having quashed the notion of my psychic inability to perform my duty at this stage and in such a self-evidently outre manner, I had divorced the definition of my sanity as Captain from acts performed outside that official role. That I was irrevocably in command had become axiomatic. Like Ahab, I had made myself an object of fearful mystery whose very darkness enhanced his charisma, a figment of inevitable destiny.

Naturellement, such clear self-awareness informed not the deed in the doing; indeed, at that point I could not have been more indifferent to the social perception of my image, for my central concern was to encapsulate myself in solitude so as to confront my own tormented being.

For truth be told, I *was* tormented by perceptions and their corollary temptation which from a social definition rendered me unsane, though from a more absolute viewpoint what I might be said to have been suffering from was an excess of insight. Social morality requires a shared matrix of communal reality to which to relate thought and deed, and the illusion of an objective ethical esthetic requires at the very least the conviction that objective reality is more than a contradiction in terms.

But I had passed over to a realm of perception where all that could be said to have objective existence was the conundrum of unknowable chaos out of which our quotidian relativities spring. And the only phenomenon of the dance of maya which touched any absolute ground was the Jump itself. By this instrumentality alone was the veil parted, revealing the trace of the Great and Only in the ship's translation through it.

Had my mind therefore not accepted through a form of reason that which my spirit could seek but not touch? Did I not then comprehend that in the most absolute sense only this Void beyond the void was real and that I myself existed as a shadow in a world of shadows?

This conviction grew within me as I went through the motions of the next Jump ritual, exchanging stiff orders and affectless phrases with Mori and Argus, who remained, like myself, sealed within duty from any emotional acknowledgments of the tension on the bridge.

In retrospect, I do not think that I could have been unaware of the odor of psychic ozone which had pervaded the ship as I marched from my cabin to the bridge, nor of the uneasy greeting I received upon entering, nor of the carefully unacknowledged pregnancy of the Jump countdown itself. Rather did I simply not deign to pay it heed, for was this not a mere shadow play itself?

Tambien do I now believe that I could not have been unaware of the ultimate implication of this logic, though by some functionally protective psychic mechanism I succeeded in hiding the knowledge from myself.

Which is to say that even then I saw that from what had become our shared weltanschauung, Dominique's ruthless indifference to all but the absolute goal could not be judged against any system of merely human morality. If only the Great and Lonely was really real, then only it was absolute, and any ethical esthetic which denied this truth was a formal failure.

In a sprach more terribly plain, I had reached the point of no way out but through, though I dared not admit this to myself.

Au contraire, I sought to use the Jump ritual to deny this unacknowledged inner reality, to mechanize the experience, to purge it of its erotic charge.

Indeed, as I went through the motions in a detumescent disconnected trance like some ancient manual laborer moving to the rhythm of a collective worksong, outer reality made no connection to my inner realms until Argus spoke the words "Vector coordinate overlay on your board."

Then, abruptly, inner and outer reality snapped into congruent focus at the glowing red point of tangency between decision and mechanism, perception and morality, the Captain and the spirit—the command point beneath my fingertip.

It all came down to this act or its exclusion. Duty demanded that I touch this glowing point and dump the vector coordinate overlay into the Jump Circuit Computer, thereby ensuring the safe passage of my ship through the Jump and back into the world of men. Temptation's fulfillment required only that I omit to will its denial.

I could never face this moment again without this awareness of its true meaning.

And as I achieved this chilling satori, my finger came down like a reflex hammer, as if to avoid the awful responsibility of this conscious choice. "Dumping vector coordinate overlay into Jump Circuit Computer," I fairly sighed in relief.

So doing, I then erected the Jump Field aura and commanded the Jump itself without any psychic connection to these acts. And in the moment of the Jump, I felt nothing at all.

For I now knew that my fantasies were fraudulent and empty if I had not the courage or moral monstrousness to act, mere masturbation when the means to true mutual fulfillment for myself and Dominique were mine to command.

At this point, naturellement, I had long since passed the point of inevitability as I slid down the geodesic of my lifeline toward my present destiny, but the acceptance of such a conclusion was still anathema to the Captain of the *Dragon Zephyr*, the Genro who had been, still loyal to his command.

Thus in a mode of abnegating and slowly eroding denial, I determined to relegate myself to isolation, both from the temptation and irresistible influence of any congress with Dominique, and from the milieu of social consequences, which for me had become a shadow play in which my role was Flying Dutchman at the fete.

Like that ghostly Hollander, I haunted my cabin, or, daunted by my own unwholesome company, wandered the corridors of my ship in an ectoplasmic phase that allowed no connection to protoplasmic beings.

"All else," Dominique had said often enough, "is waiting." Now I experienced the true vacuum implied therein, a state in which no event was meaningful, in which no figure stood out from ground to mark the slow crawl of time.

Thus was I reduced to measuring its passage by conventional instruments, becoming a watcher of timepieces and schedules, running a mental countdown to the next Jump as I waited for hands to move and digits to change. Twenty hours to the next Jump, and Dominique was being transferred from sick bay to her cabin. Sixteen hours, and by now her coma would be lightening to a more normal sleep, and consciousness would be slowly coalescing out of the Great and Lonely dream. Fifteen hours, and by now I should be on my way to her cabin. . . .

Of the venues of previously mechanically passed hours I remember only a gray generality, but the moment I realized that I was now making the choice to eschew our by-now-regular assignation engraved itself with painful clarity on my memory track.

It was precisely fifteen hours till the next Jump, and I can recall this datum with such precision because I was eating a solitary meal in my cabin, staring at a down-counter I had set with the Jump as zero point and watching the digits change. As they did so, I felt a coldness in my limbs, whatever I was chewing turned to paste in my

mouth, and for the first time since Dominique had presented me with her ultima thule and my terrible temptation, the faint uncoiling rustles of my kundalinic
serpent.

Sense memories of our previous erotic encounters were
released by this missed beat in our rhythm, and with
them the memory of the state of being produced by her
descriptive and erotic ministrations, and with that, the
lust to regain it, transcending the morality of lesser desires. But with that frisson of arational temptation came
the realization that this aching throb of nerve endings
was directed not at the flesh of Dominique Alia Wu but
through it to what lay beyond, to the state I had denied
to both of us when my finger had reflexively dumped the
vector coordinate overlay into the computer.

I wanted to do this thing. I could no longer deny the
reality of this terrible lust. I could no longer pretend that
powerful components of my psyche which might be
called my essential spirit did not long to commit it in
defiance of all other considerations. I was horrified by
the presence of this monster within me; at the same time
I despised the coward crucifying the highest impulse of
his spirit upon an ethical code.

Nevertheless, I was gripped in the bounds of both a
denial-stiffened determination of Captainly will and a
karmic equation of far greater puissance. Just as my role
in this transaction as commander of the Jump had been
revealed as both engine of ecstasy and ultimate denier of
its highest fulfillment, so did I now perceive that the
being denied was both Dominique and myself. Thus I
knew that I could no longer seek the illusion of my true
desire in her flesh any more than she was able to delude
herself with mine.

Between us now, only a truly mutual act was possible,
and that was the act of sublime criminality which I both
detested and sought, the only meaningful event remaining in the repertoire of our destiny.

Our lifelines therefore must be sundered if such an

enormity was not to be, the status quo ante must be regained, and I must proceed as if that chance meeting on the sky ferry and all events consequent had never occurred.

Upon such an improbable feat of mental judo was my forbearance based; such was the absurdity to which my moral calculus was reduced in its combat with fate. Moment by moment, hour by hour, I held myself at bay with this foredoomed false mantra.

Never did it occur to me as I watched time squeeze slowly by that the will of another would never permit such denial, that my failure to appear long after the customary hour would cause Dominique to commit some escalatory act.

Ten hours and thirteen minutes until the next Jump, and as the digits changed, there was a thumping and a shouting at my cabin door.

There stood Lorenza, vibrating with outrage, wild-eyed and clench-jawed. "If you are not a madman, Genro Kane Gupta, you are sin doubt the poorest excuse for a Void Captain that I have ever seen!" she said shrilly. "You have a duty to my Honored Passengers as well as to your machines! The public disharmonies between us may be laid to personal pique, and despite all appearances, your sanity has been certified by your own Med crew, but this occurrence is evidence that you've lost all control of your own command!"

"What are you talking about, Lorenza?" I snapped. "You're the one who's making no sense."

"This beastly Pilot of yours! Like a fool, you permit this creature the cuisinary rights of an officer, indeed you squire her at her repast, and as a result, she now has the presumption to attend our fete."

"What?"

"She holds court in the grand salon even now, attempting to engage Honored Passengers in discourse and refusing to leave on her rights as an officer of the ship."

"By no authority of mine," I told her.

"In any event, you must order her to leave. My clients are in a fever, and the damage to my reputation as a Domo I think has been more than sufficient for one voyage!"

Unable to calm Lorenza, I followed her distraught footsteps to what I perceived all too well was a tableau of confrontation arranged by Dominique for my regard. There was no other person aboard whom she saw as other than a shadow and no purpose animating her actions save the One. She would as soon have invaded the grand salon for the purpose of vexing Lorenza or her Honored Passengers as she would have forborn the same out of consideration for their tranquillity. Sin doubt, what she sought was what she had achieved: to force me thither.

When we reached the grand salon, Dominique was sitting alone at a cafe table across the floor from the entrance, where the ascending spiral balcony began its climb to the vivarium; thus she was both of the generality and perched about four feet above it, on the first shallow turn of the ramp.

As we stood for a moment on the elevated landing overlooking the fete, the ripples this apparition had created were visible in the geometric configuration of the would-be revelers. The distribution of Honored Passengers within the levels of the sculptural room was flattened like an amoeba flowing around the invisible obstacle of Dominique's sphere of influence.

Then Dominique perceived our entrance from her vantage below. "Good abendzeit, Genro," she called loudly over the heads of everyone in the grand salon. "We've all been waiting for you to arrive!"

A hush descended upon the room as heads swiveled back and forth between Dominique and the object of her greeting as I stood there naked upon the stage.

"Why have you come here?" I called back reflexively in a voice whose projection was no less thespic.

"You are contributing to this sorry spectacle," Lorenza

muttered and, gripping me firmly by the wrist, fairly dragged me down the steps and out of this highly involuntary limelight.

"You must remove this creature without further discussions," Lorenza hissed as we made our way through the throng towards Dominique. The press of bodies parted before me as if fearing contamination, and I was the object of a plethora of fearful sidelong glances.

A semi-circle of onlookers had already formed beneath Dominique's balcony table, creating a stage beneath upon which for me to perform, like a foil, below her. There was no way I was going to avoid further contribution to Dominique's spectacle; certainement, I was not at that moment able to remove this creature without further discussions.

Dominique was dressed in a plain yellow bedrobe. Her feet were unshod, her hair a tangle, her eyes hollow and bloodshot, and the mottlings and marks of the Jump Circuit machineries were still evident on her skin. She was an apparition of the postcoital price of congress with the Great and Only, and she spoke to me as if no other beings of consequence were there.

"Where have you been, mannlein?" she said from on high. "As you can see, when I missed your company, I thought enough of the lack to seek you here, in the tropical fish tank. No higher proof of my regard for you is needful, nicht wahr?"

"Dominique! *How could you?*"

Never in my life had I experienced a moment of public exposure of such enormity so cavalierly delivered as if from Olympic realms, such a total disregard for the social surround, such an act of psychic terrorism, such a sea of stunned faces, such a feeling of nude unwholesomeness as might only be remembered from primal childhood dreams of appearing pantsless in a crowd.

"With the Pilot?"

"—his secret amour—"

"—demented verdad—"

"—explains his cafard—"

"—quel horror—"

The uproar spread in growing ripples, then rebounded from the outer confines to fill the entire grand salon with a shrill, scandalized, horrified, rolling-eyed babble. Bodies eddied and swirled as the mob pressed closer. Lorenza, her body bent backward as if at the sudden release of a vile odor, snarled at me under disbelieving eyes.

Dominique stared down at me, her bloodshot eyes twin tunnels of overlapping images; opaque and fathomless, fatigued and burning with feverish energy, clear, black, and infinite as the void behind them. "Look at them, Genro," she declaimed in a voice of withering thespic scorn. "Watch the shadows caper and dance. See how they become terrified when you rattle the bars of their cage!"

"Stop it! Stop it!" I shouted at her, choking on the miasma of rage and fear in the air.

"The power to stop the dance is yours alone, mon cher," Dominique said evenly, transfixing me with the truth of her unwavering gaze.

"Genro Kane Gupta, have you been conducting an affair d'amour with this creature?" Lorenza shouted. "As Domo of this ship, I demand an answer. If such a monster is in command, we all have a right to know."

Silence fell like a curtain behind the figure of Lorenza confronting the miscreant with hands on hips and outraged eyes.

"Tell her, Genro" Dominique said with a thin little smile. "Tell her as little or as much as you like. It is a thing of no consequence."

I was psychically paralyzed, frozen on the interface between persona and being, logic and emotion, social reality and inner impulse. I was literally incapable of response, for none could conceptualize itself out of my utter chaos.

"It is a thing of the greatest consequence," a familiar voice called out, and Maestro Hiro, accompanied by Healer Lao, elbowed his way through the press to Lorenza's side. "Argus Edison Gandhi, are you here? Your presence is required."

A moment later, Argus emerged from the crowd to join the phalanx of my judges, all regarding me with a cold, horrified contempt.

"Med crew Maestros have been rendered unfit for duty by congress with Pilots, as you and I, mein Captain, have had occasion to discuss," Hiro said. "If you are the unlikely victim of such a cafard, you must be placed under medical supervision and your command remanded to your Second Officer. I am willing to stake my reputation on the necessity for such action, and I am sure all present would concur."

A guttural rumble of righteous agreement greeted his words, a low feral sound overtoned with the subsonics of fear. A strangely anomalous feeling began to seep into my bones, a cold, clear counterpoint to the nauseous helplessness of my position.

"Au contraire, all present do not concur," Dominique snapped sardonically. "And since I do not, this foolishness is at an end."

In the dead stillness that followed, Dominique—pale, unshod, frail creature in tangled hair and bedrobe—seemed yet to speak with some unsheathed queenly authority, her voice as clear and sharp and gleaming as a naked blade.

"I am the Pilot of this ship until it reaches Estrella Bonita, nicht wahr, for there is no other. And Genro Kane Gupta is your Captain until then too, for I will accept no other. Come, Genro, come up here beside me where you belong."

To the angry murmurings of all and sundry, I mounted the balcony as if in a trance and stood beside Dominique's table surveying a mob that bayed for my blood. Daunting as such a tableau might be, from this vantage the cool tendrils of calm creeping along my bones began to make connections with my main spinal core, and I seemed to be looking down on this melee as if from some mountaintop height.

"For the Jump is required the clear, untrammeled willingness of the Pilot, verdad?" Dominique said, fixing her gaze on Maestro Hiro. "Tell them, O Maestro of my worldly machineries!"

Hiro stared back at her in the confounded terror of a man of urban civilization weaponlessly confronting a wild beast.

"Tell them! If there is resistance in my spirit, there will be no Jump. If I do not freely offer myself up, this ship will hang here in the long light-years forever. If another's hand but Genro's touches the Jump command point, I promise you all that nothing at all will occur. In this regard, my will is absolute. Can you deny this, Maestro Hiro?"

Hiro glared back at her for a moment; then polarities reversed, and he was the one who averted his gaze from the more sapient eyes.

So too did the gazes of the others transmute from red ire and hot fear to a sullen, smoldering evasiveness, crusting over this volcanic flow with the ash of frozen destiny. A vast shrug of nervousness seemed to twitch around the room. From my viewpoint on the balcony, I could see the rear edge of the mob eroding away as hunch-spirited figures slunk toward other venues. Lorenza, Hiro, Argus, and Lao all seemed to flow backwards as if to lose themselves in the generality of the now beaten and dully terrified throng.

"Genro Kane Gupta is Captain of your destiny as I am Pilot of your fate," Dominique declaimed grandly. "So it is written, so it shall be."

Turning slowly to me, she stared intently but said softly, with an almost fey smile, "You are the Captain of the *Dragon Zephyr*, cher liebchen, please be so good as to dismiss these churls." Her expression hardened as if challenging me to exert my puissance as nakedly as she had displayed hers, to seal us here together on our Great and Lonely throne.

"This public forum is ended," I declared in my voice of command. "As Captain of this ship, I will brook no further interference with my authority."

I glared down at Dominique with as much outrage as I could muster. "As for you," I said, "I will return you to your cabin."

Dominique's eyes became opaque and unfathomable, mirrors of amusement tossing back a reflection of my ire distorted into an intimate jest. "Certainement, liebchen," she said, loudly enough to be well overheard. "You are the Captain as always, and I am yours to command."

Guiding the shaky-legged Dominique before me like a toddling child, I removed us from the grand salon with as much dispatch as the hysteria that formed in our wide wake would allow, and deigned not to speak to her until we had escaped into the nearly deserted environs of the central corridor, where I grabbed on to her arm and, fairly dragging her forward toward her cabin, demanded: "Why did you deem it necessary to commit such an atrocity?"

"To teach a lesson that you must learn, mannlein," she said harshly. "To strip away the final veil."

"Revealing what?" I snapped back.

"Revealing what was already known."

"That you and I have been lovers?" I said, dumbfounded.

"Known to *you*, Genro, not to those poor shadows. To me, you are the only other one who matters."

"Is that some bizarre profession of love?"

"It is a statement of our karmic configuration, mannlein," she said, pausing to regard me with an expression seemingly devoid of any tender emotion. "Have you still not accepted the truth?"

"Your truth?" I said. "The truth that has caused you to destroy my career?"

"Forsaking all else, liebchen. You know that is the price."

"And now that you've forced me to pay it, I have no choice but to continue to the end, is that it?"

"That," she said, "is what was already known."

I glared at her. Our eyes locked in some ultimate contest of will, but as my spirit drifted into the bottomless depths of her orbs, I was forced to admit that this combat existed within my own soul.

"Was it not you who first came to my cabin?" she said insinuatingly. "Was it not you who chose to return more than once? Was it not you who walked the hull of the ship so as to bring this very moment into being?"

"Was it not you who seduced me down every step of this path?"

"Certainement," Dominique admitted freely. "It was my destiny to do so, as it was yours to be seduced. We would not do what we do if we were not who we are, ne? And who we are is the Pilot of the Great and Only and the Captain of the *Dragon Zephyr,* and we both know what we want. And together we have the power to attain it. Have you finally not the courage to acknowledge the nature of your own being?"

"I acknowledge the true nature of my desire," I told her. "I acknowledge that I have the power to attain it. I acknowledge that I have become all but convinced that nothing else is real. But unlike you, Dominique, this single reality, puissant though it be, does not totally define the nature of my being."

"Doesn't it?" she said coldly. "What else is there?"

"The social realm, the responsibilities of duty, the—"

"Shadow games in a shadow realm," she said flatly, daring me with her eyes to deny it. "Did you not experience it as such but a moment ago, mannlein?"

In my silence I could read my answer on the thin smile that twisted her lips. Still, I could not accept myself as the mirror of what I saw in her eyes and nothing more or less.

"The spirits of other human beings," I said with much greater conviction. "No less real than our own."

"And no more, Genro," she said assertively. "You speak of violating the spirits of other humans, but have they not violated yours and mine? They fall upon you, do they not, like a dog pack upon a strange animal, and for what? For not fulfilling your duty? Nein! For congress with the pariah. For seeking vision beyond the bounds of their egg. For things that are the rightful province of your spirit alone."

She wrinkled up her nose and nodded contemptuously down the corridor toward the grand salon. *"That* is the lesson I sought to impart with my little theater," she said. "What moral obligation do you have to those who willfully refuse to open their eyes and deem you mad for seeing?"

"And what about you?" I said in inwardly evasive anger. "Am I more to you than another shadow, Dominique? Another means to the only purpose, which, as you say, is its own?"

"You are the only other one who matters to me, Genro," she said. "As I am the only other one who matters to you."

"Because we each need the other to attain our desire. . . ."

"Yes."

"And nothing more?" I said, studying the muscular ideogram of her face, the shifting surface of her eyes, for any new emotive response.

"There is nothing higher, so there can be nothing more."

"Sophistry," I said.

"You ask if I feel for you l'amour humaine, the caritas of personal treasurement?" she said much less certainly. "I have caritas enough to erect no easy untruth between us. And the truth, liebchen, is that this is a question I cannot answer. We are what we are and our karma is

inextricable. This may not be enough to you, mi mannlein, but it is everything to me. If this be self-serving
sophistry, mea culpa, mea maxima culpa."

We had reached her cabin door. She cocked me an in-
quisitive look.

"You would grant me your favors even now?" I said
with a certain incredulity. "After this contumely? Even
though I forswear the reciprocation you seek?"

"Perhaps that is the measure of my affection for you,
mon liebchen," she said, not without a certain warmth,
but not without a certain irony either. "I grant you all
within my poor powers sans reserve against reciprocation, and I ask only the same from you. Is this not the
essence of the true unselfish amour humaine?"

"I know not any more," I said, opening the cabin door
and ushering her through it. I stood in the doorway for a
long moment regarding Dominique as she regarded me.
Many things had passed between us, but none of these
could ever have simply been called love. Indeed, to enter
her boudoir now would only result in another act of masturbatory fantasy in which the image of ecstasy would
become a mocking reminder of the true desire, the only
true sharing of which destiny had rendered us capable.
This too had become a meaningless shadow.

"You wish not to come inside?" Dominique finally said.

I shook my head. "There is no longer any point to it."

She nodded her agreement. "There is only truth between us now," she said.

"Or nothing at all."

Her eyes widened in quite ordinary alarm. "You do not
mean that, ne," she said shakily. "You merely hide from
your own lack of courage to do what must be done. . . ."

Vraiment, from her viewpoint, this no doubt was so,
but in truth I sensed then no connection of our spirits, no
mutuality of emotion beyond a shared passion for that
which I perceived was not declared the Great and Lonely
as less than an ultimate jest.

"Perhaps," I said, "there are things which in your infinite wisdom you have yet to understand." And left her standing there in the doorway, struggling to digest this ambiguous food for thought.

In truth, the meaning of my words was as much a conundrum to myself as it must have been to Dominique; I only knew that ours was an amour shorn of all caritas, a force of nature, a passion noir sharing only the same object, and, certainement, it could not be said to be generative of nobility of character in any quotidian sense. And yet . . .

I had not proceeded thirty paces down the corridor when my dark musings were interrupted by the apparition of Maddhi Boddhi Clear, bustling up the passageway toward me like some pursuing demon, his white mane of hair an aura about his distractedly determined face.

"Captain Genro," he said, fairly grabbing me by the elbow, "I must talk to you, and I think you are a man who now must talk to me."

I attempted to regard him with detached bemusement even as he peered earnestly into my eyes. "How so?" I said.

"You need not dissemble to me, mein Captain, for we are brother spirits," he said. "Do we not seek the same goal?"

"Do we?"

Annoyance clouded his features. "Have I not to you revealed the darkest of my secrets?" he demanded in a somewhat whining voice. "Is the Pilot of this ship not your lover? Do you imagine that a man such as myself cannot perceive the inner meaning of such congress, having experienced the psychic equivalent on the planet of We Who Have Gone Before? We can speak freely, you and I, as each of us can to no other."

Shamed by his intensity and by the terrible but undeniable truth of his words, I softened my expression.

"Very well, mon ami," I said not without a certain rush of relief, "perhaps we *should* speak."

We had now reached more habited environs, and those passing back and forth across the corridor between the Grand Palais and the stateroom module scuttled across our path like frightened crabs; skittish, sidewise, and clickingly brittle.

"Let us repair to my stateroom," Maddhi said softly. "A surfeit of ultimately private matters have already been made public."

Maddhi's stateroom was strewn with stacks and piles of word crystals, antique leaved books, vials of arcane substances, holocubes, and mandalic paintings, and his bed showed the evidence of recent amorous use. Eschewing the chaises, we seated ourselves across the small dining table, littered as it was with pipes and wine goblets and an assortment of learned detritus.

"Let us speak plainly, mein Captain," Maddhi began. "You have been engaged in a sexual relation with a Pilot, as is now publicly known, and such congress reveals you as a fellow seeker of the ultimate moment."

"You speak in riddles . . . ," I protested queasily.

"Please do not evade me, Void Captain!" he said sharply. "Who better than I to understand that such congress is as close as we mortal men have come to that which only such as my dying lover and your Pilot have achieved? Not to my face can you deny that we both do know what you truly seek to taste in her embrace! I, who have fruitlessly sought this shadow in all possible feminine flesh . . ."

I met his gaze with an openness born perhaps of fatigue d'esprit not uncomplicated with a certain pity, or perhaps it was merely plain that his age-hollowed eyes saw too obviously through my defensive facade.

"Since you know all," I said, "what then is the purpose of this conversation?"

"But I know not all, my friend," he said. "Vraiment, it

is *you* who know more than I. It is *you* who have experienced the sexual truth of a Pilot, a deed which I never dared to conceive, an impossible dream, or so I had thought. You must tell me all. I must know what you have found in the center of this ecstasy and how you have achieved it."

"What I have found," I said bitterly, "is but another shadow, and as to how our affair was conceived against all custom and reason, you would do better to interrogate Dominique on that score."

"*She* seduced *you?*" Maddhi cried. "Quelle chose! Everything I have ever heard about these creatures has led me to believe that none of them seeks or obtains fulfillment from the phallic prowess of any man."

"This, alas," I said, "is quite so."

Maddhi's eyes widened at this, then narrowed. For once, he studied me with a quiet, receptive calm, as if politely inviting me to bend the ear of a kindred spirit in the service of my own, rather than hectoring me for his own enlightenment. By so doing, naturellement, he achieved that very end.

"Dominique and I share no mutual fulfillment in the flesh," I said, lowering my eyes a few degrees. "Through the oral tantric arts or other noncopulatory means does she simulate the true experience in my spirit as she titillated my body to orgasm," I blurted, feeling unmanly and unclean. "She herself eschews all fulfillment save the Jump itself."

But Maddhi displayed no pity or revulsion at this admission; au contraire, on his visage I read only an unexpected sense of confirmation. "Of course," he said, "this must be so."

"It must?"

"Naturellement. You speak as one whose erotic cusp has been revealed as an unsatisfying shadow of that which floats beyond our grasp; how much more so for one who has truly for fleeting moments Gone Before?"

Maddhi paused, his brows furrowing. "But why then

did your Pilot conceive this affair?" he asked, perplexed. "Surely not out of tenderness of the heart? Her actions cannot serve another purpose but the One . . ."

The moment seemed to hang there for a very long while. What did I know of this man? That he made his way through life as a parasitic organism of the floating cultura. That he sought the ineffable whose beatific countenance he had glimpsed in a dying lover's eyes. That nothing I had broached to him thusfar had been received as either admission of mental dysfunction or heinous act. That there was no one else aboard save Dominique with whom I could even admit to the existence of these ultimate matters.

Was this enough?

Au contraire, from what other quarter could I expect more?

"How the affair started, whether through chance or design, seduction or pheromonic congruence, is a moot matter," I said quietly. "Mayhap it started out of dreadful guile and evolved into some kind of demonic affection, mayhap the reverse. In any event, in realtime, my friend, you are right. Dominique wants a service from me indeed, a service which . . . which . . ."

I began to gag on my words. How could I even voice such a proposition? Would not the mere fact of revealing such a thought to another fellow being reveal its own ghastliness to my eyes through his horrified reflection?

But why did I fear to reveal this to myself? I suddenly realized as another part of my psyche observed this thought moving through my realtime mind. Because I would then be prevented from succumbing to the temptation?

Without further inner dialectic, it was this satoric aspect which then spoke, determined that I would commit no act that could not bear the light of day.

"She wants my collusion in Jumping this ship Blind," I blurted.

Maddhi's eyes bugged, fairly rolling in their sockets;

his jaw gaped; and in a certain sense his expression was the expected ideogram of outraged horror. But behind this mask, I sensed, lay something else, something already overruling the socially programmed moral reflex.

"This would entail failing to dump the vector coordinate overlay into the Jump Circuit computer," I went on doggedly but not without a certain sense of relieved tension as I spit the whole thing out. "The ship would then be translated into the nonbeing of the Jump along with the Pilot as usual, but neither would return to this quotidian realm, leaving us all either expired or Gone Before into the Great and Only, the existence of which we poor mortal men can only deduce through logic or faith."

Maddhi's expression became truly unreadable. His face slackened, his eyes seemed turned inward, his mouth seemed on the verge of muttering to itself. "You comprehend the meaning of this technical sprach?" I asked.

"Of course . . ." Maddhi mumbled slackly. Then more forcefully: "Of course!" Then, amazingly enough, he fairly beamed at me.

"Ah, mein Captain, I *knew* that it was time for us to speak truly," he said. "So much that was occluded now stands so clearly revealed!"

"It does?"

"Jawohl! That is how they did it! They never intended that which we call the Jump Circuit as a stardrive. Mayhap the thought never even trammeled their minds. It was our human scientists studying that which they could hardly comprehend who perverted the purity of purpose of the ultimate instrumentality of We Who Have Gone Before into a mere propulsion system, a beast of karmic burden. But for We Who Have Gone Before, the *only* way to Jump was to Jump Blind!"

He clapped hands upon my shoulders. "Do you not understand what this means?" he demanded in some consternation at my puzzled expression.

"It is no less than the answer to the ultimate question,

the revelation I have sought all these long decades," he said. "Why we have never encountered the expected abundance of sapients in our starfaring and how our species entire may at last follow We Who Have Gone Before into the higher realm."

I regarded him not without a certain confusion, but a part of me was already beginning to encompass the meaning of his words.

"Most sapient species which survive a sufficiency of their own history to achieve the necessary level of knowledge must discover the means to produce the transcendent phenomenon that we call the Jump. Mayhap this independent discovery requires a far more advanced state of knowledge and wisdom than our species had achieved when it stumbled on the clue to the Jump's premature development. Thus, we, in our youthful ignorance, created a stardrive therewith, whereas the general course of galactic evolution was for this secret to be discovered by older civilizations, which would comprehend its full purpose."

"That which is no other purpose but its own . . ." I whispered as the vista opened up before me.

"Exactly," Maddhi said, correctly reading my expression. "It is the grand and noble paradox of the universe of mass and energy—that out of its very substance evolves the generality of sapient spirit and, out of that sapience, the means for transcending the very matrix which gave it birth. Your Dominique has conceived of the Jump Circuit as evolutionary destiny intended, and in this ultimate incarnation the full experience should not be limited to any biological specificity."

"And as proof of this we have the dearth of other sapient species—most of whom have Gone Before!"

Maddhi nodded his excited agreement. "We ourselves have *always* had the means for all to Go Before," he said. "We but hid this from ourselves with our guidance machinery, anchoring ourselves to maya by act of twisted will. All of us can Jump freely into the Great and Only—it but requires the courage of spirit to be willing to Jump Blind!"

"You mean . . . you think . . . ?"

"Of course," Maddhi Boddhi Clear said with finality, for there was no dissembling or ambiguity between us now. "You must do as you have been given the knowledge and power to do, mein Captain. You must summon up the courage to do it for all of us. You must."

"Would it not be better to go on to Estrella Bonita and there inform the scientific commonality of this discovery . . . ?" I stammered foolishly. "For if we do not, will the knowledge not vanish from the universe with this ship?"

Maddhi snorted contemptuously. "Inform the scientific commonality of *what?*" he said. "If this conversation were reported, we would both be judged mad, nicht wahr? You would never command a Void Ship again, and Dominique Alia Wu would be retired as a Pilot forthwith. Can you deny this?"

I lowered my head almost imperceptibly, for surely I could not deny the truth of his words. Indeed, neither could I deny that the likelihood that another command would be entrusted to me at the end of this voyage was vanishingly slim in any event, in light of events aboard, which had already cast a heavy public cloud over my sanity.

"I see your spirit is troubled by what you must do, my friend," Maddhi said softly. "But knowledge inherent in existence itself can never be lost. Mayhap the generality of our species will not be ready to accept it for generations to come. But by then, you and I and the denizens of this ship will have long since expired in vain. For us, the only thing that can be lost is this opportunity. For us, the only time is now. You must seize this moment, for you will never be vouchsafed another."

I shook my head in soul-deep weariness. "How," I

asked plaintively, "can I believe that I have the right to decide such ultimate questions for the unknowing passengers on this ship?"

"Believe what you like about your *right* to decide, Genro," he said with an edge of ruthless knowingness in his voice all too reminiscent of Dominique. "Destiny has placed the *power* to decide in your hands, and in yours alone. And to decide *not* to use it, that too is to make a decision that must haunt you always, nicht wahr?"

I sighed. I hung my head limply. I could bear no more. Indeed there was nothing left for me to bear as heavy as this ultimate moral load.

"I can hear no more of this," I told Maddhi without censure or rancor. "there is nothing left to know."

He nodded his agreement. "Of knowledge," he said, "there is now at last a sufficiency. It remains but to act."

XV

I LEFT THE CABIN of Maddhi Boddhi Clear in a strange sort of daze—not a clouding of my clarity but an excessive sharpness of same; a cold, hard, black, ultimate knowledge of the ideogram of karma in which my spirit was frozen, and of the impossibility of seeking freedom from its inevitability through the intervention of forces beyond my will.

My existential options had been reduced to a clear duality. I must either surrender to entropic fate or will my own destiny via the only path left open. There was no middle ground. Either I would fail to act and this temptation would be gone, or I would screw up my madness or courage and Jump Blind. Either I would become a purposeless hulk deemed unfit for command and doomed like Maddhi to wander hopelessly, longing to find the Path once more, or, having already forsaken all else, I would seize the unknowable prize for which I had already paid the price.

Stated thusly, the proposition becomes a tautology, leading inevitably to the very event which has now come to pass. As I sit here encoding this onto crystal and contemplating what now must be done, I could no doubt find facile justification in the self-serving notion that all I have done and will do has been pre-determined by fate.

But as I returned to this very cabin where I now sit in self-judgment, I was still then struggling with the ethical conundrum, there was still a social creature inside me protesting against amoral destiny with the voice of the tribe.

And in the dialectic between the psychic construct and the amoral spirit a certain anger of conflict found form; as a man of duty and human emotion, I found it not difficult to conceive a certain hatred for Dominique.

Had I not met her on the sky ferry, would I not now be existing in the relative tranquillity of innocence? Had she not used my spirit as an instrument, bending it, and sharpening it, and baring it to its own self-awareness, all in the service of her own solipsistic purpose? Her pity on my poor maya-bound masculine state and her unselfish-seeming granting of orgasmic simulation of that which supposedly lay forever beyond my reach, was this not too a seduction, a dance of veils knowingly crafted to lead me on to this final naked moment?

Did she not disdain me both as a fellow spirit and a natural man? Was it not impossible for her to truly share so much as a simple mutual act of love?

Was she not a monster of inhuman obsession? And if I now shared that transcendent monstrosity, was it not Dominique Alia Wu who had knowingly captured my soul for purposes not its own?

I lay on my bed trying to force my consciousness into sleep, unwilling to bear the torture of experiencing the hours of endless contemplation before the next Jump, both hoping to escape into nothingness, and willing the time till that moment not to pass.

As a result, naturellement, I hovered on the interface between wakefulness and sleep; slipping into blackness only to awake with a start, tantalized by unremembered dreams, my consciousness fragmented into jagged jig-saw shards.

In such a hypnogogic state, half awake and half asleep

230 · Norman Spinrad

in the semi-darkness, did I suddenly bolt upright, staring into a human face not more than two feet from my own.

It was Dominique. She must have slipped soundlessly into my cabin during one of my flashes of sleep. Now she was standing beside my bed looking down at me, a Dominique transformed.

I had never seen her this close to her pre-Jump psychic and physiological peak before; nearly a full day after the last Jump and only a few hours till the next, she was radiant compared to the sickbed lover I had previously known. Her skin was pale, but even of color. Her hair was neatly combed, her simple blue jumper freshly laundered, and her body seemed to vibrate with nervous energy. The dark eyes staring down at me were clear, powerful, and only slightly shadowed by fatigue. Until this moment, I had never fully comprehended how severely the Jump drained her animal vitality, for I had never before seen how much there was to drain.

"What are you doing here?" I said, sitting up in bed and checking the bedside timepiece. "We Jump in less than four hours."

"Perhaps that is why I have come to you, liebchen," she said, joining me on the bed without solicitation. "Since it was obvious when last we spoke that you would not come to me again."

My mind began to clear of fog. When last we spoke, she had accused me of lack of ultimate courage, and I had left her with a rejection of her further favors, and in fact my ire toward her had fallen asleep aroused.

Yet somehow this seemed like another time and another place, perhaps because Dominique seemed such another woman.

"You told me when last we parted that there were things I had yet to understand," she said, crouching like a catamount on the bed, staring at me with eyes that seemed to luminesce opaquely in the semi-darkness. "I wish to understand them, Genro, truly I do."

"I wish I could believe you," I said.

She laughed; a strange, feral, snorting sound, yet not untinged with a sigh of some inner sadness. "Why should you not believe me, mi mannlein?" she said. "Have I held anything of my least politic aspects back from you? You believe that I have seduced and used you for my own ultimate end, ne, without tender regard for the free will of your spirit. You believe tambien that I have granted you sexual favors for service rendered with utter indifference erotique. You believe that I have done all this to achieve my own Great and Lonely goal without care for another fellow spirit."

"Well put," I said dryly.

She rose slightly higher on her haunches, looming toward me as she spoke. "If you believe that much, mon cher, then, nicht wahr, you must believe that I know it too. I admit to all. I deny nothing. Believe me when I say that I know what I am and what I have become."

She duck-walked closer to me, touched a hand to my knee. My flesh drew not back. "Verdad, I did all that I did in no one's service but my own. True also that even now I will not deny that my highest desire is for you to do what must be done, and perhaps I am even now exerting my wiles toward this end."

Slowly, she began fumbling with the catches of her jumper, parting the garment down her breastbone and wriggling out of it like a moth emerging from its chrysalis as she spoke.

"But if I thought only to bend your will to my ends, I find that by so doing, I have freed an inner spirit whose nature matches my own. Mayhap all who see beyond the veil become at bottom one; perhaps there is but a single dancer to step outside the dance. This is a thing I do not understand, Genro, for you are the first such creature I have met or made."

Naked, she hovered above my body supported on her elbows and knees, the tight brown nipples of her breasts arced centimeters above my chest like twin electrodes, her mouth close enough for me to taste her rose-perfumed breath, her pubes poised to lower themselves onto my detumescent loins, her eyes staring openly into mine with what seemed like simple truthful clarity.

"Am I supposed to believe tambien that you now truly seek to know me as a man for the sake of amour erotique alone?" I said. "That all at once you are consumed with fleshly lust?"

She lowered herself upon me; I neither resisted nor returned her touch, and though I felt my body begin to stir under the pressure of her naked flesh, my psychic life-blood ran thin and cold.

"Tonight I admit all, mon cher," she said, kissing me lightly on my unmoved and unmoving lips. "I wish us to truly make love, Genro, I wish you to share a moment of ecstasy with me, I wish us to come together in the only way we can in this shadow realm, so that perhaps our spirits may touch beyond it. . . ."

"So that having once shared such a lesser moment of bliss, I cannot gainsay us the greater . . . ," I said knowingly.

"I admit *all*, mannlein," she said, undoing the front of my tunic. "Such is my goal, such is my passion, such is my hope that I will make it yours. I want to take you as close as you can get, I want to feel your ecstasy as you feel mine, I want to bridge the final gap between us, I want us to come together in a place where each can know the other does not lie."

I saw no guile in her eyes as she said this, rather, the ruthless openness of spirit that denied all possibility of dissembling, the artful yet artless clarity of purpose beyond all such dances of veils, the essence which had first drawn me to her, and which, in some sense, I admired in a fearful way that might be called love.

Hesitantly, I moved my arm about her. Tentatively, I cupped her cheek in my hand.

She smiled with soft passion at me, a smile which for

once touched her eyes, but beneath it still was something of cold steel, the purpose whose primacy she did not even in this moment conceal.

"Be naked to me now, Genro," she said. "As I have made myself naked to you. When next we embrace, it will not be in this flesh, nicht wahr?"

Slowly, I began undressing, never taking my eyes off her face. "I make no such promises," I said.

"None need be made, liebchen," she replied. "Now that we are naked to each other, what will be cannot be denied. What will come out of this moment I willingly trust to fate. Can you not do the same?"

So saying, she stretched the full length of my body, and seized my lips in a kiss of such depth and passion as to take my breath away, molding her soft flesh to my contours, filling me with her untrammeled breath.

Her hand reached into the quick of my manhood, and as it surged into that embrace, I felt a shockwave of electricity surge up my spinal chakras and into my brain, opening a channel of clear kundalinic energy between our spirits via the instrumentality of our flesh.

"It has been a long time," she breathed in my ear, "but in a previous incarnation, I was considered an adept."

This was uttered in a tone of jocular challenge, but behind it I sensed the serious truth. Our dialectic had at last reached beyond words or thespic actions to the ultimate plane where being confronted being in the meeting of flesh, and even here did she challenge my manhood to command, even here would our spirits contest in a combat of wills for the ultimate stake.

Vraiment, did this merely serve to whet my energies as she mounted my steed, drawing it within her with a startlingly muscular grasp, then slowly kneading my passion with rolling and surging grindings of her hips. I felt myself flowing into my phallus as it seemed to float free in an infinite cyclonic eye within her, drawn down my spine from my roiling brain into that nether intelligence of my kundalinic serpent; at the same time, my gaze was locked into hers as if each sought to see their own interior reflection from within the other's eyes.

Slowly, without a flicker or waver in our mutual stare, without a word or gesture, I began moving within her energies, first as a minor note, and then, as I raised us into an ideogram of equality, sitting in each other's laps still locked eye to eye and pube to pube, meeting each inward roll of her hips with a slow burning thrust of my phallic lance.

This mutual tantric asana is a configuration of long duration, of the slow, even feedback of kundalinic energies, the roll of the yoni and the thrust of the lingam combining in a dance of smoldering fire, an even, calm rhythm through which the energies build not fiercely but with a rising oceanic swell.

She was adept, vraiment, and so was I, verdad; I knew I had never had or been a lover like this before. Eye to eye, lingam to yoni, spirit to spirit, we performed this exercise for a timeless eternity, until it ceased to be an exercise, until our eyes seemed to meld into endlessly reflected images of each other; until thought, and challenge, and purpose were all subsumed into the void whence they came, until all that remained was an interface of ecstasy oceanically throbbing and rolling in a space beyond space.

"Be a Captain to me now," she sighed, "and let me be the Pilot of your soul."

Clinging to my neck, she drew me slowly down on top of her, wrapping her legs tightly around my waist, and drawing me down, down, down into her with every muscle of her body, with her rhythm and with her eyes, which seemed not to blink or flicker as they stared up at me with the cold black clarity of the perfect void.

I was a lance of energy and nothing more, a glowing nerve trunk from spirit to spine, and from spine to phallus, as if a lightning bolt through the fabric of reality had pierced me to the core.

Like a leaping diver, I thrust myself into the ecstatic void of free fall, soaring and plunging down the geodesic curve into the whirlpool of her center, a demon rider on an eldritch steed.

I watched her lips part and compress, part and compress, part and compress with the rhythm of my spirit until it seemed that I was synced into the very breath of her body and she into mine as we moaned into a single endless ecstatic shout, a mantra of clear energy that went on and on as reality dissolved in a timeless flash of sweet nothingness that seemed to pour out of my spirit down the endless tunnel of her open orgasming eyes, and in that moment of utter release, we were Gone–Before, and together and into the All.

We lay there silently in each other's arms for a long, long moment, as my consciousness slowly reformed into awareness of time and space and fleshly reality, as my spirit clung longingly to the fading glory, and when I finally reluctantly returned, it was longer still until I could speak.

"That was . . . that was . . ."

Dominique kissed my lips briefly, then stopped them with her finger. "Only a shadow," she said, her eyes burning brightly. "Even *that*, liebe Genro. You know it as well as I."

I lay there supinely, still empty of all coherent thought, as she disengaged herself from the memory of our embrace and donned her jumper.

"Think of this when next you sit on the seat of command, mein Captain," she said as she drifted like a fading succubus toward the door, "and I will trust my spirit to your command gladly. In my own strange way . . . I think I love you, Genro Kane Gupta."

Then she was gone.

XVI

Aɴᴅ sᴏ ɴᴏᴡ I reluctantly approach the end of this tale; soon the recounting of the past will merge into the present act of its telling, and then I will have reached the moment when reflection must give way to action, when self-justification, if such this word crystal be, must give way to the judgment of others, when I must leave the venue of the past and emerge from my solitude into the world of my ship to face the future.

I find it strange addressing this account which logic declares will likely never be found to a theoretical audience whose future existence I am hard put to find credible. But of course the true audience I have been addressing all along has been myself, as if by recounting my past incarnations to the Genro that now is, I may re-arrive at my present state of being in a fuller awareness of how I got here, how I became what I have become.

Of what practical use such knowledge may be to the Captain of this marooned ship may seem a moot question. By all logical analysis, the *Dragon Zephyr* and all aboard it are doomed to drift in the interstellar abyss forever. No one will ever decode the apologia of Genro Kane Gupta, the Void Captain under whose command a Blind Jump occurred, and so no outside viewpoint will ever exist to judge whether he was monster or saint. Nor will an enlightened Genro survive a moment longer than the man who first sat down to tell this tale when the ship's air finally runs out.

And yet . . .

And yet I have been to a place beyond place where all such considerations were irrelevant. As I arrived there contra all conventional logic, in defiance of anything that might be called human morality, beyond the timebound realm of the universal egg itself, beyond, in short, anything called law, so has my passage through it all but convinced me that, against all rational expectation, there is a way to return.

So perhaps more than a testament to some theoretical posterity or an exercise in self-justification, this coding of my tale onto word crystal has been a ritual purification for what is to come. By admitting all and in the end perhaps justifying nothing, I bring myself to the present with the ruthless clarity with which Dominique Alia Wu sought and achieved her apotheosis. By so doing, I free myself to act with the same ultimate dedication to my only remaining purpose.

And perhaps tambien to make my peace with She Who Has Gone Before.

Even to the end of our congress on this plane of maya, the heart of Dominique Alia Wu remained a mystery; indeed, as men customarily use this word as metaphor for the human tenderness of the spirit, the question is whether she had such a thing at all. And whether such to me remains.

Certainement, in that first and only temporally mutual act of what men call love, our spirits touched, and merged, and stood revealed in the searing white light of our shared moment of ecstatic nonbeing.

But undeniable too was the truth she spoke that even this was but a shadow of the Great and Only desire we now both so completely sought.

No higher union of spirit may man and woman through

flesh and destiny attain, but if amour humaine can be nothing more, mayhap it must be something less. For in truth does not such sentiment require a dedication absolute to a kindred being, and not to a shared vision of that which lies beyond the very realm of thought and form?

But the being of which we had become kindred avatars knows no purpose other than its own, and in the end we each in our own way served it above any mere heart's desire.

Was I animated by the tender afterglow of love as I made my way to the bridge for our last Jump? Had I then already fully surrendered to the destiny that we shared?

Quien sabe? In memory's eye, I had fallen into a black and perfect sleep after Dominique slipped out my door, so that upon being awakened by the annunciator from this time-slipping state, she seemed to have faded into a dream but a moment before.

Argus' voice blared at me through the speaker. She and Mori had long since activated the bridge machineries, the Jump was scheduled within the hour, the Pilot was already in her module. Where was the Captain of the *Dragon Zephyr*, or was he ready to give over his command?

"I'm on my way to the bridge now, and I'm still in command of this ship, Interface!" I snarled in angry confusion.

And so I woke into a frenzy of bustle and tension as I drew on my clothes sans grooming or ablution and stormed like a juggernaut of purpose through the terror-ridden corridors of the ship.

Faces formed and dissolved like mist in my field of vision as I hurtled through the atmosphere like a bolide. The beauteous and fatuous Sar, cringing from sight of me. Lorenza, her eyes spitting sparks. Bocuse, companion of other voyages, regarding me with disgust. Twitterings and scamperings and raucous dismay as I charged through a cage of frightened parrots.

They passed through my sphere of perception, but in truth I saw them not. My vision was fixed at another point in time, in the ecstatic void of transcendent nonbeing, from whose heights I had seemingly just fallen into this vile quotidian realm.

Only briefly did another truly perceived being intrude, that being Maddhi Boddhi Clear, whose visage passed for a frozen moment across my trajectory, riveting my gaze for a timeless instant with sapient eyes that seemed to mirror Dominique's and my own. Therein did I read both an assent and a plea, the longing touch of a brother spirit upon my own, a beseeching camaraderie calling to me to do what must be done, a final moment of vrai connection humaine before I passed on.

In such a state did I arrive on the bridge, bursting in with a clatter of footfalls that snapped Argus' and Mori's heads around to gape at the arrival of the madman on the bridge.

"What are you staring at?" I said sharply, planting myself in the Captain's chaise without further ado.

What were they staring at indeed? In the eyes of my crew, I saw the reflection of my own distracted apparition: touseled hair and stubbly beard, tunic donned in rumpled haste, eyes that these two intrepid farers of the starways dare not meet.

"See to your duties," I ordered. "I'm still Captain of this ship!"

"By whose command?" Argus snapped. "By the will of your Pilot and lover!"

What then arose in my eyes must have been sufficient to cow my Second Officer, though what I felt bore little kin to feral rage. I had become what I had become and other beings were what they are, and each of us was our own reality. And I no longer cared what impact my persona made on theirs, for that construct had been stripped away to reveal the naked soul within, to whom all this was but vanity and maya.

In truth, I cannot judge whether this was what Argus

Edison Gandhi beheld, or whether her own subjectivity constructed another fearsome Genro out of what she saw. Be that as it may, what she perceived restored through terror the obedience I had once commanded through station and respect.

She returned to the perusal of her instruments, and Mori, naturellement, followed suit, and so the final ritual began under a dark canopy of stars veiling the reality of its destined outcome.

"Jump Drive generator activated on standby . . . parameters nominal. . . ."

The first of my ready points glowed an expectant amber.

One by one, in a tense and utterly mechanical voice, Mori ran down her checklist. In this opening act of the ritual, the Captain had no speaking part, and so I sat there staring up into the simulated starry blackness, into the imagined firmament beyond the tele's illusion, into the utter conundrum of spacetime itself which I had perceived beyond the hull of the ship, into that which lay beyond even that final veil, detached in spirit and function from the instrumentalities of the bridge.

"Primer circuit activated on standby . . . parameters nominal. . . . Pilot in the Circuit. . . ."

Only with the sound of those words did my awareness snap back into the here and now, or rather to the only point of tangency between instrumentality and essence which remained. I imagined, if such is the term, Dominique, floating there in her amniotic nothingness, awaiting the moment when her spirit would be released—to soar free forever into the Great and Only, or to be tantalized once more like myself by only a glimpse.

At that moment, I do now truly believe, the deed was done, in the sense that the decision of the will is the true essence of the act.

"Checklist completed and all systems ready for the Jump."

"Take your position, Man Jack," I said in a voice that sounded hollow and distant even to myself, a voice that seemed the ghostly generalized echo of those oft-repeated words and which therefore had somehow achieved an archetypal absolute. The mantra of this transtemporal chord moving through my being seemed to leech me of all feeling save a cold, clear, indifferent grandeur, the calm that comes with the final surrender to inevitable fate.

Mori hesitated at the arcane intonation of this familiar order, glancing at Argus before repairing to her chaise. But Argus had retreated into the world of her console, and Mori, after perusing my expression, dared not step outside the ritual's pattern.

"Ship's position and vector verified and recorded," Argus muttered tightly. "Vector coordinate overlay computed and on the Captain's board."

Now at last all my command points were active. I had reached the moment of total command once more, but now I felt nothing—a sweet, calm emptiness as I passed into true union with the rite's inner secret, as I myself became the act and the void.

"Jump Field aura erected," I said, touching a command point.

"Captain Genro, you haven't dumped the vector coordinate overlay!" Argus shouted, bolting from her chaise as my finger poised above the Jump command point, stabbing at my board with a trembling hand and wild eyes as it came down.

"Jump!"

How to describe the inherently indescribable? How to render an account of events in sequence when neither "sequence" nor "event" is a meaningful term? Words themselves are a linear sequence; this account, no matter how decoded, must be perceived as a series of images along a skein of time.

But what "occurred" when I touched the Jump command point, what "I" perceived or became in the "interval" between one nanosecond and the next bore no relation to "time" or "sequence." Nevertheless, I am now reduced to a system of translation which must force the illusion of linear sequence onto any attempt to describe the "experience."

I was still "there" on the bridge with my finger on the Jump command point and Argus' perhaps touching the one beside it in a certain sense, in that my consciousness still had access to that slice of spacetime, just as it had similar access to any other event along the geodesic solid of my lifeline.

So I did not "disappear into another continuum" in the sense that my consciousness did not translate into another timebound matrix at some remove measurable in space and time; rather did I abruptly gain awareness of "myself" as a mutating, unfolding standing wave pattern of spirit moving through the mutating, unfolding mass-energy matrix in which it arose. Which is to say my consciousness diffused down my lifeline via the annihilation of the illusion of sequential time, and I not only "experienced" but became the total spacetime pattern "perceiving itself" from outside.

My "body" frozen there with its finger on the command point was merely an arbitrary section of a flux of microenergies in the eternally unfolding macrosphere, which itself existed within the matrix of nonbeing as pure pattern flowing through its own forms, thus creating the illusion of energy and matter as interference phenomena of the intersection of "space" and "time."

To say that the "physical sensation" was akin to "endless orgasm" would be a reversal of field and ground. For the human orgasm consists of the release of a certain narrow spectrum of bioelectronic energies whose momentary free-flow through the synapses mimicks in miniature the universal untimebound reality of forms flowing "freely" out of the true Void, just as timebound notions of "paradise" and "nirvana" must be visions of this eternal universal now.

The boundaries of figure and ground, space and time, "personality" and "existence," being annihilated, "I" existed as "my" own awareness of the standing wave pattern known as Genro Kane Gupta extant as a completed and eternal subconfiguration of the completed and eternal Great and Only, the four-dimensional explosion of raw existence out of Void, the universal flow of massless, particle-less pattern itself, the Great and the Only, the One and the Lonely, the eternal sustaining orgasm itself whereby being is conjured from nothingness, creating the quotidian illusion of time.

Before me spread the "vista" of my true body as the spacetime mandala itself, the Great and Only conundrum of nothingness redoubled into being, the orgasm of the Void.

From this vantage, all things were revealed, and yet in another sense all things were occluded by an excess of light; for all things were events of the simultaneous moment, and that which perceived them was the pattern of the phenomenon itself, the figure was the ground, and its awareness dissolved into the totality.

Was Dominique "there" with "me"? Did "I" confront the spirits of We Who Have Gone Before?

Meaningless verbal paradoxes. There was no other "place" than "there" in all space and time, and every particle and event in all and eternal existence existed nowhere else. Yet since all was One and the One its own illusion, none of "us" were "there."

Nevertheless, it cannot be denied that in another sense our spirits met, since beneath the dance of forms all sapience was One, the means by which "reality" evolved a viewpoint beyond the nothingness of the Void and thus conjured itself by its own illusion into being.

Thus was it perceived that the Jump itself was no anomaly in the matrix of space and time, no intrusion of chaos through a rent in universal law, but a phenomenon of the totality of the orgasmic All itself, not of any part or locus, but of the interaction of the universal moment filling space and time with its relativistic illusion and the ground of nonbeing in which it arose.

The matter of the ship and all within it was but a standing wave of pattern in the hologram of space and time, a segment of the universal chord, no more and no less than the "consciousness" of the Pilot was a pattern hologrammically distributed throughout the Great and Lonely All.

Contrariwise was the One hologrammically distributed through all segments of itself, for no pattern conjured itself into existence save the totality itself.

To "go" from "here" to "there" in an interval of temporal "duration" was an illusion of the timebound mind.

There was no "there" that wasn't "here" and there was no motion of consciousness through time; rather did time exist as but another interference pattern in the universal mind.

At last I understood the true extent of Dominique's despair at being dragooned back into occluded consciousness by the instrumentalities of man, for now "I" and "she" *were* the purpose which knows no other than its own.

The vector coordinate overlay guided not the Pilot and the ship through the Great and Only and back into another configuration in space and time; rather did it warp itself a dimple in the eternal sentient All and suck a segment of awareness down a nullity of time, fragmenting a subconfiguration of the totality and drawing it down a whirlpool of subjectively reforming maya into a new illusion of quotidian here and now.

But "We" were Jumping Blind.

We Had Gone Before.

We were that which existed, the One and the All, Great because we were everything, and Lonely because there is no other.

But even as this vision exploded into existence in an augenblick, so too, with a rending and a tearing, did it just as "swiftly" fade, did a suction of the spirit whirl "me" down out of my unity even as another "me," with torn parting salutation, watched itself Go On—

"Jump!"

Genro Kane Gupta sat in his chaise on the bridge of the *Dragon Zephyr*, his finger touching a red command point on the board before him. Beside the Captain's throne, Second Officer Argus Edison Gandhi was in the act of crumpling to the deck, her hand still sliding off my console. As it thumped against the floor, I emerged from "I," as it were, or rather awoke to the awareness that no time had passed since the previous moment, that I had watched Argus grab for my board as I touched the Jump command point, and then—

—and then here I was in my seat of consciousness, and there Argus was, falling to the floor—

—and in between—

"Captain, Captain, what's happened?"

Mori, her eyes glazed and blinking, her countenance leeched of coherence, was staring at the prone form of Argus, at me, at the ideogram we made together.

"Don't you remember, Man Jack?" I sighed, forcing words to once more animate my throat.

"I— We—" Mori's facial features spasmed into a moment of contortion, as if gagging on memory, or discovering the presence of an illusive hole therein. Then her gaze darted about nervously above and behind, scanning the overarching starfield like that of a small frightened child in a large dark cave.

"Where *are* we, Captain Genro?" she asked me shakily. "Did we Jump?"

"You felt nothing, Mori?" I said in a cool, tranquil voice, which, under the circumstances, sounded passingly strange chez moi, even as it spoke through me. "You don't remember?"

As for Mori, I finally began to register awareness of the fact that she was balancing on the razor edge of hysteria, and that my behavior thusfar had hardly been well calculated to cozen her toward equilibrium. Moreover, a member of my crew lay unconscious or worse at my feet while I attempted to retain the unretainable.

"Summon Healer Lao to the bridge forthwith, Man Jack," I said briskly, slapping Mori gently across the face with my voice of command. "Then check the ship's position."

This had the desired effect of snapping the distracted consciousness of my young Third Officer back into duty's persona and sent her scrambling to her appointed tasks, not without a certain grateful subsumption of self-awareness into ritual.

Smartly, she summoned help from sick bay, and smartly still did she repair to the chaise of the stricken Argus and set the computer to overlaying its starry memory patterns on the realtime firmament presented to us by the tele. It took a somewhat anomalously long time for the computer to find a matching configuration.

"We *did* Jump, Captain," Mori said, as digits flashed across our artificial heavens. "But we're far off course, the vector was all wrong . . . there's a deviation of 76 degrees, and . . . and . . ."

Abruptly, she turned to stare at me in cowed and disbelieving horror. *"What have you done?"* she said. "What really happened?"

"I have done what I was destined to do," I told her from a cosmic distance. "As for what really happened—"

"The ship has Jumped Blind, and the Pilot is dead!"

It was Maestro Hiro himself who announced his presence on the bridge with these words. Behind him came Healer Lao, who made straight for the corpus of Argus without acknowledgment of the presence of those in less obvious need of his immediate attentions.

But Maestro Hiro, oblivious to the immediate medical exigency, could not take his eyes off mine.

"This is where you have led us," he said angrily, but not without a certain horrified compassion. *"This* is the terminal phase of your unwholesome cafard. . . ."

"You didn't dump the vector coordinate overlay. . . . Argus . . . you . . ." Mori began stammering at me in a fit of returning quotidian memories. "You . . . you killed the Pilot. . . . You've marooned us here to die!"

While these phenomenological accusations could not be denied, my spirit felt cool and not unclean; least of all could I be chastened as the foul murderer of Dominique Alia Wu. Au contraire, au contraire.

"And you, Maestro Hiro," I said somewhat dreamily, "do you too remember nothing? Did you not feel . . . the Pilot as she . . . Went On?"

Hiro glared at me. "Do you feel no remorse?" he demanded, somewhat hollowly, it seemed.

"Remorse?" I said distantly. "Perhaps . . . But not in the sphere of discourse you likely comprehend. . . ."

He goggled at me blankly. But behind the blankness erected before it like a mask, I sensed a discontinuity, a psychic twist of denial around a half-remembered void, and mayhap a strange sort of homage to he whose eyes had seen and willed not forgetfulness. As our eyes locked, I felt an arcane exchange of energies, which, in the next moment, seemed to leave him subdued, cowed, uncertain of the ground upon which he stood.

"We've . . . we've survived a Blind Jump," he said softly and with no little wonderment. "At least for the moment we are still alive. . . ."

"So we have, Maestro Hiro, so we are," I said. "And perhaps we have not yet seen the terminal phase of what you choose to diagnose as my cafard."

And so I have reached the end of my tale, the point at which the present grows out of the past and the future awaits in which reflection must act.

Beyond the door to this cabin lies the reality of this marooned ship, no less a shadow than he who now closes this account, yet, nicht wahr, no more. Of those under my stewardship who pierced the veil for an augenblick in my company, one is dead, four have lapsed into dreamy stupefaction, a dozen remember what they can only recall as a moment of utter madness and presently doubt their own sanity, and the rest remember naught.

Argus Edison Gandhi, suffering no obvious organic impairment, nevertheless cannot remember whether or not she succeeded in dumping the vector coordinate overlay from my board; but in any case has become a subdued personality, lacking any further impulse to challenge her mad Captain's authority.

Nor do any of them dare to move against me. The terror of slow asphyxiation far from the worlds of men stalks the corridors, and while they may deem me mad, a deeper wisdom tells them that only a madman can lead when the sane know themselves to be doomed.

So, finally, has this been the autobiography of a madman? Certainement, it would ill serve as a moral fable for the social edification of children. Certainement tambien that I am the only person aboard whose memory track retains the true vision of the Great and Only, who believes that the Captain of the *Dragon Zephyr* is as in command of his full faculties as he is of this ship's destiny.

There *was* another whom I might have rightly accepted as my sanity's judge, but he is gone from this realm, and, mayhap, it has been his final good fortune to have Gone Before.

Maddhi Boddhi Clear was found in the vivarium by Sar. Far from being disgusted or horrified at discovering this expired corpus, this apparently empty-headed and simpleminded creature reported that, after a moment's start, she experienced a frisson of unreal peace.

Maddhi had seated himself on a stone bench under a willow tree overlooking the pond. Arms stretched out across the back of the bench, his head lay back on his shoulders looking up at the simulated sky.

"Like a statue, I tell you," Sar had said, her eyes dreamy and far away. "Like a holocine. Looking up at the sky with his eyes open wide and the most beautiful happy smile on his face. Ah, who could ask for more in one's final moment, nicht wahr? Sehr romantic, no? I do believe I shall remember the old roue far more fondly than I would have believed possible."

And so, indeed, shall I. If not without a certain arcane envy.

And with the example of Maddhi Boddhi Clear before me, I shall now leave my cabin to address my Honored Passengers and crew in the grand salon, where I have assembled them to hear my next course of action.

As Academy procedure for a doomed Pilotless ship prescribes, and as expectation would have it, I shall call for volunteers from among the female passengers to serve in the stead of Dominique Alia Wu, even as Dominique herself received her name and her destiny in similar circumstances aboard the *Feather Serpent*.

Considering the certain doom of the alternative, there will be no dearth of fearful trembling souls to come forth. Nevertheless, I can hardly expect to simply pluck another Dominique from among the denizens of our floating cultura, another such terrible and glorious spirit born to ride the Jump.

But as Dominique seduced me into the final unresisting surrender through its cognate in the flesh, mayhap may I not now mold another in her image through my own preternatural knowledge? As Maddhi Boddhi Clear did on the night he took his name, may I not serve through a synergy of fleshly and electronic instrumentalities as the vehicle of another's passage, as I did for my Dominique?

Each volunteer for the Pilot's module will submit to my tantric ministrations, first in my cabin, and then in the chamber of the voidly dream. Each will walk the hull of the ship by my side. Only those who follow this path to its end will then be deemed worthy to face the ultimate test of the Jump Circuit.

Though many may at first reject this as an outrage of lecherous intent and a scandal under the ship's doomed circumstances, others, such as Sar, will assent for that very reason. Certainement, few will attain to the Pilot's module with the hope of success, but certainement tambien that in the end, as air and hope dwindle, none will gainsay this desperate and bizarre attempt at rescue.

Mayhap all of this is vanity and such a quest is doomed to fail, as all quotidian logic and sanity would no doubt contend. But as Maddhi pursued his grail longingly through years of feminine flesh, must I not pursue that purpose which is its own by the only means available?

May not my tantric puissance and my Great and Only knowledge with unlikely fate combine to create for us a Pilot who will take us to safe harbor, thereby rendering me the equally unlikely hero of an outre romance?

Or perhaps I dare to hope that a Captain and his Pilot shall Go Before together, leaving none to complete what has been no moral tale.

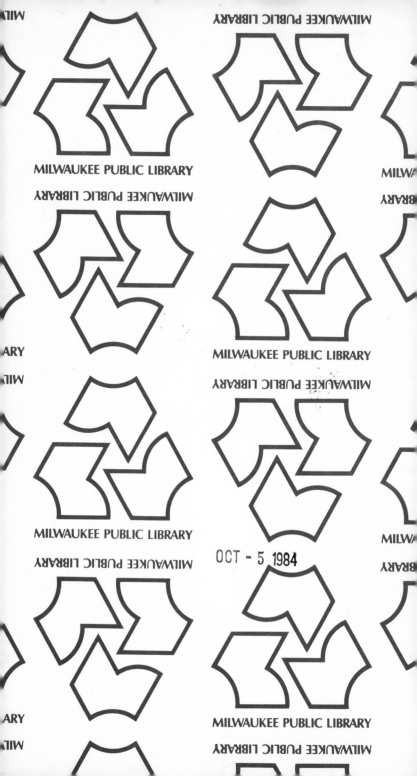